The
WHITE
FEATHER
MURDERS

Books by Rachel McMillan

HERRINGFORD AND WATTS MYSTERIES

A Singular and Whimsical Problem
(ebook-only novella)

The Bachelor Girl's Guide to Murder

Of Dubious and Questionable Memory
(ebook-only novella)

A Lesson in Love and Murder

Conductor of Light
(ebook-only novella)

The White Feather Murders

The
WHITE
FEATHER
MURDERS

RACHEL McMILLAN

HARVEST HOUSE PUBLISHERS
EUGENE, OREGON

Scripture quotations are taken from

The Holy Bible, New International Version®, NIV®. Copyright © 1973, 1978, 1984, 2011 by Biblica, Inc.® Used by permission. All rights reserved worldwide.

The King James Version of the Bible.

Cover by Nicole Dougherty

Cover Image © Kristina Smirnova / iStock

Published in association with the William K. Jensen Literary Agency, 119 Bampton Court, Eugene, Oregon 97404.

THE WHITE FEATHER MURDERS

Copyright © 2017 by Rachel McMillan
Published by Harvest House Publishers
Eugene, Oregon 97402
www.harvesthousepublishers.com

ISBN 978-0-7369-6644-3 (pbk.)
ISBN 978-0-7369-6645-0 (eBook)

Library of Congress Cataloging-in-Publication Data
Names: McMillan, Rachel – author.
Title: The white feather murders / Rachel McMillan.
Description: Eugene, Oregon : Harvest House Publishers, [2017] | Series: Herringford and Watts mysteries ; 3
Identifiers: LCCN 2016046260 (print) | LCCN 2016054678 (ebook) | ISBN 9780736966443 (paperback : alk. paper) | ISBN 9780736966450 (e-book)
Subjects: LCSH: Women detectives—Canada—Fiction. | Murder—Investigation—Fiction. | BISAC: FICTION / Christian / Suspense. | GSAFD: Mystery fiction.
Classification: LCC PR9199.4.M4555 W48 2017 (print) | LCC PR9199.4.M4555 (ebook) | DDC 813/.6—dc23
LC record available at https://lccn.loc.gov/2016046260

Printed in the United States of America

17 18 19 20 21 22 23 24 25 / BP-CD / 10 9 8 7 6 5 4 3 2 1

FOR
TANTE SYLVIA

Who loved this magically wonderful city as much as I do.

Acknowledgments

My thanks go to…

Gerry and Kathleen McMillan, for the constant support.

The Harvest House team. I so enjoy working with you.

My lovely Maisie. Tante Rachel loves you.

Allison Pittman and Sonja Spaetzel. I am so blessed to have friends like you. Thanks for talking me off many a ledge with this manuscript.

Kathleen Kerr, for many a golden moment.

William Bell, who once included me in the acknowledgments section of one of his books, and who I wish were here to experience my returning the favor.

Thanks also to Jared and Sarah McMillan, Leah and Ken Polonenko, Ruth Samsel, Maureen Jennings, Melanie Fishbane, Tim Jolly, and Lin-Manuel Miranda.

*There's an east wind coming all the same, such a
wind as never blew on England yet. It will be cold
and bitter, Watson, and a good many of us may
wither before its blast. But it's God's own wind none
the less, and a cleaner, better stronger land will
lie in the sunshine when the storm has cleared.*

Arthur Conan Doyle, *His Last Bow*

*It is our duty to let Great Britain know and to let
the friends and foes of Great Britain know that there
is in Canada but one mind and one heart and that
all Canadians are behind the Mother Country.*

Sir Wilfrid Laurier

CHAPTER ONE

War was on the tip of Merinda Herringford's tongue. The longer the Cartier Club meeting droned on, the more frequently her gaze wandered through the large windows of the third-floor meeting room of the Arts and Letters Club in hopes of catching a glimpse of the clock on the red tower shooting straight up from the grand, redbrick building at nearby City Hall. When she first joined the club, at Jasper's request, she was chuffed to be the only female in a conglomeration of well-meaning and socially progressive men. Now she stifled a yawn derived from boredom rather than exhaustion. How could one be bored when the world was shifting on its axis? She decided to play at observation.

"If tonight's ultimatum's result is war—" Horace Milbrook's small voice clashed with his large glasses and wide eyes, "then we can expect that Mayor Montague will use this as an opportunity to extend his power even further. I am determined to use his almost certain precautions—which we can guarantee will see his Morality Squad in full force preying not just on women, but on any immigrant with a tie to one of the enemy countries—to further my own campaign." Merinda noticed the arm on the right side of his spectacles was attached to the frame with string. Then she noticed the cuffs on his suit had been recently retailored. Milbrook needed to win the election when he ran against Montague in the coming months if only to keep himself and his family above water.

"An election during the inevitable war." Constable Jasper Forth gave a low whistle, reclining in his chair. Merinda couldn't credit Sherlock Holmes for her deciphering the message in Jasper's body language. She was too familiar with the mannerisms of her longtime friend. He leaned back to overcompensate for the uneasiness he felt at the looming changes before them.

"It will skew everyone's decision on our candidates thus far," said Reverend Ethan Talbot. Merinda noticed nothing different about the minister. He maintained his level, pragmatic tone.

"What might that mean?" Jasper asked, studying the stern countenances of the men around the ornamented oak table.

"I suspect that will mean some sort of illegal enterprise with Thaddeus Spenser."

"Arms smuggling and munitions?" Merinda positively twinkled. "How exciting!" She traded playing Sherlock Holmes to paying close attention.

"I should think rather devastating," Dr. William Alexander countered.

"I have recently met our new British war agent." The editor of the *Globe and Mail*, Alexander Waverley, entered the conversation. "His name is Philip Carr. He was sent here to assess how fit Canada's largest city is for war. He's often seen with Sir Henry Pelham."

"I've seen his name in the papers," Jasper said.

Every paper, including the *Hogtown Herald*, the lowest on the rung of the city's journalistic hierarchy, had been fascinated with the Boer war hero Pelham and his wife, Lady Adelaide, especially during the construction of castle-like Pelham Park, their home built on a high vantage point over the city's core. The *Hog's* photos, in particular so varied and alluring, had been gaining photographer Skip McCoy a lot of attention.

"He has an office at City hall," Waverley said.

"Not the Armories?" Horace Milbrook's eyebrow shot up.

"Montague decided it would be better to have him nearby. Especially if he decides that he needs to put extra measures in place. You know how much Montague respects Pelham."*

"It's exciting to speak about the potential of war," Dr. Alexander said, intervening. "But I would like to direct us back to the tuberculosis encasements and children's nursing stations on Elizabeth Street."

Merinda noticed, as per usual, that the doctor was well prepared to share his tactics and opinions. While her gaze kept drifting, she kept one ear attuned to the conversation around the table and became especially interested when Alexander spoke to the care they were taking in preventing Ward families from providing their children with diseased cow milk. He spoke of methods of pasteurization and the testing facilities and laboratories he was establishing. Conditions in the Ward were slowly progressing with his free seminars on sanitation and his footing the bill for several initiatives for clean water, but the men in the flophouses on Frederick Street still suffered while the immigrant women and children were placed first.

Alexander was still speaking of further improvements when the club turned at the sound of the heavy mahogany door creaking open on old hinges. Behind it, Ray DeLuca stood dabbing at his perspiration-sheened forehead with his rolled up sleeve. "Sorry I am late."

"I suppose the *Hog* is busy with a contingency plan should we declare war this evening," Jasper said, looking at Ray.

---

* Montague's respect of Pelham was greatest when the affluent war hero contributed to City Hall's coffers. If Pelham had suggested his cook be the war agent, Merinda would not have been surprised if he were offered the job.

Ray dropped into a chair adjacent to Merinda. "We are doing what we can, but we all know that the *Globe*, the *Star*, and the *Tely* (here, Ray looked pointedly at Alexander Waverley) will doubtless be the immediate source."

Ethan Talbot smiled. "We all started somewhere, Ray."

"Your choices are the brave choices," Waverley said. "Your prose runs a bit hyperbolic at times, which I think you know, but do not underestimate the readership you have, nor the voice that speaks for a part of Toronto's infrastructure. Reporting will change during the war. I guarantee it." Alexander chuckled and reached for his water. "For example, I have recently hired a young woman. With so many men promising to enlist, including some of my own reporters, I need to ensure that I have a contingency plan. Her name is Martha Kingston, late of the *Montreal Gazette*. She has a reputation for being a bit of a corker. Suffragette and all that. But she'll go after a story. Trail it. And it will be nice to get the ladies' perspective." He looked at Merinda. "Home front charity and all that. *If* we go to war."

Ray's eyes had widened the moment Waverley mentioned an anticipated change of staff, and Jasper must have noticed, for he said with an encouraging nod at his friend, "You know, sir, Ray cannot enlist on account of his having lost part of his hearing."

"Is that right?" Waverley said, shifting as if cornered.

"Left ear," Ray said. "When on assignment in Chicago."

Jasper and Merinda exchanged a look. Ray wasn't necessarily on assignment so much as looped into foiling an anarchist plot and a bank robbery involving his brother-in-law. *

The clock ticked several moments longer until the attendees were far too wired with the looming ultimatum to think of the rest of the day's business.

Jasper, Merinda, and Ray soon spilled out from the Arts and Letters Club and into the blazing sun.

Alexander Waverley intercepted them, a folded newspaper under

---

* The astute reader will recall these escapades as part of a previous adventure recorded as *A Lesson in Love and Murder*.

his arm. "I thought you might enjoy this, Miss Herringford," he said with a kind smile before handing her the paper, tipping his bowler, and crossing Elm Street.

Merinda unfolded it and noticed a picture of herself and Jem on the front page under the magnanimous headline: TORONTO'S WARD DETECTIVES BECOME NATIONAL CELEBRITIES.

"Impressive," said Ray. Since Jem and Merinda had returned from Chicago two summers previously, they had found a growing celebrity, and no longer were their stories exclusives to the *Hog*. While his own paper still sold, Ray missed the increase in sales whenever his lady detectives were responsible for solving a particularly prolific case. They had been appropriated by the city as a whole.

"What a picture!" Jasper said, looking over Merinda's shoulder.

It was, indeed, a rather striking preservation of a triumphant moment. Merinda, in a tilted bowler and loose cotton shirt and trousers, looked straight at the camera with just a phantom of her Cheshire grin hovering over her curved lips. Jemima's light eyes blazed through the image, her high cheekbones and bow-shaped mouth perfectly captured by the photographer's lens.

"Now there's a woman," a voice said from behind Ray's shoulder.

"Russell!" Jasper turned in recognition. "Merinda, Ray, you must meet Russell St. Clair. He's been newly assigned to my station. He transferred from Hamilton. The best part of his being here is that we might finally win the policeman's baseball pennant!" Jasper playfully slapped Russell on the back. "He's a cracker jacks short stop!"

"Well, I wouldn't go so far to say—"

Merinda cocked her head. "I assume when you said, 'Now there's a woman,' you were of course referring to myself?"

St. Clair was unfazed. "Of course. But I also meant the rather striking Miss Watts. I must confess that my interest in your amateur detective agency is heightened whenever there is a photograph of your lovely associate." (The way he said *amateur* made Merinda wrinkle her nose.) He extended his hand. "Miss Herringford."

"Clearly *I* am known to you." Merinda said, giving his hand a quick shake. "But you must meet the lovely Jem's *husband*," she said pointedly, tugging Ray into clearer view.

"Ray DeLuca," Ray said pleasantly, extending his hand.

Russell St. Clair blinked. "DeLuca. Of the *Hogtown Herald*?"

"The very same."

"Surely you are in jest." Russell turned to Merinda. "It's my understanding that Miss Jemima Watts is, like you, a bachelor girl detective."

"Miss Jemima Watts is actually Mrs. Jemima DeLuca," Jasper supplied.

"But—"

"Upon Jem's nuptials, I made an executive decision—" Merinda began.

"One of many," Ray interrupted under his breath.

"I made the decision," Merinda resumed, "that our clients would be more familiar with Herringford and Watts. Besides, we'd already had the sign made."

St. Clair looked to Ray. "And how did a muckraking reporter find himself so fortunate as to wed such a beautiful woman?"

Ray laughed softly. "I am sure I do not know."

"Nonsense," Jasper said. "Ray is the best fellow in the world. In fact—"

"Listen, Jasper," Russell cut in, clearly uninterested in Jasper's appraisal of Ray. "I only came by to see if you wanted to grab a bite of lunch. Kirk told me I might find you here."

"I must be off," Ray said with a tip of his bowler. "Nice to meet you, Mr. St. Clair."

"Constable," St. Clair coldly corrected.

"*Constable* St. Clair." Ray enunciated the title carefully before turning back to his friends. "Jasper, Merinda, shall we plan on meeting near the northwest corner of City Hall tonight?"

"Half past six?" Merinda asked.

"Half past six," Ray agreed, swerving in the direction of Cabbagetown and his home on Parliament Street.

"So that was Ray DeLuca," St. Clair said, watching his retreating figure.

"Shall we go to the Wellington?" Jasper didn't respond to his colleague's comment, but rather pointed to the restaurant directly across from City Hall.

A short stroll later, they were settled in the diner, and over messy corned beef, Jasper and Russell bored Merinda with talk of baseball and the policeman's pennant. Not one to feign interest where she had none, Merinda leaned her chin on her hand and watched the usual lunchtime rush filter in. After droning on about plays and scores, and waxing loquaciously about the details of his recent transfer, Russell drew Merinda's attention back by harping on his perception of Toronto's real problem.

"Germans and Italians," he said with a pronounced thwack of his hand on the table, sparing his company from the racist slurs Merinda was sure he usually used in conjunction with his diatribes. "You watch." St. Clair's voice was almost a hiss. "They will turn on us so quickly. Staying true to their sordid motherlands and all that nonsense." He looked at Jasper. "You think this DeLuca is a friend of yours. He'll use that paper to drum up support to overthrow law and order. I guarantee it." He took a big bite of his sandwich.

Merinda snorted. "You have no idea what you are talking about, Mr. St. Clair. When the anarchists were blowing up trolleys in the city not two years ago, DeLuca was using his influence to stop the exuberance for anarchy from spreading in the Ward."

"He saved my life," Jasper said, his water goblet poised in his hand. "There's enough corruption in our own department without focusing on perceived and unfounded prejudice against people like Ray DeLuca." Jasper took a sip before saying, "Really, St. Clair, I love having a new mate on the squad, but I don't agree with your views."

Russell looked at Merinda. "Surely you, a forward-looking woman, can see the tidal wave that will overtake us the moment Britain declares war."

Merinda almost squawked a laugh. "Tidal wave? I think war will offer more opportunities for women! Why, just last week the *Globe* ran a piece on how women will be allowed to participate in target practice! I have waited my entire life to shoot a rifle!"

"She has," Jasper affirmed, stabbing a bite of coleslaw.

"And your beautiful friend will join you?" St. Clair asked, his eyebrows raised as if attempting to envision what Herringford and Watts might look like handling rifles.

"She will." Merinda nodded.

"I am surprised Miss Watts…erm…Mrs. DeLuca—" (Merinda didn't like the way he said her name) "—is not a part of this Cartier Club endeavor."

"When we formed the Cartier Club, little Hamish had just been born," Jasper explained. "Jem was quite preoccupied."

"I keep hearing it around the station." St. Clair shoved his empty plate away from him. "The Cartier Club."

"Some men and *woman*," Jasper said, nodding toward Merinda, "feel Toronto has been given a great responsibility to serve those who have chosen to make it their home." He expounded on the work of their group and its advocacy for women and immigrants, fair wages, and a desire to impart the promise of acceptance and morality of the century before. He then used the earlier meeting to give Russell a taste of what was occupying their time that very morning. Merinda was preoccupied with waving a waitress over to take her order of pie.

"But all of what you say is what Mayor Montague has been trying to do," St. Clair said. "That was part of the reason I was so eager for my Toronto transfer. To experience firsthand his vision for the city's progress."

"But at the expense of so many!" Merinda countered, her eyes widening at the large slice of apple pie and cheddar cheese set in front of her.

"Do you feel the same way as Merinda, Jasper?" Russell turned to the other constable, who was watching Merinda tuck into her pie with admiration.

"I truly believe we could be making a lot more effort to find 'the least of these' comfort, clean lodging, and opportunity for gainful employment."

"But is that not what Spenser is doing with making jobs available to the newest immigrants and Montague's homes for working men?" St. Clair asked.

"Flophouses," Merinda said through a mouthful.

"The longer you stay in Toronto, Russell," Jasper said sadly, "the more you will be privy to the abhorrent conditions and unfair wages Spenser passes off as 'charity.' The Cartier Club is dedicated to helping change the city's concept of reform."

"But surely," St. Clair said, beginning on a second cup of coffee, "you're in favor of the close partnership between Mayor Montague and Chief Tipton."

Merinda, knowing Jasper had several thoughts on this alliance, none positive and most exclaimed in sentences that painted their relationship as one of a puppeteer and puppet, waited eagerly to see what her friend would say.

Jasper gave him a typically diplomatic response. "Of course I believe that all leadership should work together seamlessly to ensure the success of our city's infrastructure."

Merinda knew, in that moment, that while Jasper enjoyed Russell's company and their camaraderie on the baseball field, he didn't trust him.

"Spoken like a true politician," St. Clair said with a chuckle, rising and placing a few coins on the table. "I must get back to the grind." He tipped his cap. "Miss Herringford."

Merinda, again interested in her pie, gave him a limp wave without looking up. After finishing their meal—Jasper reaching for the check—they strolled up Queen Street.

"Now you can tell me what you really think," Merinda said brightly, sensing his eyes studying her profile.

With her chin tipped up and green eyes blazing forward, she took in the usual bustle of the day. Trolleys rumbled, quaking the ground with their speed and weight, while a lone constable directed traffic as horses and carts and automobiles flowed around him. Spenser's customers were spilling out of the grand department store, holding their parcels and wares. Newsies hawked their headlines all about the War Ultimatum on either side of the street, bellowing promise of a special edition on the deadline for war declaration.

"Chaos will erupt," Jasper said as Merinda recognized a familiar face and pressed a nickel into Kat's palm for a copy of the *Hog*, whose headline declared: TORONTO ON THE BRINK.

If Germany failed to meet the ultimatum and pull back from their invasion of France and Belgium by eleven p.m. Greenwich mean time that evening, there would be war. Toronto was a supremely British city, and Jasper and Merinda knew its population would trip over itself to help the motherland. It was all anyone had talked about all summer, and despite the ripples of excitement and fervor, Jasper couldn't help but look ruefully at the changes erupting around him.

"Are we going to go to war?" Merinda asked as he led her across the street.

"The signs have been pointing that way all summer," Jasper said gravely. "Ever since that poor chap Ferdinand."

"What does that mean for us?"

"I can't rightly be sure. But we have to make certain that if we go to war for England, we have done all we can to make our world worth fighting for—"

"A Toronto worth fighting for?" Merinda interpreted.

Jasper nodded. "I love this city, as do you. But we're fighting our own battle. How can we expect to give our all to a conflict a world away when we can't keep men like Montague and Tipton from waging battle against the people trying so hard to make a life here? Women, immigrants…"

"That fiend Russell St. Clair isn't helping," Merinda said drily.

Jasper couldn't disagree. "I saw a different side of him today."

They walked without speaking for a few moments. Then Merinda broke a settling silence. "Things are changing, aren't they?"

"That's all you've ever wanted, Merinda. Change."

"I love change!" She recovered. "But I fear it all the same."

"Fear? This from a woman who begged her parents for a roadster that could out-speed most of the automobiles in Toronto!"

"Is this your asking for a ride back to the station, Constable Forth?"

Jasper laughed while Merinda tugged him in a slight detour from their stroll, backtracking to Elm Street and to where her car was parked.

"I cannot believe your parents bought you an automobile," Jasper said as he again admired the sheened veneer. He opened the passenger door and slid in. "Did they never hear about your reckless adventures on a police motor bicycle?" He winked.*

Merinda pressed the heel of her brogan to the pedal, and they drove off into the afternoon.

"TORONTO ON THE BRINK."

Jemima DeLuca read the *Hog* aloud to Hamish, who was watching her with interest, his knees under him and his bright blue eyes looking up at her, comprehending little but enamored with the rise and fall of her voice and her animated expressions. Jem set down the paper, leaned forward, and kissed the fourteen-month-old on the forehead, directly under the fringe of his black curls. Hamish responded by grabbing one of her fingers in his pudgy fingers and holding on tightly, babbling about something in a language that was sounding decidedly more like English by the day.

They turned simultaneously at the jangle of keys in the door. Ray walked in the parlor a moment later, swept his hat off his head, and ruffled his hair. "Hot out there," he said, leaning down to kiss Jem before swooping up Hamish and kissing him. "Reading the paper, I see," he said to Hamish, who reached up to grab his father's nose.

---

* This adventure is mentioned in the case entitled *Of Dubious and Questionable Memory*.

Ray sat his son down near the window, where the boy occupied himself with blocks before lifting himself up, balancing with a hold on the window sill, and watching the bustle in the heart of Cabbagetown.

Ray joined Jem on the sofa and stole another kiss. "How are you?"

"Hot and bored," Jem said, fingering a sticky errant curl at her neck. "How was the meeting?"

The eagerness in her eyes told Ray exactly how much she hated being left out of the Cartier Club. Since Hamish's birth, she had adapted to numerous limitations. While she relied on Mrs. Malone and Jasper's mother to take Hamish while she assisted on Merinda's cases, Ray could see that a part of her wanted to be a part of their enterprises. She was pulled in two directions, much as he had long been when still responsible for financially supporting his sister, Viola, while beginning to build a life with Jem. Though the tragic consequences of a case in Chicago resulted in Viola becoming estranged from him, he was able to fill his days (and some late nights) with the *Hog* and his nonworking hours with his beautiful wife and too-fast-growing son. He sensed Jem wanted to find a bit more balance. A long convalescence after Hamish was born, the inevitable sleepless nights, and constant care a baby required made certain that it was several months before she was able to resume her detective adventures with Merinda.

"Dr. Alexander is doing some wonderful work with hygiene, especially in children's tuberculosis prevention." His eyes drifted toward Hamish, who was talking and pointing at something through the window. Ray couldn't understand him, but he knew his son's mind was working a mile a minute as he took in every sound and sight of the street.

"I bet everyone was talking of the war."

Ray nodded. The war unsettled him. He wanted to keep to lighter topics. "Alexander Waverley has hired new reporters to compensate for the men he feels will enlist."

"So he feels that the war is a certainty?"

"Most everyone does, my love."

"Then perhaps he has a job for you." Jem brightened. "Did you tell him you would not be eligible to enlist?"

Ray nodded. "I did but…" He shrugged. "It's no use."

Jem grabbed Ray's hand. "Don't give up your one dream, Ray DeLuca. The world is changing. Indeed—" she reached for the discarded edition of the *Hog* and held it up to him. "A rather brilliant piece in the *Hogtown Herald* believes that Toronto is on the brink! I choose to believe we are on the brink of something exciting, and one of the many changes will see people being able to step into worlds they have dared not go to before. Maybe a *Hogtown Herald* reporter finding employment at the *Globe and Mail*! Once and for all."

Ray gave her a half smile. "He offered Martha Kingston a job even before me."

"That must have stung," Jem said with a click of her tongue.

"It did, but—" A knock at the door interrupted him. He rose to answer it.

A moment later, Ray ushered Mouse into the sitting room. The girl first ruffled Hamish's curls, much to his delight, before turning to Ray and Jem.

"Telegram, Mrs. DeLuca."

"You can call me Jem, Mouse."

Ray pressed a coin into Mouse's hand for her trouble while Jem read the telegram.

"Client at King Street," she said as Ray returned from seeing Mouse out the door. "I suppose I will just follow Merinda to City Hall this evening." Jem stood and went to the hall mirror, where she affixed a cap to her curls.

"What about Hamish?" Ray asked as the baby ran to him, holding up one of his blocks for Ray's approval. Ray DeLuca's usual half-moon smile always surrendered fully when Hamish was in view, and it spread wide now.

Jem turned in the archway separating the front hallway and the parlor. "I'll arrange for Mrs. Malone to mind him."

"Mrs. Malone has been minding him quite a lot lately, Jemima,"

Ray said, still smiling at Hamish and passing the block back to him, only to have Hamish toddle to the window again, find another, and present it in a similar fashion.

"Ray, I don't want to bring him tonight. It will be crowded with people, and he might get tired or scared and flustered."

"Nor do you want to stay and mind him."

"Do you?"

"You know I have to be there in case McCormick needs me for a last-minute assignment." Though Ray had an independent streak at work that often found him butting heads with his boss, Oliver McCormick, he wouldn't dream of missing the opportunity of the biggest story of the year.

"You told me you had done what you can, and that you wouldn't be required at the office until after the event so long as Skip was there."

"I am just saying—"

"Ray, you knew from the moment Hamish was born that I would be taking care of him while still assisting Merinda."

"I know, and you have done a lot of assisting."

"You never expected me to stay at home."

"Jem…"

Jem strode over to Ray, brushed his hair back from his forehead, and kissed his head. "You know I will take care of him. No harm will come to Hamish. He is the most important thing in my life other than you, you frustrating man. But I also want to enjoy the fact that the city has finally embraced us! That our celebrity is keeping the Morality Squad off our heels! That Merinda and I can wear trousers and hats freely as a sort of uniform rather than a deterrent from pursuit."

"You want both."

Jem nodded. "As long as Hamish is safe with Mrs. Malone, I will be dashing off to assist Merinda!" She brushed her lips over his before turning to Hamish, who was in the midst of selecting another block. "Goodbye, duckling!" she said, picking Hamish up and kissing him on both cheeks. "I will see you this evening."

"When the world ends," Ray added drily.

Chapter Two

*Jemima Watts and Merinda Herringford's celebrity
is on the rise. At a baseball game at Hanlan Point
Thursday last, it was not uncommon to see women
in trousers and caps in broad daylight nodding
to the lady detectives or pumping their hands in
solidarity. When I asked one woman whether she
was reproached for her scandalous attire, she shook
her head. "Every woman wants to be them. They
are the face of Toronto, and it is changing so fast!"
First it is trousers in the street and women
detectives. Next, the vote or public office?
Time only will tell...*

Excerpt from the *Globe and Mail*

After a trolley ride and a sticky stroll, Jem entered the familiar King Street surroundings, wherein Merinda sat across from a thin young woman, whose pasty complexion was striped with greasy strands from a disheveled chignon. Jem smoothed her trousers and removed her hat. The girls' growing popularity had made it surprisingly acceptable to be seen in male garb even in daylight. As the muggy August heat showed no prospect of dissipating, Jem was happy for the excuse to trade corsets and stays for cotton shirts and loose-fitting pants.

"Ah, Jem!" Merinda said brightly the moment her friend crossed the Persian carpet to sink into her usual chair. "This is Miss Heidi

Mueller." Merinda waved at her guest as Jem sank into her usual chair. "Miss Mueller, my partner, Mrs. Jemima DeLuca."

"I've lived in Canada my whole life," Miss Mueller said after Mrs. Malone set the tea service in front of them, a timid tremor rippling through her voice, her eyes wavering between Merinda and Jem. "My family too. Horrible words have been painted on the sides of houses. At the Community Center. Even churches. The police will not help. We are going to war, and it will become even harder." She shook her head. "A young woman, my neighbor, was admitted to the hospital when she was hit by a rock thrown through the window."

Jem gasped.

Merinda cursed under her breath. Then she said, "And what do you think Jem and I can do?"

"Find him. Find this person who is bullying my brother and who beat him behind Spenser's. He works in the shipping department. Find the person who is terrorizing us every night! There are boys in the Ward who are just coming home from late shifts, and he waits for them."

"It won't be just one person," Jem theorized sadly. "These petty acts of vandalism will be nearly impossible to trace."

"They have to start somewhere, and if you can find this man, you can find the others. They are most likely working in a group. Like the Morality Squad.* They want to drive us out of our home!" She shook her head. "This is not my war. We have nothing to do with it. We don't have any relatives left. We are Canadians."

Jem and Merinda exchanged a look. Merinda shrugged helplessly. "Have you seen anyone around your home?"

"It's always too dark. My father has been waiting up, but whoever it is skulks around in the shadows and throws things. There's no one else who will help us. You are famous. You assisted with that big case

---

* The Morality Squad was a band of plainclothes detectives who had long acted as Merinda's personal nemeses. Under orders of Mayor Tertius Montague, they had the power to arrest a woman for loitering at a street car stop or wearing a hem deemed too short or supposedly canoodling with young men.

in Chicago. Everyone wants to be you. My little sister wears a hat just like yours, Miss Herringford."

Merinda cleared her throat. "I can try to look into the matter. Do you know of anyone else who has experienced trouble at Spenser's?"

"A few of the lads have been roughed up. Usually at the end of the shift. Please do what you can."

Merinda called for Mrs. Malone, and Miss Mueller thanked them profusely with a sad smile.

Once the front door clicked and Miss Mueller was on her way, Merinda kicked at the floor with her heel. "Hopeless!" She flopped back into her arm chair. "It will only get worse, and I suspect Chief Tipton will pay little attention to any complaints."

"Then it will be up to Jasper to ensure that these poor people have someone to turn to."

"I think he will try, but I doubt he'll have much support from the station. I met one of the new fellows, Russell St. Clair, and his views were quite antagonistic toward...well, everything."

"The fellow Jasper plays with on the baseball team? He's talked so much about him."

"He failed to impress me," Merinda said, deciding to keep St. Clair's obvious disdain toward Ray to herself.

"Well, we have to do something," Jem said, fingering the small retainer Miss Mueller had placed in her hand.

"Fancy a drive?" Merinda brightened.

The girls climbed into Merinda's Cadillac roadster, Jem still unaccustomed to the jolts as Merinda slowly sputtered the vehicle into gear. Merinda never did anything slowly or calmly, thus her steering left a lot to be desired. She swerved and skidded, barely missing a streetcar and then a horse and buggy, and finally deposited the vehicle at Queen Street. From there Jem and Merinda walked the last two blocks to the back of Spenser's, where the warehouse and delivery area were conveniently attached to the back of the grand department store.

Having previously been employed in the mailroom, Jem was familiar with the layout of the store and knew where the entrance to the delivery area was. They wove behind delivery vans with the department store logo brandished on the side.

What met them at the mouth of the loading area was a surprising commotion of policemen and medics.

Merinda and Jem made out a tall figure commanding the situation with a firm voice and stern direction. Jasper. They sidled nearer to him.

"You can't be here!" Russell St. Clair bellowed, skeptically eyeing Merinda.

"Fiddlesticks. We're on retainer for a case." Merinda lifted up on her tiptoes, attempting to see around St. Clair's prepossessing frame.

"I don't care whatever lost kitten or cigarette case is keeping you employed," St. Clair hissed. "This is a murder scene!"

"Murder?" Jem said.

Jasper pivoted toward them with a grimace. "Hans Mueller. Eighteen years old. Waste of life." He looked to the ground. "Bludgeoned on the head. No weapon we've seen thus far."

Jem and Merinda looked at the figure on the stretcher, shrouded with a white sheet. Merinda swept her bowler off and over her heart. Jem followed suit.

"Hans Mueller," Jem said sadly. "That poor boy!"

Merinda turned to Jasper, her brow furrowed. "His sister just hired us to find out who was bullying her brother and vandalizing her house. Not a half an hour ago she was in our sitting room afraid for him."

While St. Clair surveyed the scene, Jasper took Jem's elbow and Merinda's elbow, steering them to a quieter space in a brick alleyway to the right of the loading bay.

"I hate that St. Clair," Merinda muttered, seething.

"He's doing his job. You shouldn't be here."

"Jasper, Miss Mueller told us her family has gone to the police," Jem said. "And they have done nothing to stop this brutality. Her brother went home beaten the other night. Now—"

"And it's not just the Muellers, Jasper," Merinda tripped in. "Heidi said a neighbor is in the hospital because some brute threw a rock through the window, injuring her as she sat unsuspecting in her home."

A shadow crossed Jasper's face. "I know." He shook his head. "But Tipton was given orders from Montague to stay away from Ward troubles. They feel that, with the war announcement, things will reach a breaking point, and all of this petty violence will eventually play itself out. He doesn't feel it worth our resources to, and I quote, 'Skulk around the Ward at night.'"

"But that's horrible!" Jem said. "Who is to protect these innocent people?"

"This girl's brother was murdered. You think Henry Tipton is going to care about some little *Kraut* boy"—Merinda wrinkled her nose as she used the derivative term—"who worked in the loading area of a department store?" She shook her head. "I don't know what to do."

"Neither do I. The prevailing theory at the station is that as of this evening we will be at war against the Muellers and any other family from the enemy powers aligning with Germany. To them, Merinda, this young man is our enemy." Jasper exhaled. "It took a murder for us to finally be given leave to look into whatever prejudice is plaguing these people. But even then, I know I am on a short leash."

"They're just trying to make a life here," Merinda said, waving her arm toward the coroner, who was leaning over the limp body. "Like DeLuca is and half the people we know and help are!"

"I know that." Jasper sounded exasperated.

Merinda's eyes darted back to the scene. The young man's body was being moved into the back of a van for transport to the morgue. "Do something, Jasper," she entreated.

"I'll try, Merinda. But I have to follow orders."

"Not when the orders are daft!"

"Has the family been notified?" Jem asked, trying to imagine what it would be like to receive such hopeless news and blinking away the horror of it.

"No." Jasper scratched his neck. "I was just about to get Officer Kirk to take St. Clair and me to their home."

"Tell Miss Mueller we will persevere even if the police won't," Merinda instructed.

He nodded.

Merinda pulled Jem from the alleyway and back toward the loading bay. Any work that had been stalled on account of the discovery of the corpse had resumed. Once the ambulance and police automobiles backed away, leaving but a few officers in their wake while St. Clair and Jasper went to notify the family, more vehicles trundled in. Large vans and trucks with crates full of bounty.

"When I worked here," Jem observed, "Tuesday was not such a large shipment day."

They watched as large crates and barrels were unloaded and moved toward a shed on the edge of the pavement. "And this is definitely a new method of receiving goods," Jem said, narrowing her eyes. "Usually a foreman is here to inspect them." Merinda followed Jem's intense gaze at the piled and opened crates being moved to a space adjacent to the warehouse.

"So this is strange?" Merinda wondered, eager for any unusual circumstances that might eventually prove helpful to the case.

Jem, focused on the deliveries, shrugged. "It has been quite some time since I worked here."*

Merinda and Jem edged toward the side of the loading bay to take a sweep of the scene now evacuated by Russell St. Clair, Jasper, and their men, but a leftover policeman held up his baton at them, and they were forced out in the direction they came.

---

* Jem lost her job at Spenser's two years previously on account of her marital status.

Upon Jasper's instruction, Officer Kirk parked at the edge of the Ward. Jasper thought it would be faster and less disruptive if he and St. Clair walked through the small alleyways rather than lumber the automobile through, disrupting the usual bustle of the crowded tenements, cottages, lean-tos, and all manners of mercantiles and taverns. St. John's Ward was a pocket of Toronto guarded ironically by the grand City Hall, a composite of mismatched and decrepit slums that helped newly arrived immigrants eke out some semblance of existence as they picked their way through to establish a new and better life.

Better life. The words haunted Jasper as he led St. Clair to Center Street. On either side of the upturned, gravelly road sat ramshackle houses, bound together by sagging clotheslines in a rainbow of colors. Children played with sticks and rocks and jacks while men sauntered, shoulders sunken and exhausted, their smudged faces and bearing stamped by work on the Roundhouse or the viaducts. A peddler dragged his rickety wagon full of strange and wondrous wares through the dry dirt, while an organ grinder eked out a creaking and sonorous tune nearby. Women in homespun aprons, muted brown skirts, and soiled shirtwaists hoisted dirty-faced babies on their hips.

St. Clair was visibly uncomfortable as he consulted the address he held in his hand.

"Let's ask someone," Jasper suggested.

St. Clair shuddered. "These people probably wouldn't understand us."

"Nonsense." Jasper looked around, and his eyes settled on a familiar face. "*She* would." Jasper strolled toward a rather striking Italian woman with a little boy tugging at her skirts and escorted by a tall, Nordic-looking man. "Excuse me!" Jasper called. "Viola."*

"Constable Forth!" Viola Valari's face lit up. Her son, Luca, also

---

* The careful reader familiar with Merinda and Jem's earlier adventures will remember that Jasper Forth had aided Viola Valari *nee* DeLuca several times in the past when her brother, Ray, was on a muckraking assignment in the Don Jail and in providing her transport back to Toronto after her husband died tragically in Chicago.

recognizing Jasper, smiled and stretched out his small hand, which Jasper eagerly shook.

"It's so lovely to see you," Jasper said, formalities long dissolved between them.

"And you." Viola smiled.

"This is my friend Constable Russell St. Clair."

St. Clair, disinterested, mumbled something while skittishly looking about him.

"Nice to meet you, Constable St. Clair," Viola said. She tugged on the arm of the man aside her. "This is Lars Hult."

"Lars!" Jasper's smile beamed with recognition. "Ray speaks of you fondly from your time together at St. Joseph's home for working men when he was on assignment there."

Lars pumped Jasper's hand. "I did not know then that he was a reporter."

"And this is your beau?" Jasper said, smiling as he looked between them.

Viola nodded and ducked her head bashfully, while Luca seemed to find interest in a nearby dog chasing a squirrel across the uneven ground.

St. Clair shot Jasper a quick look, bringing him back to the task on hand.

"Viola, might you be familiar with the Muellers?" Jasper asked.

"Yes! Sometimes Heidi minds Luca."

He leaned in and showed her the scrawled address. "Would you be able to show us where they live?"

"Trouble?" Viola's face darkened.

"I really can't say, but I would very much appreciate your assistance."

Lars pointed to a house with cement panels and sagging windows not a block away. "Just there." He inclined his head. "They've had a horrible time of it."

"Have they?" St. Clair asked pointedly, looking up and finally studying Lars as if seeing him for the first time.

Lars nodded. "All manner of vandalism. Smashed windows. Violence." He shook his head. "A shame. And not uncommon."

Jasper and St. Clair took their leave then, Jasper turning his head over his shoulder for one last look at Lars, Viola, and little Luca. He knew Ray would want him to relay how she and Luca looked and that they were happy and taken care of, even as they had resumed habitation in the Ward.

Moments later, Jasper straightened his shoulders and breathed a prayer for strength. The most difficult part of his job was relaying heartbreaking news.

Led by Miss Mueller into the drawing room with St. Clair at his heels, Jasper noticed the hodgepodge of furniture and fabrics decorating a clean if shabby space. A photograph of the family above the mantel caught his eye. Miss Mueller was captured well with her corn silk hair and bright eyes. Mr. and Mrs. Mueller, whom now he faced, were preserved in the photograph with a measure of strength in their postures. In present, they seemed smaller, their shoulders weighed down with an invisible burden. To the right of them in the picture Hans Mueller, the young man he had just seen shrouded in forever slumber, looked directly at the camera with an intelligent gaze and almost smile.

While Jasper was drawing the breath and courage needed to break their hearts, St. Clair spoke. "It's probably best if we give you the news in a straightforward fashion. Your son was found dead at Spenser's."

Jasper, infuriated at St. Clair's callous and cold manner of delivering the news, stepped forward to lead Mrs. Mueller to a chair.

"How?" Miss Mueller spoke, her parents rendered mute.

"Trauma to the head," Jasper said softly.

"There may have been some altercation," St. Clair said plainly.

"Or it may have been murder," Jasper said, frowning at his colleague. Turning again to the young woman, he said, "Miss Mueller, you have led me to believe some people here are causing difficulties for your family."

"I have gone to the station. I have been told that we must solve these problems by ourselves! But how can we when my brother ends up dead at his place of work?" Her bottom lip trembled.

Jasper nodded solemnly. "I know. I want to help."

"You cannot." She shook her head. "None of you. I have gone to the lady detectives. They will assist us. They do not have the same *principles* as you."

"I am revisiting this. The chief will want to—"

"It is too late to revisit. The police do not care."

"We will send someone to patrol," St. Clair offered. "Every night. A policeman in uniform. So you know that we are watching."

Heidi Mueller bit her lip. "It's not good enough." She turned to her mother and father, who were holding hands, stunned, probably not hearing the conversation wafting around them just as the carpet of their lives was tugged from under them. "It's not good enough," she repeated. "It won't bring him back."

"No," Jasper agreed. "It won't."

"Nothing will bring him back, and you didn't even try to help us!"

"You are being unreasonable, Miss Mueller," St. Clair said.

Jasper raised a hand. "It is we who have been unreasonable. And it is too late, isn't it?"

Heidi nodded. "Yes."

"And nothing will bring him back."

CHAPTER THREE

*Is there any more altruistic profession than that
of detective? Amid the chaos of daily life, you are
focused on the pursuit of one truth. You put others
above yourself, appropriating their problem as a
temporary guiding point in your life. No matter
how the world may shift and creak around you, so
you are set on unraveling a mystery that may shape
the outcome of a person or family for years to come.*

M.C. Wheaton, *Guide to the Criminal and Commonplace*

All the streets leading to Yonge were awash with people by early
that evening. Cars were abandoned on the sides of the road
as traffic cops turned their efforts to crowd control. The pent-
up energy that swallowed Toronto through the pervasive heat of the
unending summer fizzled and popped over the settling quiet.

After depositing Hamish with Mrs. Malone, Ray gathered Jem
and Merinda, and they joined the crowd at City Hall. They almost
immediately collided with Skip McCoy, who was finagling with his
tripod.

"Need to be a little steadier on your feet there, McCoy." Ray teased,
clutching Jem's hand as they ascended the slight hill toward the grand
redbrick building that housed City Hall.

Skip's eyes flashed with annoyance. He rejigged the tripod, balancing his levers as the accordion-stretch of the camera distanced him
from the throng.

Jem and Ray walked on, only to turn at the sound of Skip's loud curse following a loud crash.

Skip emitted a string of curses directed at an unsteady young man who had doubtlessly jostled his camera. Jem, Ray, and Merinda watched him pick up the apparatus, which had crashed to the ground in the brief kerfuffle.

Merinda was the first to swerve. Ray clicked his tongue. "All right there, Skip?"

Skip's brow furrowed in consternation. "Loose plate," he deduced after a moment.

"Still work?" Ray asked, concerned.

Skip pressed his eye to the lens and shifted the stand. They heard the familiar click, tang, and pop of the camera. "Seems to," he said with relief.

Ray gave him a fleeting smile, and they turned again toward the slight hill. "I'll watch from up there and most likely see you at the *Hog* later if we need to print an emergency edition."

Toronto's russet-bricked Big Ben pierced the cloudless sky, its face ticking the moments onward while Jem, Ray, and Merinda found a slight opening in the throng. Reporters from the *Globe*, *Star*, and *Tely* wandered through the crowd, notepads at ready, stealing snatches of statements from those who had gathered to hear the news.

Ray simply watched. He could string together the general fervor into a story later.

Jasper arrived, clad in civilian clothes and wearing a tired expression. "Finally found you!" He gave them a wan smile. "Awful day. The Muellers are devastated."

"A truly horrible thing," Jem said, looking away.

"Wish we'd get this turnout at one of our ball games." Jasper tried to lighten the mood. "Or at one of the Cartier meetings." He winked at Merinda. "Speaking of, I saw Horace Milbrook a few moments ago. Just a split second near his automobile. He mentioned your piece in the *Hog*, Ray. He said he meant to talk to you about helping with his campaign speech."

"Really?" said Ray with interest. "When's the next meeting?"

"Tomorrow. But I move that we wait to hear what happens now before deciding when and how the Cartiers will transition with the war effort."

"The entire city is out tonight," Merinda observed, taking it all in.

"Would you enlist, Jasper?" Jem wondered.

"Uh...I..." Jasper scratched his neck and looked to Merinda.

"Half these lads need a paycheck," Ray interrupted, indicating the hopeful faces of young men staring up at the clock. "It's a free uniform and guaranteed means to send home to their family. Better than finishing school here just to beat the pavement for a job."

"Especially with the economy as it is," added Jasper

Ray nodded. "They'll either go to war or find themselves in Spenser and Montague's web."

"Ha!" said Merinda. "What web?"

"This new British agent. This Carr. I've been interested in him since he arrived. Remember in Chicago how easy it was for the anarchists to get bombs through Spenser's warehouse? What better way to supplement our city's income in a time of war than profiteering?"

"Munitions?" Jasper chewed on that for a moment.

Ray shrugged. "It is early speculation, but it would be a corker of a story!"

Silence spread over the hundreds gathered—some clutching their hands, some their prayer books or Bibles or rosaries. They watched as telegraph operators stood ready at their posts and newspaper offices awaited word flurrying under the waves of the Atlantic Ocean at a frequency exemplary of their progressive age. Later, the quartet learned that it was a newsboy who screeched, "Let out the war cry!" before it rippled and spilled and heaved over the crowds crammed into every crevice of the downtown core, finally reaching City Hall as Big Ben marked 7:15.

Silence stirred heavily thereafter as the citizens of Toronto processed the news that had been on the tip of their tongues and buzzing through their worried brains for months. Then a celebration erupted, and Jem, Merinda, Jasper, and Ray were whirled into jingoistic, patriotic chanting amid the humming din.

It was difficult, to be sure, to imagine men in khaki wading in bloody mud in faraway Europe while the Union Jack was proudly bannered, and Yonge Street, like an overturned vessel, spilled people every which way. A brass band played "The Maple Leaf Forever," and children with flags and drums appeared like apparitions from across the lawn, waving and stirring a palpable hope.

"A free trip to the motherland!" cried one young man before raising his harried voice in an off-key belt of "Rule, Britannia!"

Jasper was stunned silent. Merinda was taking in the scene at large with intent interest. Ray intertwined his fingers with Jem's.

"Will it come here?" Jem asked, her voice a decibel higher to compensate for the noise around them.

"It's already here, Jem," Ray said, tightening his grip and settling a kiss on her cheek, while Jasper sidestepped a flurry of teenagers rallying all men to the Armories to wait for the sign-up sheets.

"We're not officially in the war yet," Jasper informed one of the teens.

"But we will be!" a boy said triumphantly. "We will be very soon!"

A police whistle shrilled, and the rambunctious crowd surprisingly stilled awaiting another announcement.

"Forth!"

Jasper recognized the voice as belonging to St. Clair, who was frantically searching the crowd.

"St. Clair!" Jasper called, finally finding him in the throng.

"Looked everywhere for you," St. Clair panted, parting their quartet. "You'd better come with me." He crooked his finger. Jasper nodded and bid his goodbyes, but Merinda kept at his heels. "You too, DeLuca," St. Clair added.

"Pardon?"

"Just come."

Ray exchanged a helpless look with Jem before matching Jasper's faster stride. Jem and Merinda fell into step together not far behind.

They shoved through the crowd in the direction of Bay Street, stopping when St. Clair did in front of a black automobile.

"I don't want to disturb your feminine sensibilities," St. Clair snarled to Merinda, who was inching closer.

"Piffle," Merinda said dismissively, leaning in.

In the front seat of the convertible, Horace Milbrook was slumped in an unnatural position, his white shirt stained with blood.

Jem, at Merinda's shoulder, gripped her friend's arm.

"When did you find him?" Jasper asked, his eyes surveying the automobile. A few other constables arrived to keep the general population at bay.

"Not five minutes ago." St. Clair turned to Ray. "I wasn't alone in finding him. Your photographer, Skip McCoy, was also here. You'd figure he'd want to snap some of the real action, not a lone man in an automobile," St. Clair mused.

"Why was he just sitting here when all of this was going on?" Merinda asked. She'd removed her torch from her trousers and was moving the light back and forth over Milbrook's body.

"Maybe he never had the opportunity to get out of his car," Jasper said.

Merinda passed the torch to Jem, instructing her to keep the light on the corpse. Then she took her magnifying glass from her pocket and held it over the stain on Milbrook's chest before pausing above something slightly peeping out from his lapel. "Jasper! Do you have tweezers?"

Jasper shook his head.

"St. Clair? No? Fine. Jemima, a handkerchief." Jem extracted one and passed it over. Merinda wrapped her fingers in its lavender-scented folds and gingerly extracted a small white thing from Milbrook's lapel. She held it up.

A white feather—perfectly shaped, fanning out, and only slightly blemished with Milbrook's blood.

Not long afterward, Ray left for the *Hog* offices after finding a cab for Jemima to ride in to King Street so she could properly see Hamish to bed. Jem's first instinct was to follow Merinda, but watching Ray's eyes glower darkly let her know this wasn't the time for an argument. She promised to pick up Hamish and keep the taxi until they were both safe home in Cabbagetown.

After a rendezvous with other station officers, Russell St. Clair apprehended some suspects. Jasper stayed mostly silent as to his personal opinions on level of probable guilt, instead simply watching and, every few seconds, reining Merinda in with a steady hand every time she lunged toward St. Clair.

Jasper's approach to the law was to assume every party innocent until proven guilty. St. Clair, however, seemed to be working in the reverse of that. Nonetheless, Jasper stood stoically, minding Merinda and glancing carefully over the crime scene. If he was going to spend the night questioning suspects, he needed to have a lay of the land. Indeed, the only time Jasper intervened in St. Clair's preliminary roundup of suspects was when his colleague reached out to grab the collar of a bystander who, not yet seventeen, had little comprehension as to what the large officer was saying.

Afterward, officers led the suspects toward police vehicles, leaving St. Clair to turn to his partner with an angry spew as to the state of violence in the city.

Seeing that Merinda was still very much present, St. Clair scowled.

"Come, Jasper. We've a long night ahead of us," he said, his eyes still boring into Merinda.

"Head home, Merinda," Jasper said with a slight smile. "It might get dangerous later. If there are riots and so on."

Merinda shook her head. Sighing heavily, St. Clair pulled Jasper in the direction of the station house on foot. It was only a few blocks away, and the vehicles were full with possible suspects: some legitimate, and others, Jasper was sure, apprehended on St. Clair's whim. Throughout their walk, they did a poor job of shaking Merinda from their trail.* If St. Clair turned on his heel even slightly, he nearly collided with her. That continued until they reached the front door of the station house.

"Go home, Merinda," Jasper said again.

"No thanks," she countered.

"Merinda!" Jasper entreated.

"I'll just stay right here." She gestured toward the broad station steps.

"Merinda."

St. Clair scowled once more before dragging Jasper inside. Jasper, resignedly, shrugged once more in Merinda's direction before disappearing after him.

Alone, she worked the scene over and over in her mind, sitting on the steps and ignoring odd looks from passersby. She tented her fingers as she imagined the Great Detective had done at Baker Street.

Her first guess was that Milbrook's death had something to do with Montague. There was opportunity and motive. But Sherlock Holmes said guessing was "a shocking habit—destructive to logical faculty," so she tried to expand her deductive horizons.

She remained thus, formulating a half dozen scenarios, many of which came back to someone wanting Milbrook's car, and then she yawned and turned at the sound of footsteps on the stairs directly above her.

"You're idle," Jasper joshed, lowering himself to sit beside her. "I thought you would be prowling Toronto."

"Are you making any progress with the suspects inside?"

He shook his head. "I needed some air. One poor fellow obviously has nothing to do with it and can't even trip through English. We released Skip. He was just in the wrong place at the wrong time."

"It stands to reason a murderer could easily slide off into the night. Anyone else?"

---

* It is worth mentioning that Jasper wasn't trying very hard to lose her.

"Not of consequence, though St. Clair is still questioning hard. He believes everyone is guilty until proven innocent."

Merinda chortled. "And you?"

"I can't think of anyone who would want to dispose of poor Milbrook. Most of what he rallied for has been well received. Most Torontonians would say he had a sure shot at the next election."

"Then it was clearly one of Montague's cronies," Merinda seethed. "Get him out of the way."

Jasper nodded. "That seems a common theory."

"Or perfect. It's so easy to leave undetected." Merinda chewed her lip.

"Tipton brought in a foreigner. Someone he has had his eye on in the Ward." Jasper ran his hand over his face. "I have a feeling some of these men are facing a tribunal of officers like Tipton and St. Clair who need them to be guilty." Jasper sighed. "I've said too much."

"Surely Tipton had some reason to investigate." Merinda ironed out the fight in her voice. Jasper was looking disconsolate enough as it was.

"Tipton's man was seen earlier with a bird, of all things. Just at the edge of the Ward near City Hall and Milbrook's parked automobile."

"There's certainly a dozen good reasons a fellow would have a bird. But that feather...it was so...perfectly shaped. I highly doubt some fellow just plucked it from a bird!"

"I don't know much about plumage myself," Jasper said resignedly. He sighed. "I'd best be back in. Are you going to act reasonably and head home or keep watch on our steps in the middle of the night? I must admit that having you here is slightly safer than your wandering about unaccompanied."

Merinda ignored that. "Any mention of the murder of that poor fellow at Spenser's this afternoon?"

Jasper shook his head. "I doubt anyone will keep that incident at the forefront of other duties. A poor German immigrant and possibly an enemy now that we've thrown our lot in with the Brits. But most likely just another innocent in a scuffle that Tipton will decide a shame but not worth police resources."

"I'm not the police." Merinda stood.

"Be careful," Jasper said, stretching his arms out.

For a silent moment they used their vantage on the station steps to take in the last dregs of the evening's commotion.

"Maybe their deaths are connected," Merinda mused, distracted by an impromptu posse of revelers with loud, raucous voices rising in a lubricated ballad to the home country.

Jasper shrugged. "Maybe." He smiled and squeezed her shoulder. "Safe home, Merinda."

She looked about her, a slight smile tickling her cheek. *Safe home. Her* home, the city stretched in a kaleidoscopic flurry of Union Jack flags and leftover snatches of music from a revel that would either signal the dawning of an incredible new era or the final droning toll of a world about to end.

During her tenure on the steps, Merinda had turned an idea over and over in her brain. M.C. Wheaton would advise that one must never prematurely anticipate a connection. Yet, Merinda most decidedly subscribed to the Ray DeLuca school of "Montague, Spenser, and Tipton Are Responsible for Nearly Everything." And, if this were the case, who was to say that the two corpses from completely different rungs of the social ladder couldn't indeed be tied with an invisible knot?

Merinda skipped down the station steps and set off in the direction of Queen Street.

She suspected that the night crew at Spenser's, its location at an intersection still bustling with the now just-waning action, would likely be late to their shift, caught up in the revelry. Along Yonge Street, under the winking of the electric billboards and marquees, great banners unfurled, announcing: GREAT BRITAIN DECLARES WAR ON GERMANY.

Merinda was swung into a group of men kissing their girls. "We should all be married before we ship out!" one said, grabbing at her arm. Merinda shoved him off with a scowl.

She kept her head high and her shoulders back. Love and energy flittered around her, preventing her from reaching her destination at the speed she desired. She employed her walking stick a few times to either rap on the pavement to the surprise of an embracing couple or threaten a kid tripping into her path.

Turning onto Queen, she elbowed her way through the rollicking crowd leaving City Hall and retraced her steps to the back loading bay. She reached into her pocket and extracted her torch, flicking its light over the pavement and around the dark vans.

A surprised gasp from the boot of one vehicle drove her buttery light northward and exposed two young people in a tight embrace.

"Cracker jacks! Scurry along, you vagrants! Want me to whistle for the Morality Squad?"

The kids set off. Of course, they'd had no idea it was a crime scene, but Merinda winced nonetheless at the hapless state of the place a likely innocent young man took his final breaths.

As she flashed her light over a large grated door and the ground nearest her vicinity, she reminded herself that Russell St. Clair, though undoubtedly a fiend, was most likely perfunctory in his tasks. Jasper seemed to respect him, but Merinda had once referred to Jasper as a human golden retriever, liking and befriending everyone, so his instincts were admittedly drawn toward blind affection.

She crouched down and took a swift look around over the tarmac and near the hubcap of one of the van's tires. Not finding what she had hoped for, she expanded her perimeter in a semicircle, to no avail. Frustrated, she thought of turning toward home, but some inkling kept her brogans on the ground. At the sound of a sudden shuffle and thud, Merinda's catlike eyes blazed, and she stiffened. Was that a footfall? She froze, waiting several moments before calling up the courage to move on.

Merinda looked up, scanning the broad, gated door with careful eyes. And thus she saw it, a little flicker of white under the dusky starlight. Wishing she had Jasper's height, she looked around for something to elevate her enough to pull at the protruding item, which was a whisper of ivory against the dank, black grate of the warehouse.

She kicked over a box, stood on it, and then extended her arm to flick at the object with her walking stick, dislodging it.

A white feather floated down.

Chapter Four

*There is never real freedom in this new life. It is just
another type of bondage. Worries creep incessantly. If
you are not worried about securing passage, then you are
worried about where your next meal will come from. If
you are not worried about finding employment, then
the roof starts to leak. If you are finally settled, then
you and your family are the brunt of the scowls and
yells of masses that would see you back where you came
from. There is no freedom in this our new promised
land. Rather, just the promise of nagging worry.*

An excerpt from the *Hogtown Herald*

"What kind of trouble are you dragging us into?" Ray asked,
looking up from a desk full of paper as Skip McCoy rambled into the *Hog*.

"They just wanted to question me." Skip shrugged. "Not my fault.
I was doing my job." He retreated to his desk and finagled with his
camera.

"Was it damaged?" Ray asked, remembering the jostle from earlier in the evening.

"Just the plate," Skip said, not looking at Ray.

"Good. But your job was to capture the mood of a city going to
war, not to skulk near Bay Street and Horace Milbrook and arouse
police suspicion," Ray continued.

"I don't know what you're accusing me of, Mr. DeLuca, but the police found nothing they could use to hold me. They arrested the perpetrator. Some lumbering Swede."

Ray wanted to continue the conversation, but McCormick broke in, throwing his arms around frantically. His globed forehead bore a shiny sheen of sweat. "Why are we *always* behind?"

He kicked the press.

"Because every piece of equipment here is from the past century," Ray said sourly. Try as he might to focus on his boss, his eyes involuntarily sought out Skip in the small working space of the dusty *Hog*.

Ray raked his fingers through his hair. He was frustrated and tired.

He sank down in front of his Underwood, ignoring Skip's rants about how Ray should be more supportive of him and McCormick cursing the fate that had dealt them the hand of a second-rate newspaper. Ray worked on an article about the sights and sounds of the evening. The war. The cheers. The interminable wait as the clock ticked incessantly onward. The crowds and music and fervor. The Armories, now doubtless overrun with eager men willing to throw themselves into the fray.

But while his fingers tapped almost with a mind of their own, his brain spiraled back to Horace Milbrook, slumped in his automobile with that eerie white feather atop his chest. That symbol of cowardice was from the war against the Boers years before.

Ray ripped a half empty page from the Underwood and fed a fresh one in its place.

Milbrook wasn't a coward. Milbrook was one of the few men who had boldly and loudly spoken against Montague's brand of corruption. He came *this* close to winning the previous term by exposing Montague's campaign platform in its use of misappropriated funds.

Ray wrote and wrote and wrote. When he looked up, McCormick was there, arms folded and watching him.

"DeLuca?"

Ray passed him the article. "I can draft up something about the war now, but we are running this first."

"You run this, and Montague will shut us down. He's been threatening it for years."

"Montague was getting scared. His term is up again, and he knows this war will come with its own brand of pressure and expectation. Milbrook was gaining on him. I am willing to bet that Montague hired one of his cronies to—"

"Anytime anyone is murdered in this city, you think Tertius Montague is behind it!" McCormick interrupted. "You're never right."

"It may not be his hand that clasps the knife or pulls the trigger, but we have the opportunity to say something. Change something. The city is rattled. This can be a platform for real action. Fear. Commotion. Violence. That's all we've been seeing, and a murder just upsets people more. Scared people are angry people, McCormick."

"I won't run it," the editor said, at least humoring Ray by flicking his eyes over the piece before shoving it back.

"McCormick, with all due respect—"

His boss stopped him with a raised hand. "I've always given you free rein, DeLuca, but not this time. We have a real opportunity to expand our readership. They don't want more of your political spiels on Montague. They want patriotism and a community coming together."

Ray opened his mouth to protest further, but then he resigned himself to a nod. The sooner he finished up, the sooner he could see Hamish, smell his hair, and let his son seek out his father's face with his little fingers. The sooner he could fall into bed. Ray fed his previous sheet of paper back into his Underwood and tapped out his firsthand account of the evening's commotion.

Jem retrieved Hamish from Mrs. Malone, asking the cab driver to wait while Merinda's kindly housekeeper enjoyed one last caress of his cherubic cheek before he was transferred to Jem's arms and subsequently to the taxi. Hamish was fast asleep as King Street swooshed by. The cabbie attempted to speak of the events of the night, but Jem was distracted until they neared the edge of Cabbagetown, one patch of neighborhood sewed up in the quilt of Toronto. The driver swerved over to the curb at her direction and parked outside of her townhouse.

"Thank you," she said, reaching into her handbag and offering payment, which the driver declined.

"Something's not quite right, ma'am," he said, squinting through the window.

"I am quite sure it's just some raccoons or kids. If you think—"

The driver held up a restraining hand and asked Jem to wait. He exited the vehicle, leaving Jem puzzled as she hoisted Hamish to a more comfortable position in her arms. He returned a moment later and opened the door to the backseat. "Your front window has been smashed."

"Pardon me?"

"I'm very sorry."

Jem slowly stepped out of the vehicle and pressed Hamish closer to her shoulder.

"Would you like to go somewhere safer?"

Jem shook her head. "No. I should be here when my husband gets home. Would…would you mind accompanying me to the porch while I take a quick look around?"

The cabbie nodded. "You just wait here on the walk while I go inside and make sure it's all clear."

Jem thanked him profusely, pressing her house key into his hand. She watched him walk up to the porch and strike a match on his shoe and hold it up. She caught its flicker through the now noticeably jagged opening of the window as he made his way through the front room and into the hallway.

He returned moments later, assuring her he had checked the back door and upstairs, and there was nothing to be frightened of.

"Maybe some kids playing a prank."

Jem pressed cash into his hand. "I wish I had more."

He gave it back. "No charge tonight. You just get this little fellow to bed safely, and for your sake I hope your young man returns soon."

Jem nodded and bid him good night, walking up the porch steps gingerly and then edging through the still-open door. She set Hamish on the sofa while she turned on the gas. She walked toward the jeweled crystal of the glass shards catching the wink of the flittering streetlight outside. Spotting something out of the corner of her eye not too far from her latest knitting disaster, she knelt to pick it up. It was the rock responsible for the desecration of the window pane. She clutched it without looking at the note affixed to the bottom, preferring to wait until Ray arrived.

She returned to the sofa and tucked a quilt around Hamish. Then she skittered at every sound while huddled at the edge of a chair. Her little boy's even breathing was the one comfort she had while the cloudy night spilled in through the broken window.

When she heard footsteps coming up the walk and a rattle at the door, her heart clenched in her chest, and she instinctively moved to grab her son.

"Jem!" Ray's voice met her even before he did, calling frantically from the hallway. "Jemima, what happened?" He surveyed the room and the damage to the window before standing beside her, searching her face before peering down at Hamish and running a finger over his cheek. "Are you hurt?"

Jem shook her head. "We arrived home after it was done, and...oh, Ray! It scared me so! Hamish plays by that window. We haven't ever had any trouble here. Not with the neighbors."

"Times are changing," Ray said in a low voice.

"I found this." She pressed the rock into his hand.

Ray examined it, and she watched his eyes darken at the note on the bottom.

"I've been called worse." He shrugged. "And with European politics at a tipping point, people's prejudices are raging even hotter. Tonight almost certainly pitted us at war." He ran a hand over his face, flushed with the heat and anger Jem knew was bottled underneath his level tone. "But there's a very big difference between someone picking a fight in the Ward or a flophouse and someone smashing our window.

I can take care of myself. But…" he swallowed. He reached out and touched one of the curls licking Hamish's neck.

Jem felt sick, looking at the slight sparkle on the carpet even as she tried not to. She'd have to put a mat down. Or keep Hamish from the windows. "I can't imagine anyone on our street resorting to violence. Maybe someone is angry at you for something you printed."

Ray shook his head. "It's more than that. It will be worst in the Ward. It's the war. People are ignorant and scared."

"You're Canadian!" Jem countered. "You've lived here for years."

"Am I? I don't know what I am." He scratched the back of his neck. "The enemy, maybe."

"It could be an angry *Hog* reader," Jem repeated. "You are not the enemy."

"I don't care if people come at me with words, Jem. But a missile through the window?"

"Your job has always had an element of danger to it," she said slowly. "That's the risk that—"

"*I* take, Jem. The risk *I* take. I won't risk you or my little boy."

"So what are you going to do?" she asked after a long silence interrupted only by the persistent ticking of the clock in the hallway.

He shook his head. "Hope that the man who did this got all of his anger out of his system. I think you should gather your things. You and Hamish should go to King Street for a while."

Jem shook her head. "That's just giving in to them, Ray. We won't run away. We've done nothing."

They stared at each other silently a moment. "I want you to go, Jem."

"And I say I am staying. We do all of this together."

"Jemima, you do not need to help me fight for my right to live here."

"Nonsense! I took the risk as well. I took your name. We stay together." With that pronouncement, she kissed her baby lightly on the cheek. "I am taking Hamish to bed."

Ray followed her in the direction of the stairwell a few paces before turning to the window. There wasn't much he could do at the moment, save to grab a knitted quilt from the sofa and maneuver it over the shattered glass in a makeshift barrier from the outside elements. It was a ratty solution, and one that wouldn't even deter a curious raccoon.

Upstairs, Hamish snuggled softly and gently breathing in his crib, Jem waited for Ray's pacing in the front hall to desist. Much later, while her eyes remained open in the dark, she saw his shadow cross the room and heard his usual nightly routine. Thereafter, he gathered her up and tucked his chin into her shoulder blade.

They lay there silently a few moments, Jem certain she could feel Ray's open eyes on her back.

"I'm a little afraid to go to sleep tonight." She broke their silence. "I don't know what kind of world I will wake up to in the morning. War breaks out. People riot in the street. Milbrook is dead behind the wheel of his car. This poor Mueller girl hires us just as her brother is killed for nothing other than his family's origins. Our front window." She turned to study his face in the darkness but could make out little of his expression. "I moved to Toronto because I wanted something more. I moved here because I always thought the city connoted freedom! It's one thing Merinda and I share." Jem cupped her husband's chin. "It's one reason why I fell in love with you. This city is our anchor, Ray. It's what makes you tick like that old pocket watch I love so much."

"Canada just has to give these lads going off to war something worth fighting for."

Jem shook her head. "Montague and whatever corruption will happen surrounding the next election. The horrid conditions of the Ward. How can our city guarantee that? I know you have your voice. I know you have the Cartiers. And Merinda and I have tried our best to help women who have nowhere else to go." She bit her lip. "I guess I'm wondering if it has been worth it. If it is enough."

Ray felt for her hand in the pitch-black and squeezed it. "It's too late to have such deep thoughts, Jem. It's been a..." Jem could almost hear the wheels in his mind turning, her sense of hearing heightened in the dark, "…harrowing day."

"I don't want you to lessen what I am feeling just because it's been a harrowing day," Jem said, sighing.

"I'm not lessening anything, my love. I just know that sometimes you have to climb each mountain as you come to it. Then another and another. You can't see the peak on the other side, so you concentrate all of your efforts and strength on one. You focus on one. And then you take a deep breath and see the next mountain and find the strength to climb it." Ray exhaled.

"Just one mountain," Jem said softly.

"Just one mountain," Ray agreed.

Jasper tossed and turned the few remaining hours of the night away. Every time he drifted into some semblance of sleep, his eyes flew open to inspect his hands. The previous night, his fingers came away red with the blood of a colleague and an ally. A fellow Cartier. A man infused with the spirit of what he hoped Toronto would be.

When Chief Tipton had finally released him for the evening, keeping but two of the possible suspects in Milbrook's murder, Jasper took a walk through much quieter streets. Men snaked in long lines at the Queen Street Armories to enlist, even as they were reminded that only those with previous military experience would be required this early in the endeavor. When he finally returned home, his mind alive with a million thoughts and prospects, sleep came fitfully, and dawn broke far too soon.

Jasper returned to the station. He hoped the scalding tea he was sipping would sustain him while he looked over the messages and paperwork piled on his desk. He only looked up when Officer Kirk knocked on the door and informed him that Tipton wanted him. After Jasper crossed the corridor and walked into the chief's large office, he noticed Russell St. Clair was already seated.

Montague, Tipton informed them, was to hold a press conference to announce the results of an emergency council meeting the evening before.

"New measures and protocol." Tipton settled comfortably behind his mahogany desk. "We'll be the first to enforce them. It's likely Prime Minister Borden and parliament will dole out their own measures after the governor general gives the official word. That should come down the pipeline shortly. But Montague is afraid of the immigrant problem."

"The immigrant problem?" Jasper hedged.

"Anyone allied with Germany. Who knows what they're hearing from their families overseas? It could be chaos. Anything could be festering in the Ward. These people are anarchists. Not two years ago, dozens of people were killed and injured in heinous bombings."*

"We found that source," Jasper said. "It was one man with a vendetta of his own. David Ross."

"He represents a larger problem," Tipton said.

"So you're going to round up anyone with a German or Hungarian or Austrian surname and do what exactly?" Jasper looked to Russell to see if he mirrored his own skepticism. Instead, Russell was listening intently, nodding with the chief.

"Precautionary measures." Tipton poured himself a measure of whiskey. Jasper had half a mind to remind his superior it was nine thirty in the morning. Tipton swallowed and said, "Nip it in the bud before it becomes a problem."

"Obviously, sir, these precautionary measures should also hold for those of descent nominally involved in the conflict. Those who could go either way."

"Explain, St. Clair."

"Those of Italian descent."

"You can't just mark anyone who has at one time affiliated with a

---

* Readers can find a full report on these heinous bombings and the scurrilous antics of would-be anarchist assassins in *A Lesson in Love and Murder*.

country we *suppose* may make friends with Germany and the Central Powers!" Jasper exclaimed, looking first at Russell incredulously before darting his eyes to Tipton. "How can you possibly account for those who have married into a different nationality or who have distant relatives or who have lived in Canada more than half of their lives?"

"St. Clair is right, Forth. Is it worth the risk? I expect you to back Montague's enforcements one hundred percent."

"But you're being—" Realizing he was on the brink of insubordination in front of his superior officer, he stopped speaking and looked down at the floor in frustration.

"If you have something to say, Forth, by all means say it." Tipton crooked an eyebrow.

It took all of Jasper's restraint not to kick his chair across the room. "No, sir. I just…" He looked around, hoping to find some tick or change in St. Clair's face, something that would back him up. He had so many things he *wanted* to say but couldn't without an ally. To add, his mother had always told him to count to ten when angry.

That way anything said in reaction to a tense moment had time to diffuse and turn into something firm…but also hopefully kind.

"Then I expect you'll continue with the Milbrook case?" Tipton asked before Jasper had a chance to get to number eight in his mental count.

Jasper nodded, rose, and turned toward his office. He didn't make it three steps before he was intercepted by a ruddy-faced constable, breathless and bleary eyed.

"Constable Forth!" he erupted. "We just received a telephone call from the *Globe*. Alexander Waverley has been murdered!"

CHAPTER FIVE

Mark my words that upon declaration of war,
Montague will unleash powerful measures with
his usual tinge of illegality. He molds the city
into whatever shape he needs to keep it under his
thumb. He doesn't inspire loyalty. He instills fear.
The chaos hovering on our horizon will give him
the opportunity to take whatever drastic measures
he deems fit in order to maintain his position.

The *Globe and Mail*

Merinda leaped for the telephone as soon as its *brrrring* cut into the parlor. Jasper's voice on the other end was breathless as he relayed the news about Waverley and asked that she meet him.

Merinda dashed to the front hall, affixing her hat before flying down the steps and into her roadster, cranking it into gear and setting off an alarming pace, stopping only when she spotted Kat hawking newspapers atop an overturned cart. She swerved over with a loud screech of the tires. "Kat! Go round up Jem!" she hollered, before steering the vehicle back in the direction of Yonge and the *Globe*'s offices.

She parked and took the walkway at a jog. Once inside, her senses were bombarded with the clicking of keyboards, the bellows of the latest headline, and the clacking echo of heels over tile. This was a world in constant motion despite the devastating news that its head editor had been murdered. Its verve and spark exhilarated her even as she moved through the parted officers and concerned employees bordering the hallway to the offices.

"She's here on Forth's invitation," Kirk said by way of explanation as Merinda walked through to several looks of amusement and a few of consternation.

When she reached the end of the corridor and the large corner office, she found Jasper and St. Clair leaning over a body set back in a grand chair.

A knife was in Waverley's breast, just above the pocket square ornamenting his fine suit. A white feather caressed a congealed red pool of blood.

"Alexander Waverley," Merinda breathed, acknowledging a mannequin of a man who had once been so alive, whose low voice rumbled through their Cartier meetings, his fingers rapping on the side of his chair and now slumped unnaturally. She shuddered.

"Another one of these messages," Jasper said, accepting an offered pair of tweezers from Kirk and gently lifting the feather.

"I'll take this back to our lab." St. Clair turned toward the door. "Maybe they can find something that links it to the one found with Milbrook."

Merinda swallowed down the urge to tell them she had found a feather at Spenser's, but she didn't trust St. Clair and decided to keep that information for Jasper's ears only. She returned her gaze to Waverley, focusing on his tailored jacket and then up to the slight sweat-stained line on the collar below his neck.

"I question whether she should be here." St. Clair stopped with his hand on the door.

"It's fine," Jasper assured the other constable. "She has a good eye. I'll find you shortly."

St. Clair nodded curtly.

"I'll wait outside, sir." Kirk walked through the door and shut it behind him.

"He appears very much as Horace Milbrook did," Jasper said once they were alone.

Merinda examined a loose thread on Alexander's suit jacket. "There is no sign of surprise, which leads me to believe it was someone familiar to him."

Jasper locked eyes with her for a moment. She half expected he would affirm her supposition, but instead he lowered his gaze to Waverley's desk. He began opening each desk drawer, using his fingers to fan through various pieces of correspondence.

Merinda watched him, perching on the edge of the desk and handing him the small magnifying glass she kept fastened to her vest. "At least we know that the men being held at the station for Milbrook's murder are innocent, unless there are two men who think it's a lark to plant white feathers on dead bodies."

Jasper still said nothing, and so Merinda followed his eyes. They lit as he shuffled through papers in the top drawer and settled on a handwritten missive in Waverley's precise slant.

After skimming the lines on the page, he passed the sheet to Merinda. Her eyes flitted over it as recognition brightened over her face. "This sounds like what DeLuca was talking about last night!" she exclaimed. "All about this war agent, Carr"—she skimmed a few more lines—"profiteering from Spenser's."

Jasper nodded. "I wonder if Waverley intended on passing ideas to Ray."

"But why not just run his own theories?"

"We both know the *Globe* is controlled by Montague. Maybe Waverley felt he needed to find another to give this to." Jasper leaned over Merinda's shoulder, settling on a sentence about monitoring the "legal preparations in case of war as ensuring that the proper channels were in place for receipt of all manner of firearms."

Merinda watched Jasper's brow furrow in consternation. "This sounds like something we would read in the *Hog*."

Jasper nodded. "Exactly. I think he knew he would never publish it."

"So you think this is here for DeLuca?"

Jasper shrugged. "And there is this."

"What?"

"Look closely."

Merinda leaned in and their shoulders brushed. Jasper felt a whisper of bobbed curl brush his cheek.

"For R.D."

"I think we have our answer."

"Sir!" Kirk opened the door and stepped inside. "I found—"

"I'm here!" Jem's voice cut in.

"Jemima. You're out of breath!"

Jem shook out her curls. "I had to leave Hamish with Mrs. Malone. Not everyone has the luxury of an automobile, Merinda. Some of us have to take the trolley! And with a child—"

Jasper grinned. "Well, you're here at last."

Jem stepped forward and then paused, noticing Waverley's body for the first time since entering the office. "Oh, how horrible."

"And another one of those feathers," Jasper said.

"The same killer!" Jem gasped.

"Do you need your smelling salts, Jemima?" Merinda chortled.

Jem ignored her. "We should leave this to Jasper and continue looking after Miss Mueller's request."

"Oh, I think they're one and the same," Merinda pronounced, striding from behind the desk to join Jem.

"What?" asked Jasper.

"I found a white feather at Spenser's when I returned after the commotion of last night. It was right at the edge of the warehouse."

"Where is it?" he demanded

"In my bureau drawer."

Jasper whistled. "That certainly adds another layer."

"But how is someone like Hans Mueller connected to Milbrook and Waverley? That makes no sense," Jem said thoughtfully.

Merinda glanced her way. "The Mueller kid worked at Spenser's. If his death has to do with the profiteering—"

"There's no proof of profiteering, Merinda," Jasper said shortly. "We only have our suppositions. There isn't even an official war yet for us. Just because Britain declared war—"

"You know we will join them. It's only a matter of time." Merinda turned back to Jem. "I think we should pay a visit to this Philip Carr to see if he has anything to shed on the situation."

Jasper placed his hat on his head. "I'll be heading back to the station." He called for Kirk to pull up the automobile. "Don't do anything stupid, Merinda."

"Me?" she asked with mock incredulity.

"You," he said, smiling at Jem and taking his leave.

"Come," Merinda instructed. "I parked around the corner."

"I saw." Jem snickered. "The point is not to park the automobile directly on the curb."

"Oh, hush!"

Jem and Merinda left Waverley's office and walked down the corridor toward the building's front door.

"Wouldn't Ray be perfectly suited here?" Jem asked, her eyes brightening.

"It's a step up from the poor old *Hog*, that's for certain," Merinda said, smiling at a reporter who was eyeing her with interest. They really *had* become celebrities. Maybe Montague was right. Maybe they were an emblem of the shifting world.

"Herringford and Watts." A familiar voice met them at the door way.

"Skip, how's the camera?" Merinda asked as the reporter shoved his glasses higher on his nose.

"Right as rain." His eyes widened as they took in the *Globe* offices. "Never been in this place. Sure makes the grass look greener."

"Well, we're off."

"Did you find out anything about Waverley? Quote for the *Hog*?"

Merinda rarely passed up the opportunity to see her name in print, but on this occasion she shook her head. She wanted to beat Jasper to the war agent and find a connection before he had the chance to. "There's not a lot to say at this point."

"Mrs. DeLuca?"

Jem shook her head as well. "I was, unfortunately, late to the scene." She wondered why Merinda wasn't mentioning the white feather discovered at Spenser's, but she followed her friend's lead. "Not a lot to say."

They smiled their goodbyes to Skip and pushed through the revolving door onto the humid sidewalk. "I wonder why Ray wasn't behind him," Jem said as they strolled to the roadster.

Merinda shrugged. "DeLuca's your arena, not mine."

"We both had quite a scare last night." Jem told Merinda about the rock through their window.

"I suppose anyone could threaten DeLuca, but he hasn't printed anything of a particularly incendiary nature of late. Give him time, though. This election might mean more of the same."

Jem nodded as she opened the door of the passenger seat and sank onto the warm upholstery, branded by the beating sun.

Merinda steered with the grace of a buffalo, pointing the roadster in the direction of Queen Street.

The pavement was strewn with the evidence of the previous night's revelry. Street cleaners were working diligently, but University Avenue was yet coated with a layer of patriotism haphazardly gift wrapped in red, white, and blue.

Above the sound of the engine, they heard the newsies hawking headlines in the creaky discordance of adolescence. The names of the prime minister and governor general whistled on the breeze conjured by the movement of the vehicle.

Jem prided herself on being able to distinguish a DeLuca head-line from the others in the loud cacophony, even as Merinda steered around a fast-moving cart, the horse tugging it neighing his frustration.

Jem, though unaccustomed to all of the rules of the road,* began

---

* Many of which Merinda seemed to be creating as they swerved and squeaked along.

to notice that her friend was wandering between both sides of the pavement, and her customary jittery movements became even more erratic.

"Jemima! I think that—"

Jem saw perspiration beading Merinda's forehead. She shot a look over her shoulder. "We're being followed!" she squealed.

Jem couldn't make out anything as to the identity of the figure behind them, who wore a cap and dark glasses. She clutched the sides of her seat, knuckles white, and felt her heart rate speed up. Merinda shrieked for her to look out as the roadster frantically swerved left and jostled Jem with it.

Just as Merinda abandoned the wheel to grab her friend, the automobile behind them crashed into them. Merinda was kept from being flung completely forward by her angle in aiding Jem.

Jem had just enough time to scream before the impact flung her forward. Her forehead smacked the dashboard, and her world went black.

CHAPTER SIX

*A woman learns with the realization of her most sacred
role as wife and mother that her life is no longer her own.
She gloriously sacrifices any modicum of adventure that
would set her in the way of the slightest of harm. She is
of secondary importance to the comfort and security of
her husband and her children. And it is this beautiful
martyrdom that completes her life's fulfillment and
finds her contented and whole for the rest of her days.*

Flora Merriweather, *Guide to Domestic Bliss*

Y ou're going to need to lower your voices!" a passing doctor
hissed. Ray and Merinda ignored him, not for the first time.
"Not until you let me see her!" Ray addressed the doctor,
though his black eyes still glowered at Merinda.

"Sir, I told you. The supervising doctor will keep you informed.
We've already given you the most pertinent details."

Ray nervously fingered his suspenders, every sinew in his body on
edge. He spent the insufferable moments until he could see Jemima
for himself railing against the woman who had landed her in a hospital ward. When Ray was particularly agitated or flustered, his English was wanting, and Merinda was dealt verbal blows in a hybrid of
English and Italian, the gist of which pointed an accusatory finger at
her. They had been going in circles for several moments with both
at a near tipping point. She had been surprised how quickly he had
arrived from the *Hog* after receiving her frantic telephone call.

"I always knew one day this would happen!" Ray said darkly. "I dreaded the inevitable moment when the telephone at the *Hog* would ring, and it would be someone telling me you had finally done it. Finally gone and got her killed."

"That isn't what happened!" Merinda's voice reverberated through the sterile corridor of the hospital ward.

"Shhh!" This time an attendant scowled at them.

Merinda didn't listen. "We were driving. Just *driving*, DeLuca. That was all. And it was all fine before—"

Ray had never seen Merinda cry, and he didn't fancy experiencing it again. Her usually confident alto was a series of hiccups, and her aquiline nose was red at the tip.

"I won't let you do this again! I can't! It will kill me, Merinda. *You* will kill me."

"Unless you want to lock Jem up inside forevermore, you cannot keep her from the danger that ran into us today!"

"Yes, that's what Jasper told me. It was an *accident.*" Ray spat the word like a curse.

"It...it was," Merinda said tremulously.

Ray lowered his voice to a whisper. "You're a horrible liar, Merinda Herringford."

"Fine! Do you want me to tell you I think someone was intentionally trying to kill us? I didn't have a moment to press on the horn or slam on the brakes. That car came out of *nowhere*. I may not be the most careful driver, but you know I have never placed Jemima in danger I wasn't undertaking myself so that I could throw myself in front of her." She wrung her long fingers. "But this...this was too fast." She stopped a moment. "It was broad daylight, DeLuca. We weren't skulking around at night or chasing a murderer."

Ray fingered his collar. "I don't believe you."

"She has a gash on her head and a bruised rib!" Merinda threw up her hands. "I am dreadfully sorry, but she will live. I was more scared today than I have ever been in my life. For a split second, when I saw her..." Merinda swallowed and jerked a thumb at him. "You're not the only person who loves her, DeLuca. I would have traded seats with her in an instant. But she is going to be just fine. You can rail at me all you want, but—"

"The doctor said it was a very close call. Too close."

Merinda felt her knees buckle a little. "I know."

"I want to hate you," he said after a moment. "I want to turn you out of our lives forever. Forbid you from ever setting foot in our house or luring her away. But you are so much a part of what makes Jem who she is and..." He shook his head. "But she'll always throw herself after you. She'll throw herself into it. Whatever case you're solving. These little feathers." He nudged in the direction of Jem's room. "You think you're something wonderful. That you're helpful. That you can do things! You're just a silly girl in a bowler who has never kept a real job for five whole minutes of your life. And you take her down with you."

"Me! There was a rock thrown through *your* window the other evening. We were not pursuing anything dangerous! We were in pursuit of an interview with that war agent fellow, Philip Carr. She was safe as houses. I'm not the one who placed her in a situation where she would be attacked in her own house. The other day a young woman was hospitalized due to a similar injury in the Ward!"

"Enough!" Ray waved his hand and scowled at yet another attendant begging them to be quiet. "Enough of this," he said, lowering his voice but a decibel. "There is a side to Jem you don't have, Merinda. *My* side. There's a part of her world that is not you. That is my part of it and Hamish's part of it, and I want more of it. You are no longer the most important part of her life. You haven't been for years."

Merinda gaped at him a moment. "You're a cad, DeLuca." Her voice was quiet and cold. "I don't mind your lashing out at me. I don't mind us fighting. We always have, and maybe we always will. But you're a cad." She swallowed down the pesky lump growing in her throat.

Ray's eyes bored into her. In an instant, all of their usual banter and camaraderie was replaced by his disdain for her. It was bound to come to this, eventually. Explosives in Chicago and taking off on a whim to pursue a missing woman in Massachusetts, commandeering a motorbicycle and speeding off with Jem holding on tightly. It was a matter of time, wasn't it? Yet, Merinda only made it two steps toward the exit before spinning around and facing him. "DeLuca—"

"I don't have anything to say to you, Merinda."

She wondered if he would ever have anything to say to her again.

Later, Jasper found Merinda where he expected her. Her glazed eyes were surveying the damaged roadster. Thanks to the proximity of the hospital to the station and the help of Officer Kirk, she had gained entry to the police garage.

"Leave us now, please," Jasper said to Kirk, who gave a perfunctory bow and turned back toward the station.

The garage behind Station One was a rudimentary affair with only a few police cars and a row of motorbicycles. Merinda's roadster, surprisingly sleek and shiny under the suspended electric light, was intact for the most part, save for the passenger door and seat.

"You've been crying."

"Ray DeLuca hates me," she said, running her finger over the detailing.

"Oh."

"*Oh,*" she mimicked him. "It's my fault her life was almost ended?"

"There's nothing to say, Merinda."

"You're not the first person to say that to me," she said sourly. "DeLuca…" She paused and bit her lip.

Jasper poked his thumb at a crinkle of remaining glass in the windshield, while Merinda crossed her arms and stared vacantly at the worst of the damage. She stepped closer when she caught the slightest shape of something just under the dashboard. Extracting her small magnifying glass, she leaned forward. An instant later, she held up a white feather.

"He's our Moriarty," Merinda said, stepping back so her arm

brushed with Jasper's. "And this is his symbol. Another one of these feathers."

"We don't know who *he* is."

"Well, whoever he is, he's tied to Montague."

"Merinda, you and DeLuca always rush to convict Montague."

"But we're right, aren't we? Maybe he was trying to stop us." She worked her teeth over her bottom lip. "Maybe he assumed we would discover Waverley was connected to Spenser and—"

Jasper took her elbow. "Merinda, you're making very little sense. Stop thinking about your case for one second. You can't just shelve tonight like a book in your library. You've had a horrendous experience. Devastating and…" he paused, his eyes silently pleading with her. "I want you to talk to me. To actually talk to me. About Jem. About what you are feeling."

She circumvented him and rounded the roadster. She glared from the other side of the lowered covering. "I am not *shelving* anything."

He cleared his throat. "You are trying to methodically work through something you aren't in any way ready to process yet."

"Every time I close my eyes I see it again and again. That automobile smashing into the side and almost killing Jemima. I thought she was dead." Merinda shook her head. "It's my fault, Jasper, and DeLuca will never speak to me again. He'll never let her come over or come on a case, and that's my fault too. He'll never forgive me. He hates me. I have never seen him talk to a living soul like that."

"He's upset and scared, Merinda. He'll come around."

Merinda shrugged off his words of reassurance. "It's personal now. I never cared if Montague was promenading us around as some emblem of the strength of women needed for the home front or railing against me with threats of St. Jerome's Reformatory for Incorrigible Females. But I care now. It was the passenger side, Jasper!" She flung her hand emphatically near the decimated door. "Whoever did this knew that was Jemima's spot. They did this intentionally!" Merinda rubbed at her temples. "Whoever it was knew…How did they even know where we were and where we were going?"

"It can't have been personal to Jem, Merinda," Jasper said softly. "How would the driver know where you were going to swerve? If he meant to harm Jemima or tamper with your steering, he would maybe have hit your side instead." Jasper ran his hand over his face. "It was someone who wanted to hurt both of you." He ruminated a moment as silence settled around them. "It could be someone out to hurt DeLuca. The same fellow who threw a rock through the window?"

Merinda mulled this a moment. "It could be…" She blinked a few times under the suspended light. "I was paying attention to the road," she said forlornly, leaning against the mangled, misshapen metal.

"And yet Jem could very well have been killed," Jasper said, following her eyes over the damage.

"It was so pointed. Someone *wanted* to kill us."

"What kind of automobile was he driving?"

"It looked very much like mine, but it was green. It stands to reason it would have the same level of damage, at least to the front lights." She came back around the car and followed his finger to a scratch near the dashboard. "Look! There's just the slightest bit of glass and paint embedded just so."

Jasper extracted a pair of tweezers from his front pocket and removed the evidence, which he placed on a handkerchief.

Merinda shook her head. "He knew exactly where we were and in which direction we were headed."

Jem was finding it difficult to rest in her hospital bed. She couldn't get rid of the disturbing images inside her brain. Every time she closed her eyes, the automobile flung her forward again.

She was overcome with guilt and sadness and worry. It was enough that she hated herself at the moment. She had almost left Hamish without a mother. She could hate herself, yes. But if he did?

When she heard the door click and Ray's footfall, she readied herself.

He looked worse than she assumed she did. He was extremely pale, and matted hair fell over bleary eyes. Then his expression softened, seeing her, his whole body seeming to exhale. He scraped a chair across the bleached tile to her bedside and gazed at her silently.

A nurse held up a hand, indicating he had five minutes. Ray, who hadn't taken his eyes from Jem, didn't see.

"I-I'm very sorry," Jem said after a moment, her own eyes barely seeing the edge of bed sheet she was wringing. "I recognize you probably feel you have the right to tell me that something like this was bound to happen. That I threw myself carelessly into a situation and came so close to…" A lump filled her throat, and she blinked away the tears stinging her eyes.

"You got into an automobile," Ray said softly. "Something you have done numerous times before."

Jem nodded, her eyes frozen on her fingers. His voice certainly didn't sound angry, but she didn't trust what his face would betray. "You must be so disappointed in me. When bad things happen, you always tell me it's a close call and I should spend more time thinking about our family."

"Jem—"

"I know it doesn't make it right, but I *hate* myself for what might have happened. There is nothing you could say that would make me unhappier than I already am."

"The doctor said you should feel better in a fortnight." Ray's voice was quiet. "You just need to take things slowly for a little while. You will be fine."

Jem shook her head, her curls sweeping across her tear-stained cheeks. "But it could have been different."

She waited for him to reach out and touch her—but he didn't. She read this as a sign. She concluded it was because she had thrown her life in danger's way again, and that the cost, this time, was too much for him. He was imagining how her choices may have left him alone with Hamish. Without her. When Merinda and Jem first started into danger, she had only to worry about a lifetime of abandoned teacups and suitors. Her husband and son were new risks.

Jem finally looked at him and watched his heartbreak in his eyes. She could hear his watch ticking in his pocket. It was the only interruption to their silence. "I want adventure," she said sheepishly after a moment. He didn't say anything in response. Ray DeLuca without words, in any language, was something Jem wasn't used to. She studied him a moment under the harsh light. "Ray?"

"I know, and yet…Jem…" He struggled for words he never found.

"You should go," she finally said. "Or the nurse will come and make you leave."

He nodded. He moved at last to touch her, but she turned suddenly, and he stole his hand away.

"I didn't mean to flinch, Ray. I'm sorry." She reached for his hand, but it was already in his pocket.

"No. No. Not your fault. Take care, Jem."

He brushed her forehead with his lips while she kept her eyes on her fingers gripping the starched white sheet.

Then the ticking of his watch and the sound of his footsteps were gone, and she was left quite alone.

Ray's hand shook so fiercely that its involuntary movement shot a spasm up his arm. He dug his knuckles into his palm. He couldn't physically plaster himself to a rickety iron chair in the cold corridor of the women's ward for the night, so he set off from St. Michael's and wove through pedestrian traffic and blinking lights. When he passed the Elgin Theatre, he looked up a moment. Atop it sat the secret Winter Garden. Their place. His memories with his Jem.

For she *was* his—until a missing rooster or cat, or a jaunt with Merinda to Massachusetts, or disguised as Silent Jim amid barrels of explosives in a Chicago warehouse.

And now…

He muttered half in English and half in Italian all of the things he wanted to say to her. The words fell, unfettered, onto the shine of the pavement.

When he arrived at King Street to collect Hamish. Mrs. Malone's concern showed on her face.

"She'll be all right." He did a frankly horrible job of reassuring the landlady, running his left hand over his face while his right clenched in a balled fist. He dug his nails deeper and deeper until he broke the skin.

"Good."

"Is Hamish asleep?"

Mrs. Malone nodded. "He's just in here." She led him to the sitting room before promising tea and sandwiches despite his protests he would be unable to consume either.

Hamish was asleep on the sofa, with a pillow under him and a quilt over him that Ray tugged more tightly to his little chin. Hamish stirred a little at his touch and almost roused completely when Ray pressed his lips to his forehead, just under the fringe of curls.

Mrs. Malone returned then with a plate of lemon sandwiches and tea.

Ray sipped slowly, and then he said, "May I use your telephone?" Several moments later, he returned to the sitting room and Mrs. Malone's watchful eye.

"All right there?" she asked kindly.

"I always kept Jem's parents' telephone number in my notebook." He smiled ruefully.

"How did they take the news?"

"Her mother has agreed to take Hamish for a little while."*

Mrs. Malone brightened. "Jemima has long wanted to reconcile with her parents."

Ray nodded. "They are not ready to meet me, or so they say, but I

---

* He spared Mrs. Malone the tone of the conversation, which was even more adverse than he feared might be the case the first time he had personal contact with Jem's estranged parents.

hope you will extend your hospitality to Hamish until Jem's mother can collect him tomorrow?"

"Of course."

Ray gave Hamish one last kiss before scooping up a few sandwiches and tucking them into a napkin, slurping one last sip of his tea, and turning toward the door.

His brain advised him to set out on the familiar course home, but his feet took him instead over the cobblestones to the *Hog*. Ray stood a moment outside the door. When he opened it, what would he do? Pace? Kick things? Smash his typewriter to smithereens? His wife was lying in a hospital bed. If the doctor hadn't walked him through the extent of her injuries—a bruised rib and a gash on the head, both likely to heal in the next week and definitely within a fortnight—he might have thought her dead.

He tried to reassure himself that she was alive and Hamish would be safe in London, a city not three hours away from him. But it was little use. The night could have ended very differently. Not the fact that he had never seen her so unhappy. The light in her voice and eyes were gone, and she just stared forward. That was worse to him than any bandage. He couldn't help but think, *She has done it again! Gone and thrown herself into action at the behest of Merinda without thought to her family or safety.*

The rational part of himself knew it was just an unfortunate incident in an automobile. Just as he had reassured her in hospital. But he was certain that automobile ride wasn't just a simple trip to Spenser's or to tea.

Ray jiggled open the lock of the old office door and made his way to his desk. He scraped his chair across the grainy floor and opened his drawer, extracting the half-written piece he had worked on about Milbrook's murder. He had always championed Milbrook and had never shied away from speaking his mind, even when it came to pointing the blame at some of the higher echelons of Toronto society. And while McCormick threatened that Ray's persistence in making enemies in high places would see them shut down, Ray had always been able to counter his editor's wariness with readership. People needed to hear the truth.

His thumb absently stroked the side of Tuesday night's almost article. He knew how to jerk the press into gear. He knew how to lay the type. He knew where the newsies lined up to dole out their coins for their bundles, and he knew where Merinda's urchins, Kat and Mouse, were most likely to bellow whatever headline he gave them without question or thought.

Montague and his puppets may well be responsible for planting white feathers and running his Jemima off the road.

Assessing his lukewarm words of the previous evening and finding them wanting, he scrunched them up and threw them into the waste-basket. But the theme ran rampant through his brain.

A fresh page. A pulse so fast he thought his heart might leap out of his chest. Fingers that sped over the Underwood before his brain could keep up.

By the time Merinda arrived home, Ray's dishes had been cleared and Hamish had been transferred to Merinda's own quarters. Mrs. Malone provided a pot and a strainer for Merinda's Turkish coffee but said little about Ray's mood.

He hates me, Merinda reminded herself, pulling her knees to her chest and staring at the empty fire grate. She had long harbored a nag-ging and wholly unwelcome feeling that one day Jem would disap-pear. Jem always protested she would want to go on adventures with Merinda, and while she spent several months after Hamish was born doing little more than discussing Merinda's cases in the comfort of the King Street parlor, she eventually began leaving the baby in the capable care of Mrs. Malone and following Merinda out once more.

DeLuca had always been cautious but supportive, understanding the part of Jem that would always stretch beyond a happy home and hearth and into the city night.

Merinda tented her fingers and exhaled. Was this just one more thing shifting in her world? The sitting room was covered with articles from all the dailies praising Jem and Merinda to the skies. Bowler hats were in fashion, society's elite emblemized their enterprise, and they had been invited to numerous soirees. Yet someone had tried to run them off the road. A year ago she might have assumed it was the Morality Squad. Montague's cronies had often attempted to stop her from tarnishing Toronto's pristine reputation, silencing women in the bargain. Of late, it seemed the opposite, with Montague needing Jem and Merinda to establish a symbol of feminine strength and agility as war loomed.

On the table beside her, Merinda kept a few reference books, chemistry formulas, a copy of the *Strand* magazine with the most recent Sherlock Holmes story, Wheaton's *Guide to the Criminal and Commonplace*, and letters from Benny Citrone tied with string.* Underneath this varied pile sat a journal she had kept in her university years. It was a habit she soon lost when she settled into deductive life.

September 10, 1905
Ainsley Women's College, University of Toronto.

All of the women here are useless. They can't string two sentences together without mentioning some silly fellow from the rugby team. "Ralph has such broad shoulders." "Nathaniel has the sweetest dimples." I want to throw my teacup at them.

It's lucky Father was able to splurge for a single room. Most of the girls share.

I keep mostly to myself, though I have become quite chummy with Jasper Forth from Vic College. We spend hours in the labs on Saturdays doing all sorts of nifty experiments. He

---

* For a comprehensive exploration of Merinda Herringford's connection to Constable Benfield Citrone of the Royal Northwest Mounted Police, please consult the case documented as *A Lesson in Love and Murder.*

*thinks I will make a fine doctor. I tell him I wonder if I will
make it to the end of term without storming out.*

*The one girl I've met here who doesn't drive me round the
bend with her incessant need to speak in frippery is Jemima
Watts from two doors down. She's a pretty thing, all right, and
all the boys in the dining hall trip over themselves to see her.
She doesn't seem to have a lot of interest in them.*

*I met her one dinner hour when the gong tolled and I
couldn't find an empty seat. She looked up and smiled and
waved me over. She didn't expect me to talk a certain way
or be a certain way. I never had to be anything but myself.
What's more, I deduced she genuinely enjoyed my company.
Whatever mystery is rampant in the dormitory—a missing
essay, a purloined love letter—Jemima Watts is always up to
the task.*

Merinda skimmed ahead. These words had been written so long
ago. Revisiting them was like reconnecting with a part of herself she
barely recognized.

*Jem will follow me anywhere. Even across the quad on a
pitch-dark night, though we all know Hart House is haunted.*

Merinda snapped the book shut. Jem *would* follow her anywhere.
From the haunted quad to the darkest corners of anywhere. She
needn't fear DeLuca's threat. And yet…something settled strangely
within her. Something that underpinned her usual buoyant and brash
confidence. Whereas the Merinda of yesteryear would have pinned
Jem's blind loyalty proudly on her lapel and brandished it as one
might a prize ribbon, she didn't want to revel. She didn't want Jem to
follow her anywhere if the ramification meant DeLuca's silence and
the loss of his friendly affection. She didn't want Jem to follow her
if it meant her friend faced the same staggering danger she had that
very day.

Merinda had just made up her mind to retire when she heard a knock at the door. She found Jasper on the step and motioned for him to be quiet as Mrs. Malone was asleep in the back of the house.

He followed her into the sitting room, and they settled onto the settee. Jasper unfolded an envelope and extracted a single sheet of paper. "Every automobile owner in Toronto must register their car, as you know. You said that the automobile you saw was of a class very similar to your own?"

"Yes."

"And we know from your description and the residue found on your car that it is green." He nudged the paper closer to her. "There are only two other citizens beside yourself who own such a vehicle in Toronto proper."

Merinda looked at the names. "The Reverend Donald MacNeill and Sir Henry Pelham."

"The Reverend Donald MacNeill is nearly a century old. I highly doubt he is the one who ran you off the road."

"But Sir Pelham?"

"Whoever is responsible was driving one of these two automobiles. Your job will be to discover which car has seen damage."

"Can't you do that?"

"Tipton will never give me leave to inquire about the accident, however unofficially. When I explained to him in passing this evening about the threat to you, he said, 'That Herringford woman is a reckless nuisance.'"

"He knows me so well," she said. But she didn't have time to dwell on Tipton's slight. Rising, she saw Jasper to the door.

"I hope you decided to heed my advice, Merinda," he said kindly, taking her hand and lightly squeezing it. He seemed surprised when she didn't draw it away. "To shelve any casework tonight and get some rest."

"Yes. Yes, of course!" she said glibly. Clicking the door shut behind him, she scurried back into the sitting room to add the names of the two automobile owners to the blackboard near the mantelpiece.

CHAPTER SEVEN

*There is nothing so befuddling as our modern world,
Merinda. I can't trace an automobile as I can trace
a lynx. I cannot fathom pursuing a wanted man
throughout the maze of concrete found in the city,
whereas, when here, all I need to be able to do is
deduce which tracks are pronounced through a blanket
of freshly fallen snow. No, my friend, you have the
more arduous task. It is with esteem and respect that
I follow your adventures through the clippings you
send from your papers. Though, I must admit, the
post has been ever so much slower arriving north here
in Fort Glenbow since the threat of war began.*

An excerpt from a letter from Benny Citrone to Merinda Herringford

Merinda woke the next morning far earlier than was her custom. She was determined to take on the world. She roused from a less-than-fitful doze in her armchair with a bellow for Turkish coffee. A few sips later, she was in front of her blackboard, fingers chalky and mind spinning.

MURDERS:
HORACE MILBROOK
ALEXANDER WAVERLEY
HANS MUELLER
JEM (almost)

The morning headlines* announced the whereabouts of Philip Carr, war agent. He was apparently inspecting the automobile factory in Hamilton, a city several miles west of Toronto. Merinda chewed her lip. She had thought of beginning where Jem and she had left off before Jem's untimely accident but decided Carr would wait.

She meant to follow up on the leads Jasper had provided regarding owners of automobiles similar to hers, but Merinda knew her promise to Heidi, her paying client, was just as important as finding the culprit responsible for their accident.† The incident at Spenser's hadn't completely left her mind, despite the disruption of Jem's accident, and she assumed Mrs. Malone would happily accompany her to visit her grandson, who worked in the loading bay.

At first the mention of Ralph's name lit Mrs. Malone's face, but then she frowned. "I am responsible for transferring young Hamish to Beatrice Watts."

"That's a new development!"

"Mr. DeLuca was here last night and arranged for Hamish to spend time with his grandparents while his wife is unwell."

Merinda wondered if Jem knew about this arrangement and supposed it was a decision DeLuca had made on her behalf. She grabbed her hat and set out the door, tapping her walking stick in rhythm with her quick pace to the streetcar. Toronto's usual energy had escalated over the tense summer months, and somehow the city seemed busier and more frenetic this late morning than Merinda was accustomed to on a midweek day.

When she arrived at Spenser's and requested to see Mrs. Malone's grandson, she again considered her growing celebrity fortunate. For not three moments later, Ralph gave her a proud though meagre tour, buoyantly indicating his particular influence on the ins and outs of

---

* "Morning" to Merinda Herringford was a loose term for her own lazy descent upon the world at a much later hour than was decent or respectable.

† Some of M.C. Wheaton's advice regarding the detective-client relationship was easier to follow than others.

the stock room and loading bay. Merinda attempted to listen with interest while her eyes narrowed on every worker, seeking any kind of sign that would indicate something was going on behind the store that hid an operation worth killing for. Perhaps a man with Hans Mueller's death on his conscience might unwittingly reveal himself.

Merinda asked Ralph about Hans, but he was summoned away before she could finish the question. He gave her a bright smile and an informal salute. Merinda bade him farewell, walking back through the stockroom at a slow pace. She supposed the most interesting exchange she had with Ralph included his excitement at the prospect of longer shifts—night shifts on the weekends and being paid double. New shipments and barges were tugging in, and men were needed to meet them at the harbor so that the goods could be transported to the loading bay.

"Apparently with the war, it's imperative that we be prepared." Ralph's enthusiasm had been genuine, but she doubted whatever Spenser had up his sleeve could be labeled as mere preparedness with the prospect of war.

Sauntering back to Queen Street, she noticed a familiar figure a half block away. "Miss Mueller!" she called across the sunny street.

Heidi Mueller wrung her hands, and Merinda noticed that her face was paler than it had been before.

"I was just at Spenser's," Merinda said. "I am determined to learn the identity of Hans's murderer."

"I didn't think I could hate this city any more," Miss Mueller said. "First my brother, and now our house in near tatters." She blinked back tears. "My little garden. We had radishes and turnips. I was so proud of it. Mama helped me when she could, and—"

Merinda wanted to curse. "They ruined that too?"

"They ruin everything!" Heidi held up her hand, her index and thumb pinching a long envelope. "I am to report as an enemy alien along with my family on the fifth day of each month."

"Enemy alien." Merinda snarled as she repeated the atrocious words.

"We go to the City Hall, and they sit us in a room and then interrogate us. If they suspect we are fraternizing with the enemy—"

"What enemy?"

"Miss Herringford, I am of German descent. These people…these officials believe that my family is as much to blame for the war overseas as those fighting in the battle."

Merinda nodded. "I read something of this new protocol in the *Globe*." She sighed heavily. "Am I correct in interpreting that anyone who is relatively new to the city from a county seemingly tied to the enemy overseas will be subject to new imposed laws?"

Heidi nodded. "It's as if I'm a visitor in my own city, Miss Herringford. An imposter in my own home. Guilty of a kind of treason merely for being born in a country that opposes Canada in this horrible war."

"I can't much help with Montague and his ridiculous fear tactics, but I can continue to try to find the man responsible for your brother's death and the vandalism in the Ward." Merinda inclined her head in the direction of the warehouse. "I've been searching Spenser's."

"Have you learned anything?"

"Your brother's murder may be linked to the other two murders of the past few days."

Heidi's eyes widened. "How?"

Merinda shrugged. "That's what I have to find out. But when I do, I will let you know everything."

"I appreciate your help."

Heidi said goodbye and walked on, leaving Queen Street to enfold Merinda with its harried brand of bustle and noise. Merinda's next plan of action was to question Reverend MacNeill, one of the automobile owners Jasper mentioned the night before. His parish was St. Stephens-in-the-Field, a long, stout, redbrick building at College Street.

A matronly secretary found Merinda wandering aimlessly in the vestry and escorted her to Reverend MacNeill's office.

Jasper was right. The man appeared to be two feet away from a crypt. But his watery gray eyes were kind as he slowly issued an invitation for Merinda to take a seat.

"Young man, it is a pleasure to have you."

Merinda looked down at her trousers, and even though her hat was off, this fellow squinted at everything. She might as well play along.

"I understand you own a green roadster?" She passed him the specifics of the model, and he held them up to his cataract-filmed eyes.

"You are interested in cars!" he exclaimed with a rusty smile. "I did own such a vehicle, but I sold it only a week ago to a friend with a parish in Mississauga." The man tapped at his temple. "Not a lot up here anymore, and not a lot to see."

"And this man drove it away?"

The reverend nodded. "I got a whole new train set in exchange."

Merinda began to tell him that he was cheated, but the fellow seemed happy enough to have given the automobile to a person he was fond of.

She bade him good day and strolled westward, her brain emphatically underlining the only other person in Toronto who owned a vehicle of the pertinent make and color: Sir Henry Pelham. And as she walked along, thinking about all that had happened to her in the last twenty-four hours, the city embraced her in the harried way it had of seeming to weave around her.

How she *loved* this city! Its progress, its populous streets, its billboards that winked in a neon carousel of light at night. The organ grinder at the mouth of the Ward, the energy that thrummed through the electric wires and over the trolley tracks and settled amid the throng moving this way and that. But she also loved Toronto because it was a mélange of people and thoughts and ideas. A girl in trousers and bowler hat was lauded for her work in an international case. A fellow like DeLuca could scrape by at the roundhouse with barely a handful of English at his disposal before working and learning and finding opportunity at a city-wide level while his readership expanded.

But Montague's new protocol demanding immigrants like Heidi report as potential enemies conjoined with the already salacious enterprises of a few of the city's most powerful men soured the otherwise perfect summer day. Would they stop with citizens supposedly aligned with the enemy from their home country? Or would Montague's fear and prejudice stretch their gnarled hands out to more and more people? Women had so long been seen as potential enemies to his city, and this improper view of them inspired the brutal tactics of the Morality Squad. Now the pervasive tactics of those who would see Toronto's newest citizens return to the lands from whence they came resulted in havoc and violence.

Merinda loved her city, yes, but she also feared it.

Once home, she noticed a strange car parked on the street, its driver leaning against the door.

He met her eyes and tipped his cap.

Inside, she met Jemima's mother.

"Hello, Beatrice," Merinda said in greeting.

"I am collecting the boy." Jem's mother seemed frozen in time. Her bearing was elegant, and she barely had a line on her porcelain skin. She had the same big blue eyes as her daughter, though her hair was a silvery blond contrasting with Jem's chestnut curls.

"Does Jem know?" Merinda asked Mrs. Malone.

"Her husband had the common sense to ring me last night," Beatrice Watts answered, reaching for Hamish.

Merinda intervened, picking up the baby and holding him a moment. He babbled and grabbed for the watch she kept fastened to her pocket. His little fingers were used to seeking it out.* "Goodbye, Hamish," she said, staring into his bright eyes a moment before transferring him to Mrs. Watts. Jem's mother gave her a curt goodbye,

---

* Merinda, of course, in general had little time for children, but she fancied Hamish more intelligent than any other of his ilk.

nodded another slightly more courteous farewell to Mrs. Malone, and then she spirited Hamish off to the waiting car.

After Mrs. Malone had returned to the kitchen to see about lunch, Merinda peeled back the lace curtain to watch Beatrice situate Hamish in the taxi. The poor fellow would die of boredom in the stuffy, stodgy nursery of his grandparents' home. Merinda bit her lip. There was little chance Jemima knew about this arrangement.

In the sitting room, she crossed off the name of the kindly minister. The more likely possibility was Sir Henry Pelham or someone who had access to his renowned collection of automobiles.

Merinda had one glaring problem. One did not just walk into Pelham Park, no matter one's celebrity status as a lady detective.

She rifled through the bureau. Though messy, it contained articles and pamphlets of the sort Holmes often made Watson fetch for him.

Merinda was hopeful that something therein would inspire her next step.

Chapter Eight

*The law is a funny thing, especially for an amateur
detective. It is so easy to want to bend it or move
around it at the interest of a client. But remember,
the police are a detective's greatest allies, and the
justice system is at the core of wanting to find
resolution to the most perplexing mysteries.*

M.C. Wheaton, *Guide to the Criminal and Commonplace*

I f two murders and one attempted murder are committed while
a fellow is in jail, then said fellow is innocent," Jasper told Kirk
while walking in the direction of his office. "Yet Tipton has yet
to sign off on the fellow's release." It bothered Jasper more than he
could say that Lars Hult sat in a cell when there was no possibility
of his having committed any offense other than being at the wrong
place at the wrong time.

After Jasper had arrived at the station, he passed Russell in the
corridor, who was seeing to a complaint from a young woman whose
shrill voice painted a dramatic scene of broken windows and gener-
alized terror.

Russell looked up, and the men locked eyes. Jasper's sympathy
met Russell's impatience.

Sighing, Jasper strode to his office and slammed the door. He
rolled a pencil over his ink blotter again and again. He had long felt
alone in the department. Perhaps that was why he was so excited
for Russell's arrival and so disappointed the more he saw that, rather

than gaining an ally, he had found yet another man willing to side with Tipton.

Jasper ran a hand through his hair, plastering the front to his forehead. What was he going to do? Part of him had long thought he went along with Tipton because, even though his chief was in Montague's pocket, he still believed that Tipton's dedication to the justice system would cut a swath through the corruption. Even when he disagreed with the chief, Jasper felt he was working toward their united goal for justice. To uphold the laws so integral to the preservation of Toronto's growth and freedom as a burgeoning city.

Jasper had always thrown himself into his duty, no matter the cost. But what was his duty if he no longer followed orders or believed in the man dictating his next move in the name of justice?

Jasper rose, opened his door, and crossed the sleek tiles in the direction of the chief's office. He tapped on the doorjamb.

"Enter!" Tipton looked up over his paperwork "Ah. Forth."

"Sir, why is Lars Hult still incarcerated? We can't keep him here."

"Why can't we?" Tipton cocked an eyebrow.

"Because he is clearly as innocent as you or I."

"Forth, sometimes you need to make an example."

"An example? An example of what? So you know he has nothing to do with these murders!"

"There's too much going on in St. John's Ward. This bull of a man has been noticed for being a bit of a vigilante. Roughing up those who—"

"I don't believe it...unless he was defending someone."

Tipton shrugged. "He may *call* it defense, but our laws are in place for a reason, and all Hades will break loose if we let citizens take those laws into their own hands."

"Sir, I'm sure he had a good reason for—"

Tipton turned back to shuffling the papers on his desk. "I remember the days when you were efficient at taking orders without these pesky questions of yours."

"We have no manpower working on the Mueller kid's death, and my friends were in a very intentional automobile accident!" Jasper said in defense of his questions. "I will see a resolution, sir, to this man's death. And to the accident as well."

"I am sure you'll try," Tipton said patronizingly. "But even your altruism would concede that Milbrook's and Waverley's murders seem a bit more calculated than a kid being roughed up at Spenser's."

Jasper barreled on. "*Roughed up at Spenser's?*" He shook his head "That's a poor euphemism for murder, sir. And I will make it so that every unlawful arrest from Montague's latest tyrant brigade is found innocent and dismissed if I have to spend the next day reading through the fine print of our police code. There is a higher law than his, sir, and yours. Justice. God. And while I have done my due diligence by both, we are at war! I will not see my city terrorized and innocent blood spilt."

"Get out of my office, Forth. I am not your friend DeLuca's silly liberal paper. Forget about all of this. Focus on one of the many outstanding tasks you have at hand."

Jasper opened his mouth to say something, closed it, and then turned on his heel.

How could he possibly focus when he was employed by a force that would see women incarcerated for merely walking after dark or possessing too short a hem? Lars was an easy target. Keep whoever was really responsible out of the limelight and frame a helpless immigrant. Lars was the physical emblem of all that was wrong with the supposed streams of justice jutting through what Montague thought was Toronto's otherwise perfect sphere.

Jasper asked Kirk for access to the holding cells and for the junior officer's keys.

Through the bars he saw Lars, his shoulders hunched, staring at his scuffed shoes.

"Tipton said you are on their watch for roughing men up in the Ward," Jasper said as Lars turned his head to look at him through the cell door.

Lars shook his head. "That's not how it is."

"Can you tell me how it is?"

"You know how they are. Those brutes. Like Forbes.* They rough up girls and drag them away. The other night I heard a noise and went outside, thinking it was just a raccoon in the rubbish, but it was a man in a mask, and he was picking up things to throw at windows. I stopped him. One of Montague's plainclothes men saw me wrestling him." Lars stopped a moment. Then he said, meditatively, "I didn't think I had done anything wrong. Nothing that any citizen wouldn't have thought appropriate." He looked up at Jasper, obviously hoping for his approval.

Jasper was silent, jangling the keys he had acquired from the officer. It would be so easy to open the cell door and let Lars free. That would be justice. That would be right. Yet his conscience ticked a little. In his heart of hearts he knew this man was no more guilty of a crime than Jasper himself. Yet, Jasper always followed code. Jasper obeyed orders. Jasper knew that to obey the laws and the higher order of justice was his duty. In this case, that meant following Tipton's orders.

"I would have done the same," he admitted after a moment. "I wish I could do more for you. I promise I will try."

Leaving Lars with a genuine though uncertain promise to work toward his release, Jasper felt deflated as he ascended the stairs from the holding cells.

"Care for lunch?" Russell asked, intercepting Jasper on his way back to his desk.

"Certainly." Jasper failed to understand this man. Russell St. Clair had been such a needed addition to the baseball team, and Jasper had been eager to welcome a man of similar age and rank to his division. Yet St. Clair harbored prejudiced views that continued to shock him.

At the Victoria Room across from the station, St. Clair settled into his pork chop with a relish. Jasper stared out the window next to him and watched the bustle of Yonge Street.

---

* One of the Morality Squad's more notorious brutes.

"I have to ask," Jasper said after a long sip of lemonade. "Why are you so averse to Toronto welcoming an immigrant population?"

"Don't you see it, Jasper?" Russell said after a swallow. "They'll take our jobs. They'll bring their kind here. To Toronto. They'll stir the pot and see to it that war comes here much as to countries overseas."

"Or, alternatively, they will keep living peacefully and try to eke out a new life for themselves and their families, thankful to have made it so far from the heart of the conflict!"

"There is violence in the Ward. You know that as well as I."

"There is violence everywhere, perhaps most exacerbated by people who are hungry and driven to anger."

St. Clair dragged the tines of his fork over the checkered tablecloth. "That fellow Milbrook? Maybe he made a promise he couldn't keep. He was *their* man. Their advocate. If they didn't like what he failed to give them, they saw him dead."

"They?"

"Jasper, it doesn't suit you to be facetious."

"Russell, there is so much good we can do. Tipton is very much…"—Jasper mulled over his words carefully—"*aligned* with Montague. But we can make sure there is a balance in the station. From officers who try to see the truth for what it is beyond any prejudice or assumptions."

Russell laughed. "I'm not the idealistic sort."

"Then why are you a policeman?"

"I like to think I am cleaning up our world."

"By allowing innocent men to be incarcerated?" Jasper leaned forward. "Lars Hult is as guilty of that crime as you or I. You know that!"

Russell shrugged. "I wish I could have your blind faith in people."

"It's not faith. It's fact. The feather found in Milbrook's car was ivory white. You think the Ward is full of ivory white birds? They're a special breed. The birds for layman such as us are rummy pigeons with homely colors!"

Russell just shrugged in response and turned his attention back to his lunch. They sat in silence for several moments. Then he said,

"Jasper, you are a police officer because you like to toe the line. And following Tipton's orders and keeping this fellow for whatever reason helps us stay in the chief's good books. In case you hadn't noticed, our city is in a financial recession *and* on the brink of war. It does us well to stay gainfully employed."

Jasper merely exhaled in frustration. His appetite gone, he watched Mouse hawk the latest edition of the *Hog* beyond the windowpane. He rapped on the glass with a knuckle and she spun, a small grin lighting up her face when she recognized who it was who wanted her attention.

He motioned her inside and set a few coins worth more than the price of the paper in her palm, accepting the *Hog* in their stead. She tipped her cap at him and bounded outside again.

Russell chuckled as Jasper spread out the paper. "There's one friendship of yours I find difficult to understand."

Jasper ignored him and began to read.

> When I first came to this country, I didn't have two pennies to rub together and a sister and nephew to support. I could barely find work, and I could barely speak English. But I found solace in my belief that the strength it took to get here would somehow make it worthwhile. I still believe in our city. I still believe that the change we experience now will lead to a future that accepts us. But that doesn't mean we have to sit by and let Montague and his men continue to see us degraded. Montague as mayor has unleashed powerful measures with his usual tinge of illegality. He molds the city into whatever shape he needs to keep it under his thumb. He doesn't inspire loyalty. He instills fear.

"You look serious."

Jasper didn't look up. "Montague's war tactics," he murmured, skimming down the page. "They just give him more power to arrest and detain whom he pleases. He's been doing this for years with his

Morality Squad, but now it looks as if there will be federal support for identifying 'enemy aliens.'"

Russell reached across the table and pilfered the paper. He licked his index finger and peeled back a few pages. "Now this is something I am interested in reading!"

Jasper followed Russell's eyes over several pictures of Pelham Park, all boasting the caption *S. McCoy*. "Grand to live here, eh?"

Jasper surveyed the tennis courts, the grand promenade overlooking the city, the ballroom, library, and pool. "They're so eager to show off they even let the *Hog* in for an exclusive," Jasper muttered before the conversations turned to different channels.

When the bill came, St. Clair accepted it and paid for both meals. Jasper thanked him, but his voice was devoid of its usual good-natured tone.

Upon their return to the station, they found Kirk attempting to sidestep Skip, who was leaning against a desk, his pen poised.

"You sure are doing a lot of ground work," Jasper noticed. "Where's Ray?"

Skip shrugged. "A quote about Waverley's death, Forth?"

"I've already said all I know," Jasper lied, thinking of the folded piece of paper in his pocket, the one where Waverley theorized on a munitions profiteering act and the shady actions of the war agent. Jasper Forth had lied less than a handful of times in his life and subsequently wondered if those on the receiving end could see right through him. Fortunately, Skip took him at his word. So Jasper added, "But I will say that his death clears Lars Hult of any suspicion."

McCoy raked ruddy hair off his face. "St. Clair?"

"I am still charged with Hult's interrogation."

"He's innocent," Jasper said grumpily. He looked at Skip. "Surely that's a stale story for the *Hog*."

"These immigrants need to solve their problem for themselves," St. Clair said, stabbing Skip's notebook with his finger. "That's a direct quote. They read your rag. Tell them we don't have the time or resources for every brawl they interpret as a reflection of a war a million miles away."

"St. Clair, we just talked about—"

"No, Jasper. You're the one who wants to see Toronto as something good and separate everything into black and white."

Jasper looked between them. He was tired of this. Sick of being the only man at the station who openly took the side of people he knew were being wronged. With DeLuca silenced, these citizens would feel completely ostracized and ignored.

He barely managed a cordial nod for Skip and St. Clair before retreating to his office.

Therein he paced, balled his hands into fists, and then shoved his fists deep in his pockets. The station suffocated Jasper. The clang and clack of telephones that had heretofore thrilled him were jeering and dissonant today. He flung open his door and bellowed for Kirk. "The keys to the cells, please!"

Kirk, surprised, dislodged them from his uniform and passed them to Jasper. Jasper stomped down to the dingy basement, a solitary light swinging with the movement of his forceful steps, and unlocked the door to Lars's cell. "You are free to go."

Behind him Kirk made to speak. "Sir…"

"Quiet, Kirk. I'll take the consequences."

Lars's eyes were wide as he took a few slow steps into the corridor, eyes blinking at the sudden wash of light. "Are you sure?"

"You've done nothing wrong. I figure the chief owes me one for years of exemplary service, and I am calling in that favor now."

"The chief will have your head, Forth," St. Clair said as Jasper led Lars to the front of the station and opened the door wide for him. They watched Lars's retreating back. Skip, still reclining against the counter, looked up in between spurts of writing in his notebook.

"Is that a direct quote?" Skip asked facetiously. "Will the chief have his head?"

"He can gladly have it." Jasper spun on his heel and walked swiftly in the direction of his office. Something ingrained in him had shifted, and he didn't recognize the man he saw in the reflection of the window.

Ray DeLuca would never be pegged as someone who possessed a particularly sunny disposition. His temper flared a little too easily, and he was too often plagued with worry as to his next paycheck. In addition, he was riddled with a most inconvenient ramification from the disastrous end to an adventure in Chicago: a right hand that trembled and shook with seemingly little provocation. This symptom was exacerbated by worry or trauma, and Jem's accident caused painful and near constant spasms rippling through the sinews of his arm.

Reporting to the *Hog* to face McCormick's inevitable wrath after a sleepless night was the furthest thing from his mind. He looked at his hand. It shuddered and shook, and even if he slowed his breath or clenched his fist, its rumbles were still felt in his upper arm.

So he took to the streets aimlessly. Ray always thought that Toronto's core was its heart, and there were few things as natural as winding through its veins and arteries. As they had countless times before, they led him to St. James's. The cathedral's golden bricks almost sparkled in the sunny light.

"How are you faring?" Ethan Talbot asked, looking up from the brass candlestick he was polishing.

"You're taking on custodial duties?" Ray asked.

"It calms me to keep this lovely world in order."

St. James was indeed lovely. Rays of sunshine spliced through the rainbowed vignettes on the stained glass windows, illuminating the carved statues of Jesus, the Madonna, and the cross adorning the front of the sanctuary.

Ray settled next to Ethan in one of the polished pews, admiring the grand purple drapery, the flowers on either side of the vestibule, and the lined candles sloping from the altar.

"Terrible few weeks, Ray." Ethan shook his head solemnly.

"Everything I touch is terrible," Ray blurted out. "Everything. Tony. Viola. Jem." He tripped over her name. "Hamish is with her parents because I can't protect him from vandals who would see me run out of town. Jem is in the hospital because..." Ray squeezed his fist tightly, not able to finish the sentence. "I would run off and go with the men, you know. Prove that I am fighting for Canada. That I am part of this." Ray used his left hand to gesture to his ear. "But they would never recruit me."

"No, they would not. Is Jemima all right?"

"Car accident. Merinda was driving, of course. Who knows what might have happened."

"Ray, would you be happy doing nothing but sitting by a fire with a glass of sherry and cozy slippers?"

"No."

"You can't sit still. You need to be a part of something. So does Jemima."

"She *is* part of something. She is a mother. She is my wife."

"Oh, piffle. You of all people know she's more than that. You could have married ten other women if that was what you wanted. A mother. A wife. Yes, she is those things. But she's more. Are you just a husband and a father? Or are you also a wordsmith and an advocate?"

Ray studied his folded hands a moment. Ink still rimmed the cuticles. "I want her to be safe."

"No one is safe. Not really. Not in these times, and any layer of protection over her life comes from a much higher power than yourself."

"Well, I hurt her. She probably thinks I am angry with her. I acted angry. I couldn't think of one thing to say." Ray gripped his hand more tightly. "I love her so much. You know I don't deserve her."

Ethan looked at the candlestick in his hand. Then he passed it and the polishing rag to Ray with an incline of his chin. "Keep your hand doing something other than making your palm bleed."

Ray took the candlestick and began deftly making circles around its circumference. There was a bit of tarnish just at the floral ornamentation near the base. He put extra pressure into the task, straightening his shaky fingers so he could polish well.

"You often come here to talk to me about what happened in Chicago." Ethan watched Ray as he worked the cloth in a methodical, calming movement. "You should talk to her about it."

"She's been through enough."

"She wants to share the dark as well as the light, Ray."

"If she wants to share anything at all." Ray's voice was low.

"In the next while, spouses, friends, fathers, mothers, and children will all say things born of a world cracking at the seams. They will say things out of anger, out of hurt, and mostly out of terror. And they will cry and weep and regret their hasty words, but at heart those who truly love them know that those words are often a reflection of insecurities and fears and have very little to do with the person they are directed at."

"But Jem—"

"Jem knows you love her, Ray."

Ray shrugged, scrubbed at the candlestick a little more, and then shrugged again. "The whole world is falling apart. Our world. The one we were just building. Me and Jem. The Cartiers. How can we possibly sew together the rift in our city if we are all drawn toward a conflict a million miles away?" He shook his head. "Without Horace Milbrook," he added sadly, knowing Ethan had always enjoyed Milbrook's company. "Milbrook was a sure chance that Montague's term would end here."

"There is something better on our horizon."

"You don't know that."

"But I do. There's a verse in the Old Testament in the book of Habakkuk. 'Wonder marvelously: for I will work a work in your days which ye will not believe, though it be told to you.'"

Ray's eyes skimmed the beautiful sanctuary. He always understood things better when he was here. "How can He do anything if I have no have power to change what is happening here? If my words never make it beyond a third-rate paper?"

"Because He's used far more unexpected vessels than a man who showed up on the very doorstep of this church penniless and with broken English. So give me my candlestick back and go find yourself a way to let the world hear you." Talbot winked. "You're little use to the hundreds of people in the Ward if you're comfortably sitting here whining to me. And tell Jemima you love her. And at the very least, show her the grace of letting her into your world. This is a sacred bower." He pointed at the high triangle of the roof with the candlestick. "But so is the space you share with her."

Ray was halfway across Church Street in the direction of the hospital when he noticed a tingle of relief in his upper arm. He retrieved his hand from his pocket. The palm was creviced with garish pink moons from his tight grip, but its trembling had lessened somewhat.

Jemima was bored out of her socks. She wondered how long she could stare at the four white walls surrounding her with only a slice of sunlight finding its way through the window in the far corner. The bed had been made and she was discharged, having been kept overnight only for observation. She sat on the metal chair and ran her palms over the knees of her wrinkled trousers.

The corridor echoed with the snoring from a bed three doors down from her own. Jemima's impatience was growing when Ray finally arrived to collect her. And though he didn't mention his silence of the night before and looked tired, he seemed a little more like himself.

"Jasper has sent Kirk round with a car," he said, taking her hand. "You are sure you are well enough to come home?"

"I'm looking forward to it. And seeing Hamish." She beamed at him, but his face was unreadable. His expression remained thus as they walked through the hallway, past the doctor who had attended

Jem, and the nurses whose faces had crossed above her last night. When they reached the doorway of St. Michael's, Ray's hands, which Jem noticed had previously been balled into loose fists, were now shoved deep in his pockets. The tick of a clock nearby echoed over the linoleum and through the hollow corridors. Jem looked about her at plastic plants and uniformed orderlies, while Ray fixated on the street outside awaiting the young officer's promised arrival.

Kirk swerved over to the curb outside their townhouse, and they thanked him. Ray helped Jem get out of the car, and then he placed his arm around her back as he helped her up the walkway and toward the door.

"Oh!" she said. "I forgot about the window."

Ray had done a crude job of patching it up with boards. The post was waiting on the verandah, and amid the usual bills and notices, Jem noticed one envelope addressed to Ray from City Hall.

Once they were inside and Jem was comfortably settled on the sofa, he ripped it open and grimaced. "That didn't take long," he muttered.

"What?"

"A precautionary measure in accordance with Mayor Montague's measures of impending war. 'All enemy aliens must report to City Hall at the beginning of the month with papers in order and…'" He read the rest before capping "to ensure those late of a country opposing our allied forces are established as above reproach and dedicated to Canada. God save the King."

Jem's eyes went the ceiling, then moved toward the window, and then back to the ceiling. "It's preposterous. You have to write something about it."

"I have to choose my hills, Jem."

"You cannot pretend this isn't happening. Maybe this is your moment, Ray. The reason you have had this platform all these years."

"You were almost killed, and someone vandalized our house." He rubbed his hand over his face. "I have to choose my words carefully. I have to…"

Jem waited for him to finish his thought, knowing he wanted to say something shattering and type until his hands cramped up. When he didn't speak, she said quietly, "I'm not the only one caught between adventure and our life here."

"I'm sorry, Jem. I didn't hear you."

"Just thinking aloud." She exhaled. "I was thinking of sending round for Hamish this afternoon."

"I…I rang your mother," he said after a moment.

"Excuse me?"

"Your mother is taking care of Hamish while you recover."

"Ray DeLuca, you had no right to do that!" Jem wanted to rise and face him down, but her rib smarted. "You didn't even consult me? You want me to recover, so you take my little boy away from me?"

"You would have sent him to Mrs. Malone's anyway," Ray snapped.

"Ray…you don't have to speak this way."

"You almost died, Jem!" He found the words that had evaded him the evening before. "I felt as though I had cracked in half! You were so pale and your eyes…I never want to see you like that again. I was devastated and heartbroken and so angry at anyone who would hurt you."

"It wasn't my fault. You said—"

"You talk about family, about Hamish. If you cared more about *our family*, Jemima, you wouldn't have risked your life."

Jem watched Ray's eyes shine helplessly and his body deflate. "You think I don't care about our family?" Her voice sounded like broken glass.

"Jem, I didn't…" He reached to touch her, but she flinched away.

"Yes!" she said between gritted teeth. "You did mean it! As if I *intentionally* did this to myself!"

Ray raked his fingers through his hair. Jem noticed the gray was more prominent at his temples than before. Was it just the light?

"What do you want, Jem?"

"You will *not* ask that question of me!" Now her voice was steel.

"Jem, you are a mother. You are a wife. This is of your choosing." His hand swept the circumference of the living room from boarded window to sunken sofa. His eyes flicked to the discarded letter demanding his reporting to City Hall. He swallowed and then said, "This is *our* home, and you need to decide what you want most. Didn't it become as clear to you in that hospital bed as it did to me? Was the risk not too great this time? The consequences…Hamish could have grown up without a mother! And I had to imagine a life without you."

Jem tried to speak, but her throat was filled with a lump. When her voice finally came, it was little more than a whisper. "You said in the hospital that I had been in automobiles several times before. That…" She took a breath. "Do you realize what a contradiction you are being? I cannot be everything to you, Ray DeLuca. I cannot be the spirited woman you married and a mother and your wife and live in these rigid regulations just because you had a momentary scare. You cannot fit women into boxes. I am all of these things. And you want me at home, but you also want me at Merinda's, and you want…you…" she trailed off.

"That experience, Jemima. The one where…" He squeezed his eyes to block a million imagined scenarios where the outcome was not a safe and sound Jemima standing defiantly in front of him. "Jem, I can't do it anymore." His right hand, she noticed, was shaking. A rippled trace of the action that had sent his brother-in-law, Tony, to his death in Chicago. She wondered if he would ever be completely free of it.

He drew a jagged breath "The world is shifting. I cannot say what darkness will happen upon us next. I need you to be safe. I need you to be my fixed point. For my sake but for also for Hamish's. My little boy *will* not grow up without a mother."

Jem shook her head, at first a small movement that picked up speed. "I am not a fixed point. You cannot ask me to be something that I am not. I need to move. I might change. I have never once asked you to be anything but what you are."

"I know."

"I support what *you* do!"

"I know that."

"And here you are saying you can't do it anymore. What can't you do, Ray?"

"I think you need to leave, Jem."

"Why? Because of the window? Because of the accident? Because we're fighting? You make little sense."

How had she failed to notice that while his right hand slowly shook, his left curled around the discarded missive he had received from City Hall.

"Because I refuse to humiliate you. I refuse to drag you down with me. Can't you see?" He exhaled. "Jem, I am a proud man. I cannot have you tugged along with me while I register under Montague's orders."

"We share a last name!"

Ray shook his head. "No, we don't. Not to Toronto we don't. Not in the papers. Right now, I prefer it that way."

"I'm not ashamed of you. I went into this marriage with eyes wide open, Ray. Do not lessen my choice."

He scratched the back of his neck. "There is little for you here right now. A broken window. An empty larder. No Hamish."

"*You* are here right now."

Ray said something in Italian before shaking his head. "I am going to go to the office. And when I get back, I think I would feel better if you were at Merinda's."

"Is...is that what you really want?"

"It's not safe for you here. It's also not safe for you there running around with that woman, but at least I can count on you being sane enough to give yourself time to recover. And you'll have Mrs. Malone."

"Why are we arguing, Ray?" Jem's voice hovered just above a whisper. "I don't even understand this argument. I think you're trying to tell me what you want me to be, but it's so many different things at once." She reached out and grabbed his forearm. "I don't understand you."

"Be careful with your case," was all he said as he disappeared into the kitchen. "I'll ring Jasper to send Kirk by to take you to King Street."

Jem sat stunned a moment. All she had thought about in that cold, sterile hospital room was the safe bower of home.

She took a deep breath, straightened her shoulders, and opted to take the world straight on. She had reserves of strength. She had Hamish, and she had Ray to some extent, and she had a battle fresh for the taking in Toronto.

Jem's eyes went around the perimeters of the empty sitting room. The grandfather clock's tick unsettled her. She rose and left through the narrow hallway, taking the stairs slowly, her rib still aching with a stinging stiffness. Once in her bedroom, a ray of sun highlighted the dust shrouding the furniture, reminding her that, yes, the home she wanted was so often unattended, a transient stop between adventures.

She swiveled to face Hamish's crib. He had his favorite teddy bear and blanket, but a secondary quilt, recently laundered, was folded over the side. Jem pressed it to her nose. *Hamish.* If she were the woman Ray wanted her to be, she would be with him now at her childhood home, ensuring he had his favorite treats, singing him lullabies, and kissing the silky hair of his soft head.

She took her case from its place beside the bureau and lined it with lavender-scented sheets. Then she began packing, carefully folding in lace and tweed, brogans and stockings, as she tried to resist the persistence of her brain in revisiting the baffling disagreement they had just had. He wasn't himself, she decided as she folded a few perfumed handkerchiefs and tucked them into the lining of her case. In this occupation she recalled something Ray had said to her in a long-ago adventure.* *Empathy is the greatest gift.* She couldn't begin to imagine some of the families being torn apart. The Muellers mourning young Hans, the mothers preparing to send off their sons with knitted socks and scarves into the unknown mire of the war. She was in the middle of her own loss. Not as desperate, but still keenly felt.

She would just have to rely on Merinda and her brand of incessant hyper-energy to throw her into a case and out of self-pity.

---

* Ray DeLuca's profound statement on the human condition is documented in *A Singular and Whimsical Problem.*

Chapter Nine

Those labeled as suspicious can be held on apprehension of sedition. Their mail can be confiscated and read if from a country supposedly allied with the Central Powers. With very little provocation and with the best interests of Toronto at hand, arrest without warrant may be enforced.

From Mayor Tertius Montague's Plan of Enactment

*G*od uses broken vessels. Ray remembered something Ethan Talbot had once said. He'd remembered several things Ethan had said when he argued with Jemima. Funny that every sane, salient word that had ricocheted through his brain on his way to pick her up from the hospital disappeared when he faced her. Perhaps he was never more broken than at that moment, having just found momentary renewal with Ethan only to lash out at Jemima. What was it that made him think that he could exact things of her he wouldn't of himself? The prospect of throwing himself into work was often a reprieve when his thoughts spun as rapidly as they did at the moment.

Ray knew Skip would pester him about Jem's accident, McCormick would berate him for not being at work at his appointed time, and he would scrape together words about the plight that had just been doled out to him even as the war loomed far away and the election was near.

Nonetheless, he boarded the trolley at the edge of Yonge and transferred at King, a route he could navigate with his eyes closed.

When he finally alighted at Trinity Street, he took the last leg to the *Hogtown Herald* office amid the cobblestones and industrial structures of Corktown at a slower pace, drawing out the feeling of sunshine on his face before retreating into the dank cave of the office.

When he arrived, the door was open, ushering in the sunlight. Ray found that strange because even though keeping the door closed trapped the summer humidity inside the ramshackle building, it allowed Skip to work with his photographs.

When he walked through the doorway, he nearly collided with Jasper Forth.

"Jasper!" His voice held surprise.

"Ray…" Jasper began to explain, but as soon as Ray looked over his friend's broad shoulder, he focused only on the upturned furniture and discarded paper all over the floor.

The first time Ray met McCormick, he was told the story of William Lyon Mackenzie, the rebel leader of a failed revolution whose presses used to rail against the elite before they were dunked into Lake Ontario.

Here, amid the chaos of the ransacked *Hog* office, he could make out their skeletons.

"You're out, DeLuca!"

Ray hardly heard his editor as he surveyed the office in tatters. Newsprint fluttered about like misshapen confetti. Inkwells had been spilled, chairs were knocked over, and desks were breached. Upon moving at a slow diagonal through the carnage, Ray noticed that his desk was the most assaulted, his beloved Underwood near unrecognizable. The keys popped up jaggedly, the springs and gears spurting at unnatural angles.

"You're out, DeLuca," McCormick repeated. The little hair the editor had left was plastered to the globe of his forehead with perspiration.

Ray looked to Jasper, who had followed him. "When did this happen?"

"Skip rang this morning. I didn't know whether you were preoccupied. How's Jem?"

"Safe enough at Merinda's," Ray said absently, running his finger over the edge of his destroyed workspace. The pad of his finger came away black with ink. He rubbed it on his wrist.

"DeLuca!" McCormick stood on the other side of the desk, his watery gray eyes near popping out of their sockets. "You ran that Milbrook piece. This is on account of you! How many times—"

"You won't have any content without me!" Ray was adamant. "You will have nothing to print. You think Skip can get you your readership? Your exclusives?" Ray fingered his collar. "This piece will sell a storm. It hasn't even gone to print yet! Print it, McCormick!"

"Who cares if it sells a storm if we're shut down in a fortnight?" McCormick cursed. "Look at this office!" He flung out his hand to the carnage. "If I want to salvage anything of a paper that I personally invested in long before you stepped onto the scene, I need to do so now. This is my livelihood. I always let you get away with things! I always let you—" He raised a hand, stopping himself. "There is no sense talking to you about any of this, is there? You don't care."

"Perhaps," Jasper intercepted with a level voice, "this is not the time. Ray, what is this piece?"

"I am surprised anyone saw it. I came here last night, after…" he used his hands to draw out the rest of the sentence. "But I didn't *do* anything."

"You intended to distribute them?" Jasper asked.

"I hadn't…I hadn't decided. I just needed to finish it. How did you know about it?"

"It was plastered on the front door when I arrived this morning." McCormick was livid. "And you are *out.*"

"Maybe it has nothing to do with the article. Maybe it has to do with me," Ray surmised. "Someone threw a rock through my front window the other day. Attached was a rather nasty note."

"You never mentioned it," Jasper said.

McCormick was sourly muttering, unconcerned with the possible tie to the previous threat.

"I was preoccupied."

"Pack up what is left of your things, DeLuca."

"Mr. McCormick, this may have nothing to do with Ray's article. As he says, who had time to see it?"

"It doesn't matter, Constable. I can't afford to have this place explode. I cannot conceive what the damage here is. What the cost—"

"I need an outlet!" Ray slammed his fist on his broken desk, leaving it if possible in an even worse state. "No one else is brave enough to speak up for the corruption here!"

McCormick pretended not to hear him. "So you create your Cartier Clubs and you rail against Montague, not caring a hang for anyone else? Do you ever think that maybe I toe the line and Skip toes the line because we are in a recession and we need the money as much as you do?"

"You need me! I *am* this paper, McCormick. I have always been willing to do things no one else would!"

"Until the moment you decided to do something that would see us run into the ground! I am playing ball, DeLuca. We have always disagreed on this, and I respect your passion for reform. But I have a wife and family to feed!" He shook his head. "You're a bright writer. You're a bright man. But your temper and your impetuous need to find corruption in every corner is a hindrance! I should have done this years ago."

"I need this job. You know I do. We have a history, McCormick. You owe me one! I have a wife and family too!"

"Mr. McCormick—" Jasper interceded, but McCormick was a train on an unending rail.

"I owe *you* nothing! I never had any debt to you! I took you on because Ethan Talbot told me he had found a smart young man willing to do anything with words! I saved you from the rubbish heap. But no more. You're out!"

"This paper will not function without me!" Ray exclaimed, summoning a courage he did not feel.

"Don't have such a high opinion of yourself, DeLuca. If it wasn't your raking Montague over the coals, it would be something else.

Didn't you just say your window was smashed a few days ago? They'd come knocking to run you out of town on a rail. This is better for both of us."

Ray looked over what was left of his makeshift desk. Papers were fanned out around it, ink stickily covering the scraped surface.

He's been in a fog. He was impulsive, certainly, but he always tried to toe the line as well, and when he didn't he was perfunctorily apologetic.

The hardest to bear of the wreckage surrounding him was his Underwood. His most prized possession.

He had been so proud of it. It was sleek despite its secondhand status and broken *H* key. He knew the sound of it and the familiarity of its perimeters under his fingers. It was so much of who he was. Now, numbly, he saw the end of his tenure at the newspaper as through a film or dream.

He collected the shards of almost a decade of his life and slowly, vacantly walked in the direction of the doorway, Jasper close behind.

Then he turned, an instinct to ensure every inch of his workspace was rid of any half written article or photograph of Jemima or…

He crossed the floor and inspected it, even lurching open the desk drawers one last time. Slamming shut a scarred drawer again, he almost didn't notice Skip standing over him.

"You're out then, Mr. DeLuca?" the photographer pushed his glasses higher on his nose.

"It appears so," Ray said through gritted teeth. "Your camera?"

"I had it with me. I have little respect for a man who would try to get this operation shut down."

Ray swallowed. "I have little respect for him too," he said ruefully, turning and walking out the rickety door and onto the cobblestones a final time.

Jasper was right beside him, but Ray was drained of words in either Italian or English and sauntered silently on.

"This may be an inconvenient time, but…"

"I didn't run that article, Jasper! Whoever did this did it for some other reason altogether." He cursed in his first language and then stopped in his tracks. Jasper followed suit.

"I have no idea yet what that would be, Ray, but I need to know if the article had anything to do with munitions."

"What? No. I mean, I speculated on it, but…the point is the article…no one saw that article. I was working on it last night because after Jem…I went a little…"

Jasper nodded. He understood. He similarly had difficulty functioning after seeing Merinda so distraught at the garage.

"How closely were you working with Alexander Waverley?"

"Not at all. Not outside of the Cartiers." Ray smiled ruefully. "It's no secret I wanted to work for his paper."

Jasper reached into his jacket pocket. "This was in Waverley's desk. We found it after we were notified of his death." He handed a folded piece of paper to Ray, who took it with eager interest. Opening it, he saw several lines of thoughts and ideas that pertained to Ray and the *Hog*.

"He wanted you to do what he could not."

"He seemed to anticipate what Montague was going to do." Ray's eyes settled on the elegant slant of the editor's old-fashioned handwriting. This was not newspaperman's shorthand. "This is so neat and precise."

"He wanted it to be legible."

"Do you think it's a clue to his murder?"

"I think it's a clue to him *knowing* his murderer. His desk was neatly arranged, but the desk drawer was jammed at an awkward angle. Which leads me to think that he recognized his attacker when he saw him in the doorway and quickly shoved this piece of paper into this desk."

"And now it is an unintentional last message," Ray said, turning it over.

"This war agent held quite a bit of interest to our editor friend."

"Indeed." Then Ray sighed. "Well, there's little I can do with it now, Jasper. I don't have a press."

"You'll find something to do with it."

"I am scarcely in the mood for your unfailing optimism—"

"You'll find something to do with it," Jasper repeated.

They walked Trinity Street in silence. Around them, the world moved on despite the full stop halting Ray's life. The trees were just beginning to exhibit the first of their red leaves, the grass whistled in the slight wind, and Corktown children played hide-and-seek around the leaning cottages.

"What am I going to do, Jasper? I sent my wife to Merinda's, and my little boy is hours away. I have no means of providing for them anyhow."

Jasper crossed his hands behind his back and kept his face forward, selecting his words carefully. "I think, for now, you keep that brain of yours turning, you put one foot in front of the other, and you remember that there is always another door."

"That's a little too..." Ray reached for a word. "...vague for this moment. If you think I will go home and make a cup of tea..."

Jasper shook his head. "Immediately? No. Immediately, you and I are going to go patch up that broken window of yours."

Merinda nearly pounced on Jem the moment she stepped into the front hallway.

"Owww!" Jem cried as Merinda's arms flew around her, inadvertently putting too much pressure on her hurt rib.

"Oh." Merinda stepped backward, assessing Jem from the top of her hair, over her pale face, to her boots. "Well, you're in one piece," she said, leaning in to squeeze Jem's shoulder but opting to pat her awkwardly on the head instead.

Once Jem had given her friend a truncated account of her temporary return to the townhouse, Merinda concocted a plan for her convalescence, which Jem subsequently learned involved keeping Jem so busy in solving their unsolved cases she had little time to feel sorry for herself.

"Do you need tea?" Merinda asked impatiently, strolling in front of the mantel. She hadn't been able to sit still, opting instead to watch Jemima as she settled on the settee and drew a quilt over her legs.

"No, I'm fine."

"Ill?"

"Just a headache."

"Can you walk?"

"A little. Not at any frenetic pace."

"So you are not averse to distracting yourself of the unfortunate circumstances of the past day and a half by joining me?"

Jem shook her head. "It will do me good."

"I will convince you it will." Merinda ignored the deflation in her friend's voice, flashing a Cheshire grin before turning her head in the direction of the kitchen. "Mrs. Malone, please see Jemima's bag to her room!"

Jem slowly disengaged herself from the quilt and rose, while Merinda pointed to the blackboard and the little progress she had made in both the white feather incidents and the Mueller case. Merinda retrieved the feather from the roadster from the bureau, now wrapped in a *Papier Poudre* sheet to keep its shape and properties. "We found this in the automobile."

"How is your car?"

"Couldn't matter less," Merinda said, flippantly. "My first plan was to meet with Philip Carr, but he is out of town on business. So then I thought it would be worthwhile to attempt to find out who ran us off the road." She bounded into the hallway and grabbed her bowler from the hat stand. Jemima trailed slightly behind.

"I had a horrible row with Ray."

Merinda scowled. "So did I."

"Oh."

"And I saw your mother." Merinda's voice was somber. "She took Hamish."

"That was part of what our row was about," Jem said quietly, stealing a look in the glass, unimpressed with her askew curls and the dark circles under her eyes. With the roadster in the police garage and Merinda with no immediate desire to replace the automobile,* they set to walking to the trolley stop in the sticky sun.

"Fortunately, Jasper was able to provide some information about the automobile we believe is responsible for the accident," Merinda said, walking at a slower pace to compensate for Jem's getting her bearings straight. "There are only two owners with that type of car. I have proven one innocent on account of his being…well, aged. The other is Sir Henry Pelham."

"Sir Henry Pelham!"

Merinda reached into the pocket of her shirtwaist and extracted a small piece of paper, which she passed to Jem.

Rifle practice
White feathers
Ornithology
Automobiles—Pelham

"Ornithology?"

"The study of birds and their patterns. A subsection of zoology. Find the feather, find the culprit!" Merinda clapped as the trolley arrived with its familiar clang and ding. Not a half hour later they alighted at the edge of the wide University of Toronto campus, familiar to Merinda for her almost weekly experiments with Jasper.

They crossed over a soft carpet of manicured grass toward Trinity College, a neo-Gothic institute whose hallowed corridors housed a department of Animal Biology.

Grand, cathedralesque windows ushered in the sunlight, while Tudor-style beams crisscrossed over domed ceilings. Portraits of important chancellors watched as sentinels, their legacy bannered over the stoned walls.

Professor Paul Monroe's office was perched in a turret atop a winding staircase, which caused Jem considerable effort.

The scholar welcomed them with a crooked smile, simultaneously nudging his spectacles higher over his nose. Wiry gray curls flounced

---

* Or ever to drive again.

on either side of his nearly bald head. He was dressed in the ceremonial attire of a tenured professor, but his shoes, just visible under his billowing robes, were scuffed.

"This is quite the collection." Merinda beamed while Jem shuddered. Stuffed birds and models and skeletons were a gruesome menagerie atop tomes and folders. His walls were covered with diagrams and scrawled Latin.

"You are the lady detectives. I recognize you from the papers."

"Surely you have heard about the late Horace Milbrook?" Merinda asked.

"Ah, yes. Poor fellow run through with a knife on the night of the war announcement."

"He was found with a white feather on his chest."

The professor clucked his tongue.

"As was Alexander Waverley, the editor of the *Globe*," Jem added.

The professor was visibly taken aback. "I have not yet had a chance to see any of the papers today," he said somberly. "Such tragedy."

Merinda nodded. "Which is why it is imperative that we find a solution as quickly as we can before the killer has a chance to strike again."

"May I see the feather?" A note of urgency was in the professor's voice.

Merinda reached for the feather from the roadster. "This feather is not from either body, but it seems to match almost perfectly with those found with both corpses."

Professor Monroe accepted it and carefully detached it from its *Papier Poudre* bower, turning it over and over in his ink-stained hand. "Do you know the significance of white feathers during a time of war?"

"I remember a popular novel inspired by the war against the Boers," Jem contributed. "In that story, the feather was a symbol of cowardice."

The professor nodded. "This is a *columbidae* feather," he assessed. "Definitely of the pigeon and dove family."

"Were these the same feathers made famous in the conflict against the Boers?" Jem asked.

"I believe so." Monroe passed the feather to Jem. "They were known as a release dove or a homing pigeon in the latter part of the nineteenth century because they knew how to find their way home. Messenger birds."

"I've seen a thousand pigeons in the city," Merinda mused, accepting the feather Jem held out, wrapping it up again, and then tucking it into her pocket. "But none as white as this feather."

"Mostly these doves are specially bred for ceremonial purposes. They are not your typical Toronto pigeon hovering around crumbs and whatnot."

"Do you know of any breeders in Toronto?"

"The Pelham family keeps an impressive collection." He straightened his collar.* "The rare privilege of consultation on the family's collection was bestowed upon me before they found a resident ornithologist."

Jem and Merinda exchanged a glance.

"Indeed?" Merinda said. "Well, Professor." She grabbed his hand and shook it enthusiastically. "You've been a great help."

They left him amidst his dusty books, the stuffed birds' beady glass eyes following their exit.

"One does not just walk into Pelham Park," Jem said, as they maneuvered slowly down the spiral staircase and back into the shimmering blue.

"We'll just have to get an invitation."

"I recognize that look." Jem peered closely at her friend.

"What look? Honestly, Jemima, I am probably just squinting funnily because of the sun."

"You have an idea on how to get an invitation to Pelham Park?"

"Precisely how severe was your row with DeLuca, Jem?"

---

* And then proceeded to sound as if he had been given the parish at Rosings Park.

"Why do you ask?"

"Because we are going to the *Hog*."

Jem conceded, but only under condition that they take a taxi. Merinda happily obliged.

"Everything from tennis matches to the swimming pool to the preferred turbot sauce," Merinda said as they were underway. "Skip has been photographing all of it. He might have need of an assistant. I am sure we can convince him to return to Pelham Park."

They exited at King and Trinity Streets and walked down to the *Hog* offices.

"Take a deep breath, Jemima! I'll lead the charge."

"Ray will be furious with me for being out with you so soon, and I don't want to say anything even stupider than I did in our argument earlier."

"You are always a lady. Even when you're a man."

Jem's soft laugh rippled through the air.

Once they reached the office, they found the door wide open.

Inside, Skip was bent over his desk, snipping at photographs. He looked up, jarred, before registering them.

"Oh my!" Jem gasped at the extensive damage. It hurt her heart. It was so much about Ray and how they met and who they were and…"Where's Ray?"

"Hello, Miss Herringford. Mrs. DeLuca."

"How's it faring, Skip?"

He pushed his tawny hair back from his forehead. "Ray is no longer employed here. I was sure he would have told you."

Merinda grabbed Jem's elbow to steady her.

"They did quite a number on this place," Merinda said. Though the photographer had begun restoring the ransacked office, Jem and Merinda still took in the toppled desks and bashed presses.

Sawdust and pulp permeated the air, while bits of paper were covered in a film of the same and besmirched the floor. Jem walked slowly toward Ray's work area and audibly gasped when she saw the damage therein.

"Are they going to arrest who did this?" she asked Skip.

"Why would they? It was most likely Montague's men. Tipton won't care. We'd had several warnings." Skip ran a nail over one of his clippings. "Someone found an article Ray had been working on about Montague. Odd, even for him. Something really upset him."

"I can only imagine." Merinda looked pointedly at Jem.

"It's my fault," she breathed.

"So if you can't write about the mayor and his corruption," Merinda said, moving a fingertip in circles around the smudged surface of a desk, "what are you going to write about?"

"There's the white feather murderer."

"Clever." Merinda wanted to exchange a look with Jem, but her friend was leaning over Ray's old desk. Merinda joined her.

"Ray loved this typewriter," Jem said, her eyes misting. "It was a present from Ethan Talbot. Secondhand and not the most modern model, but it was his own."

Merinda sighed. Even she knew about Ray's love for that old typewriter. She picked it up for a moment. Its gadgets and keys were berserk, the levers and bars bent.

"Merinda!" Jem gasped.

"What?"

"Look!"

In the empty space left by the typewriter, and in the middle of the outline it had made in the old wood, sat a smushed white feather. It wasn't as pristine as the one they found in Milbrook's car or the one left in Jem's side of the roadster; but it had the same shape and ivory tint as the first two.

"What?" Skip appeared,

"Nothing," Merinda hedged, quickly shoving the feather in her pocket. "We're just surprised at how long this poor mangled typewriter was on the desk. It left its imprint. The desk will never be quite rid of it."

"You sure you're talking about a typewriter, Merinda?" Jem asked softly, caressing the edge of the desk.

"Yes, well…Skip! Business!"

Skip folded his arms over his chest. "Which is…"

"Your pulse on Toronto society. The Pelhams."

"I can't help you. Do you know how many times I was turned away? Why do you want to go there anyway?"

"A case," Merinda explained. "I will give you first dibs on the story."

"You overestimate my interest in you now that Mr. DeLuca has left," Skip said.

"Oh, please, Skip," Jem pleaded. "Ray was always helping you."

He shrugged. "If you want into Pelham Park, you're best to try your hand at something with Lady Adelaide." He returned to his desk to retrieve a paper that he handed to Merinda.

Lady Adelaide Pelham is pleased to chair the Ladies Auxiliary and Women's Patriotic League.

The inaugural meeting is to be held at St. James Cathedral

Monday, the third of August, 1914
at seven o'clock in the evening

"That's tonight!" Jem said, her eyes widening over the date.

"Much obliged, Skip," Merinda said brightly. She looped her arm with Jem's and tugged her gently toward the door. Jem swept one more lingering look around.

Outside was a study in contrast. The sun was bright, the clouds were scattered about the sky, and the tang of hops and barley flirted with the tang of summer humidity in the heavy air.

Back on the main stretch of King Street they found a taxi, which Jem was adamant they take to Cabbagetown. But when they arrived, they found the townhouse empty. They noted that Ray had been there, at least. The broken window was now boarded up in an attempt to render the home secure in lieu of replacing the glass. Jem walked slowly through her home, each wall seeming to whisper something—a lost snatch of laughter, a moment she'd shared with Hamish. Now, it was so bare. So still.

"Ray?" Jem called.

"You know he's not here, Jem," Merinda said softly.

"I just…"

"Come on," Merinda coaxed. "There's nothing for us here." She grabbed Jem's elbow and led her to the front door. "At least the raccoons won't get in," Merinda said, referring to the boarded window.

They instructed the driver in the direction of the Wellington, a diner Ray frequented.

Jem kept her nose planted to the windowpane, scanning the pedestrian traffic on sidewalks and under every striped awning, and around the large buildings at the arcade at Yonge as they trundled toward the east side of King Street. As the driver swerved outside St. James, Jem wondered if Ray even wanted to be found.

*Beyond the obvious devotion she must demonstrate
toward her husband and her family, a woman must
prove that she is also dedicated to the well-being of others,
both in her own community and her country at large.*

Dorothea Fairfax, *Handbook to Bachelor Girlhood*

Jasper's return to the stationhouse after assisting Ray with a crude and short-term solution to his front window was a somber one. He was in a wretched mood after listening to his friend's despair over everything: McCormick's dismissal of him, his inability to heed Ethan's advice, that Jem wasn't home waiting for him after all.

When Kirk informed Jasper that Tipton requested an audience, he was surprised that his first inclination wasn't to follow orders with his customarily punctilious fashion, but rather to cut and run.

He hadn't seen eye to eye with his commander for as long as he could remember. He wondered if the chief had something to do with Ray's dismissal.

"Sir," Jasper said after being given leave to enter.

"Where were you all morning, Forth?"

"Skip McCoy rang about the *Hog*. Someone has seriously damaged the newspaper office. McCormick sacked Ray DeLuca."

"I fail to understand you. You want to make sure that I am paying attention to this white feather business and to the files you have presented me on the Ward, and you, a senior constable, take half of your shift to see about a little vandalism at a rag newspaper."

"Sir—"

"We do not pull in special favors for friends here, Forth. Because you are so eager to help with such situations, perhaps it's time I reassess your duties."

"You cannot put me back on traffic duty. I—"

"Hush, Forth. For now, you can see to a skirmish in the Armories while I decide how best to use your particular *talents*."

"You know my talents."

"Right now they seem best suited to discovering who threw rocks through windows." Tipton's voice was far from complimentary. "Take St. Clair and see to this fist fight."

"If it's the Armories, I am sure military police are nearby."

"Not for two men on the outside of the facilities merely waiting to sign up," Tipton explained

Jasper wanted to say at least a dozen things in retort. Nevertheless, he counted to ten, bellowed for Kirk, and tucked his annoyance under his hat.

A short ride later, the three men stood outside of the overbearing brick structure that seemed to gobble up half of University Avenue from Queen Street. Turrets and flags lent the place a regal motif, while the half-moon windows recalled the grandeur of the city's most opulent offerings of the past century.

Jasper told Kirk to wait nearby, and he gave them a small salute. As St. Clair and Jasper walked through the front doors and toward the front desk, they were intercepted by a man draped in regulation khaki with boots Jasper could see the overhead lamp's reflection in.

"Tipton sent you, eh?" His voice was clipped perfunctorily. "Follow me. You are welcome to use one of our training rooms for your interview."

"Very kind of you, sir," Jasper said.

They entered a small classroom where, seated at a desk facing a blackboard full of military tactics, a man held a handkerchief to a bloody nose. In the seat adjacent sat another young man with a purple bruise undercutting his eye.

"Why are the police involved in what appears to be a fist fight?" one of the two seated men asked Jasper.

"Once you are in the trenches in France, we subscribe to a different law. But for here, for now, you are Toronto citizens and must abide by our laws," St. Clair began. "I expect the truth."

"What were you fighting about?" Jasper asked calmly.

"Tensions were high at the enlisting tent," the accused said. "This fellow shoved me, and now he reports me to the police."

"The lines were crowded, and you stepped out of your way to get into my space."

Jasper was remembering too many conversations of a similar ilk—men flinging blame about like snow in a snowball fight—from his demotion to traffic patrol.*

"Well..." St. Clair hedged.

"My little brother was the target of a bully on Center Street last night, and this was the bully," the young man said, jerking his thumb at the man beside him.

The other remained silent while St. Clair approached his desk. "A bully?"

"With reason, sir," the man said. "This fellow's brother was seen with a bunch of *Kraut* kids. They could have been a gang. Who knows what kind of meeting they were coming from?"

St. Clair stood back, folded his arms, and turned his direction to the accuser. "Is this so?"

"These are his school chums! He came home with a black eye and bloody nose. Just for playing stick hockey with *school chums.*"

"Stick hockey?" the accused retorted. "That can account for numerous sins." He leveled eyes with St. Clair. "Sir, I am enlisting so that I can fight the very evil I encountered on Center Street last night. I believe that their tactic is to instill this philosophy in the young and turn them against us. My father encountered enough of this with the

---

* A disciplinary measure that had occurred more than once during his association with Merinda Herringford.

Boers, sir, and he knows that Canada does not have room for those who are slaughtering our men on the field. Any day now, and they will turn on us."

Jasper stepped forward to control the situation, but he was superseded by St. Clair.

"This young man," he pointed to the accused, "makes a salient point. And we know that violence begets violence."

"Are you going to charge us?" the accuser asked.

"I would charge *you*," St. Clair mulled. "Partly for your blindness and stupidity. But for the time being, I am hoping the two of you will shake hands like men, and you will keep a closer eye on your little brother."

The men rose and limply shook hands, the accused wiping his nose on his sleeve.

"If you're truly going to see action overseas," Jasper said, halting them as they made their way to the door, "you can expect skirmishes and tensions that run far higher than this, and you will want to do your country and your mothers proud by behaving like men."

They both nodded at him and mumbled something that could have been "sir" before setting off.

St. Clair and Jasper took their time through the corridors of the Armories before starting a brisk walk toward the station.

"St. Clair, the more time I spend with you, the more I realize that we approach everything about our work and the war from completely different angles. You honestly believe that this young man's brother is in league with the Kaiser for playing stick hockey with German boys in the Ward?"

St. Clair adjusted his hat brim. "We can never be too careful, Jasper. Besides, we go round and round in circles on this point. You're a right good cop. A corker at your job. But we need our minds to be fit. We need to be able to see a few snakes in the grass, eh?"

"But children playing hockey? Bully tactics? Suspicion? That just sets us up in a web of fear and degradation."

"Or it keeps us alert."

Jasper didn't respond, and they continued their journey in silence. Jasper wondered why St. Clair was so readily accepting of an assignment that saw him dealing with combatants in a fistfight when Jasper's first skeptical instinct was that Chief Tipton wanted him distracted.

"We recognize that aid in our national crisis impresses as much of a duty on our women as it does on our men!" Jem and Merinda heard the words even as they passed through the double doors of the cathedral and took seats near the back. Merinda watched several hats adorned with feather plumes bob in agreement as the woman continued. She was dressed in the colors of suffrage imported by British supporters: purple for dignity, white for purity, and green for hope, with a Union Jack ribbon affixed to her lapel. She continued in a strong alto that reverberated to the rafters and seemed to rattle through the towering pipes of the grand organ.

"Our role is not diminished because we are keepers of the hearth. Our patriotism not subdued because we are charged with trinkets, good luck charms, teary goodbyes, and favorite songs as our parting gifts. Our sacrifice is no less important because we give our sons and husbands over to the King and not ourselves. Imperial daughters, our job is no less important and our duty no less great. I am inspired by the promise that we are keeping this home safe so that our men have something to fight for. So that our children can benefit from the sacrifice our brave make every day as they leave on trains and ships to the yet unknown horrors awaiting them."

The woman went on for several more minutes with the same cadence and conviction. Finally, she moved to the side of the podium and invited Lady Adelaide Pelham to speak. Upon rising, Lady Adelaide was met with thunderous applause.

"Ladies, I echo what our esteemed friend has told us today. We will need 'all hands on deck' in order to ensure we are giving as much as our brave husbands, fathers, and sons. To this end, I am pleased to

be appointed the chair of the Ladies Auxiliary for the Preservation of
the Beloved Home Front. Our first order of business will be to canvas
the streets to raise a collection for a most worthy and noble project…"
Lady Pelham paused for effect, "…a hospital ship!" She paused again,
and this time she was rewarded with a fervent response from the audience. "Our brave men need the best medical supplies, and how exciting is it that we Canadian women can be at the forefront of the highest
medical care as our men set off to the battlefield?"

Lady Adelaide continued with a genuine dedication toward her
cause, and while Jem was admiring her trim tailored suit and ivory silk
gloves, Merinda was eagerly assessing the way she pumped her fist in
the air and the light that gleamed through her bright eyes.

After several more speeches, a young woman well known to both
Jem and Merinda from previous cases* took the podium. "My name
is Martha Kingston, and you may know me as an advocate for wom-
en's suffrage and as a reporter. But, sisters, I am here in solidarity with
Lady Pelham. You know that until now there has been no greater
cause for me than the liberation of women and the breaking of our
chains with the woman's vote. But now, with our men fighting overseas, we must temporarily redistribute our passion and fervor for that
cause with a higher one. For how can we possibly hope for the freedom we are determined to win in our future if our entire country is
overrun with evil? No. We must devote ourselves to this immediate
cause for Canada and for Britain before we return to stomping out
the injustice afforded us by men who continue to see us deprived of
the vote!"

She finished to applause, and the congregation of women sang
"God Save the King."

"I don't know whom I want to speak with first!" Merinda said
eagerly as the throng began to exit in the direction of the refreshments

---

* Readers familiar with Herringford and Watts' adventures in *A Singular and Whimsical Problem* and *Of Dubious and Questionable Memory* will already be familiar with the redoubtable
Martha Kingston.

promised in the lower auditorium. "Martha Kingston or Lady Pelham."

"Perhaps our acquaintance with Martha will lead to an introduction to Lady Pelham," Jem said helpfully.

"Brilliant!" Merinda whispered as Martha caught her eye from the aisle and waved.

Merinda and Jem slid out of the pew to greet her. Martha was enthusiastic, pumping their hands with spirit. Her long red hair was fashionably dressed under a tilted hat, and her eyes sparkled.

"Ladies, you are a dream!" She appraised both of them. "A dream! All of the stories! Chicago! Roosevelt! And now I hear women about town are sporting bowlers and wearing trousers." Martha fanned herself with a hand. "Not that the weather has been conducive to their wear! Nonetheless, this city is one after my own heart. I cannot believe I have been here a fortnight and this our first encounter! Come, you must allow me to introduce you to Lady Adelaide Pelham! Lady P is always dying to meet the city's brightest—" She swiveled on her heel. "Lady P!"

Lady Adelaide turned, adjusted the pin in her wide-brimmed royal blue hat, and stepped toward them. "Of course I know you," she said as she extended a gloved hand to Merinda, who shook it with relish, and then to Jem, who pressed it only to the degree of social propriety.

"It's very nice to meet you, Lady Pelham," Jemima said. "We were so moved by your words."

"And I by your deeds!" Lady Pelham flashed a genuine smile. "I have been so excited to follow your adventures."

"And now we are eager to turn our enthusiasm for justice toward your benevolent cause," Jem said.

"How happy I am to have you." She appraised Jemima's eager blue eyes and Merinda's odd attire kindly. "Why, you *must* join me for a little party tomorrow evening." She turned to Martha. "Won't it be a lark to have the girls there? I'll even wear a bowler!" She clapped her hands. "I've had one fashioned. I affixed a little rose at the brim. A lark!"

Merinda couldn't stifle a sputter. Jemima compensated with a polite gasp. "That sounds delightful!" she said. "I am eager to see it."

Lady Pelham provided them with the particulars of the gathering, and they promised to attend.

"And you are both cordially encouraged to bring a guest. The more the merrier!" She looked between them. "I assume the two most sought-after women in Toronto have beaux?"

"You would assume correctly," Merinda said cheerily. Jem spluttered loudly in surprise.

"Splendid! I look forward to welcoming you to Pelham Park."

Jem and Merinda made the usual pleasantries to Lady Pelham and Martha before taking their leave of them.

"A beau?" Jem said, slyly, once they were alone. "My goodness, Merinda. Is Constable Citrone expected?"

"I am not going to Pelham Park without Jasper," Merinda explained lightly. She looked at Jem shrewdly, "And we must find DeLuca. We can't be everywhere at once on that grand estate. We'll need our men."

Merinda led Jem to the refreshment table with the express purpose of placing cucumber sandwiches in a napkin and stealing out the side door into the twilight. A swath of pink, mingled with a lemon hue, colored the low clouds, offering a glimpse of day languorously giving way to evening.

"Here I am pursuing the next step in a case when Ray must be beside himself." Jem's voice was exasperated, her head throbbed, and her side ached something fierce.

"Cracker jacks, Jem. The day is just catching up with you. Ray is a proud man. If he wanted to find you, he would."

"Merinda, it isn't that simple." But even as she said the words, Jem knew her friend was right.

"We'll go back to King Street, and you can attempt to reach him by telephone."

"If he hasn't had the service cut off." Jem worked her teeth over her lip.

"Then we'll try Jasper."

"I suppose that will have to do."

Ray had a notebook, a stub of a pencil, and a sense that the world had turned against him. He was on his fifth cup of coffee at a Chinese restaurant in the Ward. He had first made his way toward the Wellington, but he knew he might be discovered there. Worse still, sought out. He needed time. Even Jemima and her probable eager and altruistic quest to find him was more than he could handle.

On his sixth cup, he accepted the plate of egg drop tarts a small woman presented him. She spoke little English, but her smile was a strong statement.

He turned a tart around on his plate. Some part of him had known that McCormick would turn him out eventually. He had a penchant for walking on thin ice. Nonetheless, so much of his identity was constructed of his need to build what meagre livelihood he had with words. Now more than ever, he knew his voice was needed. An empathetic tie to the experiences plaguing those who were not unlike him in circumstance and fear.

Yes, fear. What if Montague's hold pulled so tightly that they were forced out of their homes altogether?

He opened a blank page of his notebook and poised the pencil over a grainy sheet.

The last time he had considered finding an alternative source of income was when Jemima informed him she was expecting a baby. He still remembered how the thought of eking out a living by any other means than words pulled his chest tightly. He flexed his fingers, spared of the gnarled and scraped contractions so common with men employed at the Roundhouse or in the viaducts. But what choice did he have? If it were only him, he could scrape by with odd jobs typesetting or writing copy for second-rate pamphlets. But there was Jem and there was Hamish, and there was a house in Cabbagetown and electricity and food.

The Scripture Ethan Talbot had so confidently quoted at him after Jem's accident surfaced with a subtle mockery. How could God be doing a work in his days when there was no work for him to do? Inasmuch as it was difficult for him to accept that particular snippet of their conversation, he was drawn back to Talbot's words about Jem. He owed it to her to let her in. To shake out of his pride for a moment and allow her the opportunity. She had, on more than one occasion, shed her resolve on his behalf, and he owed her the same courtesy.

Chapter Eleven

It is most discourteous for a woman to extend an invitation to a gentleman. A proper relationship cannot recover from a woman's audacity to inhabit a role best assumed by a member of the opposite sex.

Dorothea Fairfax, *Handbook to Bachelor Girlhood*

I need you to be my escort," Merinda said eagerly. While Jasper was delighted to accept her last-minute dinner invitation, routine dictated that because it was not his usual weeknight for a visit, her insistence was a result of her needing a favor.

And while Jasper Forth had waited a very long time to hear Merinda say something of this nature,* he knew it had little to do with her becoming suddenly desirous for his company.

"I will happily accompany you, Merinda," Jasper said, accepting the glass of water Mrs. Malone handed him. "But I advise you and Jemima to consider the honor of this invitation. It won't do to get Sir Henry Pelham on the offense."

"I am inviting you as a coconspirator! That pesky war agent Milbrook and Waverley were worried about will most likely be traipsing after Sir Henry Pelham!"

Jem, who had little appetite, was seated not in her usual place, but rather at the end of the table nearest the door leading to the kitchen, where the telephone was housed. "You are sure Ray didn't try calling the station?"

---

* Precisely 7 years, 3 months, and 22 days.

"Jem, I swear to you that if I hear anything at all, I will let you know. When Ray wants to be found, we will find him. He took a few hits to his pride today."

Jem nodded and focused on shifting peas around her plate with her fork.

"I don't mean to make an enemy of Sir Henry," Merinda said, continuing their earlier line of conversation. "Waverley seemed to be suspicious of some underhanded smuggling that could happen, and we know how close Sir Henry is to the war agent. Also, if one of his automobiles was indeed the same one that hit Jemima, I highly doubt Henry was driving it. He probably doesn't know how to steer on a city street. The rich lot always have fellows to see to that sort of thing."

Jasper had initially tucked into his dinner with a relish, but now, with Jemima's dour mood and Merinda's insistence on speaking of the case, his eyes drifted toward the blackboard, which could been seen through the open French doors to the adjoining sitting room.

"I suppose it's easy to think this man is targeting members of the Cartier Club."

"Yes, but that doesn't account for Hans Mueller," Jem added.

"Unless…" Jasper leaned over the table and motioned for Jem and Merinda to follow suit. He lowered his voice a few decibels. "Does it not strike you that Hans Mueller could have been mistaken for another young man also of the loading bay at Spenser's? Same hair color and roughly the same build?"

Merinda chewed on this* a moment before whispering, "Mrs. Malone's grandson Ralph."

Jem shook her head. "He's little more than a child. I don't understand."

"Perhaps," Merinda expounded after a rather unladylike swallow, "this murderer is not only interested in members of the Cartier Club, but those close to them."

Jem's eyes were round as saucers. "Ray."

---

* And simultaneously her third roll.

"Ray is fine, Jem." Jasper squeezed her elbow. "It was just a thought and a possible connection to explain how the Mueller kid is connected to Waverley and Milbrook."

Merinda, her head buzzing, was suddenly finished with her nearly clean plate and dashed toward the blackboard. She added the initials "R.M." with a question mark beside them, vowing to not worry Mrs. Malone by ever speaking of the theory aloud.

After a few hands of cards, in which Merinda defeated Jasper,* he took his leave. Merinda prattled on about appropriate attire for the Pelham dinner, remembering with delight what Lady Adelaide had said about her affection for bowler hats.

"You'll still have to manage some sense of propriety!" Jem snapped, cutting her off.

"Cracker jacks, Jem. You don't have to snarl just because DeLuca is out prowling the city like a fox. He has done as much before." She studied her friend a moment in the flickering lamplight mellowing the sitting room, and her features softened slightly. "Was today a little…you are not feeling too worse for wear from our adventures today, are you?"

Jem shook her head. "I'm fine. Good night, Merinda."

"It's late, Jemima. You never burn the midnight oil."

"I promise I will retire presently."

As Merinda's footfall on the stairwell faded, Jem pulled her knees up to her chest and listened to the comforting tick of the grandfather clock. The sounds of her friend's house were like an old quilt, something Jem could sink into and within its folds excavate the past. She recalled the days when she had lived here, slipping out at night in bowlers and trousers to sneak after a missing pocket watch or cat. Then, the resplendent first days when Ray DeLuca colored her world and every rosebud on the wallpaper reminded her of the terrible poetry on the sheets of the stolen† journal she tucked beneath her lavender-scented pillow.

---

* Partly because she creatively conjured up her own rules.

† For more on Jemima's uncustomary thievery, please consult *The Bachelor Girl's Guide to Murder*.

She finally turned down the lamps and ascended the stairs, performed her evening toilette, and attempted to settle into sleep. Instead, memory called, and with it her heart flurried with moments at once adventurous and commonplace in a city that was exciting and new and a life she was finally deciding for herself beyond the perimeters of her parents' expectations.

She was just beginning to drift off when she heard a rather pronounced thud at the windowpane. At first she supposed it had begun to rain and droplets were pounding on the window. But its insistent rhythm was of a stronger staccato, and it finally drew her legs from under the covers.

She tied her robe around her while striding toward the windowsill to draw open the curtains.

She blinked to adjust her vision to the waning streetlight before finally making out the perpetrator. She squeaked her delight and threw open the window.

"Where have you been all day?"

"Consuming about eighty egg drop tarts," Ray called up in a dramatic whisper. In response, a stray dog began barking, and a light from a window across the street shone through closed curtains.

"I'll be down there in a moment," she called quietly. She turned away, letting the curtain fall into place behind her.

"Get dressed!" she heard through the window.

And suddenly the night was alive and the room fizzled.

Jem quickly stepped into a pair of cotton pants and shirt, leaving her braided hair hatless. She eased from her room and down the stairs as silently as she could and then was out the front door, closing it behind her.

"I am so sorry about…I thought that…" her fragmented sentences were stopped by her husband the moment she stepped outside.

He smiled and took her hand. "Come on."

"Where are we going?"

Jem merely caught his smile under the streetlight, tightening her hold on his hand and happy to wind along dark streets with their lazy sputtering lamps and eerie blanket of quiet just so long as he was at the helm.

They took King at a pace she knew required effort on Ray's part. He had an incessant need to render the city smaller by taking it in fervent stride. She turned to whisper she loved being married to someone who couldn't sit still, but he pressed his finger to his lips, making out what he could of her visage in the half shadows before pressing onward.

Several silent moments later, Jem renewed by the pressure of his fingers intertwined with hers and the friction of his cotton shirt against her sleeve, they reached their destination on dark Victoria Street.

"I am certain this is highly illegal," she informed him, even as he kicked down the rattling fire escape stairs suspended from the back of the Elgin and Winter Garden theatres.

He motioned for her to ascend first, and she carefully held to the bars in the pitch-dark night around them, taking the stairs gingerly, conscious of the limited movement rendered by her bruised rib.

When she reached the landing, she turned and waited for him. Ray confidently raised the lever and pushed open the door.

"They really do need tighter security on this place," he said with a wink she could just make out in the shimmer of moonlight before they stepped into the building.

She knew what awaited her there: a forest, a sweet secret, a bower safe from shattered glass and enemy alien cards. Ray scratched a match on the brick wall and flicked it into a small flame, using it to light a discarded lantern. Then he moved toward the electrical switch and clicked it on, Jem's heart catching at the movement.

She could hear a smile in his voice as he said, "You would think after all this time that a celebrated female detective wouldn't jump at the slightest noise."

Soon enough they were surrounded by the theatre's forest. On the other side of a fire curtain, adorned in an elaborate pastoral set, the stage stretched toward rows of empty chairs.

"I am so sorry about what happened at the *Hog*," Jem blurted out. "I don't want you to think I didn't try to find you, because I did—"

"I didn't want to be found."

"I was worried about you."

"You needn't have been. I was..." He flipped through his mind for a word. "I was selfishly sulking and far too proud to see you."

"That's nonsense."

Ray lowered himself to the lip of the stage and then hopped off. He extended his arms to Jem, and she gingerly crouched, feeling some discomfort in the region of her sore rib before stumbling into his arms. "I remembered, fair Jemima, that this is a row we have had before." He could see the wheels in Jem's mind turn. "Before Hamish was born."

"It is a row we shall have again, Ray, and again and again."

He held her tightly, and she tucked her head under his chin. "It is a row I have with myself," she whispered into his shirt. "I want to be everything. I want to be a wonderful mother to Hamish, and I want to be everything you need me to be. But I also want to be myself. I never want to lose that little jump of feeling I get when we are out on a case or seeing my name in the paper or following Merinda."

"You are relaying to me things that made me fall in love with you."

Jem stepped back slowly, still holding on to his forearms. "But you are angry with Merinda, and you couldn't force two sentences together when I was in the hospital."

"Because you take the words from me, Jemima. You always, *always* have."

"I suppose I want too much." She felt her bruised side. Ray noticed her slight wince and led her to a chair in the front row.

"I want to be able to tell you everything that is happening. How my hand shakes since Tony's death, how I fear for you and Hamish more now than even after our window was broken. How ashamed I am that I cannot provide for you. That you are tied to my name."

Jem smiled and cupped Ray's chin in her palm. "How many men would wake me in the middle of the night and take me to my favorite place in all the world?" Her eyes traveled the theatre, from ornamented moon over latticed flowers and dripping lanterns. "You are all I have ever wanted, Ray DeLuca. At my core it is you. Even when I want to spirit off into the city and grab at a few adventures of my own. In the deepest part of me, it is you. The very center."

Ray smiled, and Jem wondered if the fake buds adorning the stage would start to bloom, or if the lights would flicker and brighten further still with the effect.

"I will stay at Merinda's as you wish, but I will not go so many nights and days without you near me." Jem was adamant. "Which is why it is rather opportune that you sought me out tonight." She straightened and clutched Ray's hand. "I would like you to be my escort to Pelham Park tomorrow evening at the personal invitation of Sir Henry and Lady Adelaide." Jem's eyes grew as she shared the details of how the invitation came to be, and Ray grinned at her enthusiasm.

Then the magnitude of her request washed over him, and he paled slightly. "Jemima, can you imagine me at a fancy dinner at Pelham Park?"

Jem cut off his deepening frown with a lingering kiss. A moment later,* she caught her breath and combed her fingers through his hair. "Darling, I can imagine you anywhere. You can be remarkably charming when you put your mind to it."

---

* In this instance, several moments.

CHAPTER TWELVE

*A proper wife must be at all times ready to
infiltrate any manner of society, even to its highest
echelons. This requires that she be versed in all
manner of social etiquette from china and cutlery
to conversational conventions. It would not do for
her to embarrass her husband on account of her
being unprepared to blend in with the upper crust.*

Flora Merriweather, *Guide to Domestic Bliss*

Merinda almost looked like a lady in her best organdy dress, but black ankle boots and a bowler interfered a little with her efforts. Strands of pearls from her uncle's costume trunk in the attic were swathed around her neck with a small Union Jack affixed on her collar.

Jemima was more traditionally outfitted in a dress of delicate lavender and lace gloves.

She gave a little laugh as she descended the stairs. "Merinda, you cannot go looking like that."

"We are celebrities, Jemima." Merinda gave herself a saucy look in the mirror and was pleased with what she saw. Jasper, too, was pleased when he arrived dressed in spit-shone shoes and blue uniform.

Ray arrived a few moments later, out of breath and attempting to smooth down his hair. Not owning anything remotely appropriate for the occasion, he was adorned in a suit he'd borrowed from Ethan Talbot. His collar button was open, and his jacket draped his shoulders in a cavalier embrace.

Jem extended her hands, and he took them both with a smile. He gave her a kiss on the cheek.

"You are radiant," he said, his eyes twinkling appreciatively.

"And me?" Merinda pouted at Jasper as she tugged a few of her blond curls from under her bowler.

"You are *you*." Jasper's congenial voice made it a compliment.

He waited while the girls walked ahead of him, stepping into the lemon light of evening and in the direction of a hired vehicle that cost Jasper more than a day's salary.

A white-gloved driver opened the door and stretched his hand to Jemima, who gathered her skirts and lowered herself into the vehicle. Merinda turned to smile at Ray, whose eyes were kept straight ahead.

"We haven't spoken two words to each other in as many days." Her voice held entreaty. He didn't move or blink. Deflated, she joined Jasper and Jem in the back, Ray settling in the front.

The driver smoothly swerved off King and onto Spadina Road.

"He's a much calmer driver than Merinda." Jem tried for a light voice in response to Ray's inquiry as to her comfort in the back.

The car slowly climbed the hill from Walmer, and soon the stone gates of the castle perched high atop a hill overlooking the city came into view.

The driver swerved right, and the magnitude of the mansion was made manifest, highlighted by the setting sun.

"Did Mr. Rochester live here?" Jem whispered to Merinda after they had exited the automobile and went through the open wrought iron gate. The imposing Gothic structure overtook the whole of their sightlines.

"It's magnificent!" Merinda gaped at the tiered fountain, the tennis courts, and the extensive gardens.

Jem grabbed Ray's arm. "Can you imagine? It's all a fairy tale! And look—"

"Ah, my lady detectives!" came a familiar voice a moment later, interrupting Jem's gushing.

Lady Adelaide appeared before them in a fashionable dress of delicate black satin with a sheen of lace over the bodice. Ebony glass beads set off her white skin at the open neckline, and a gigantic diamond ring drew the eye to violet gloves extending from fingertip to elbow. Atop her head at a prim angle was the promised bowler.

"Cracker jacks!" giggled Merinda. "That really is the most atro—"

Jem, anticipating her friend's reaction, introduced their escorts with all of the propriety her breeding could muster.

"Constable Forth," Lady Adelaide acknowledged. "Mr. DeLuca." She puzzled over Ray a moment, noticing perhaps for the first time the wink of Jem's plain wedding band and the possessive hand with which she clutched Ray's arm. "Indeed, you are not Jem Watts after all."

Jem shook her head happily, her curls dancing slightly under her glistening bandeau. "My maiden name," she explained. "But familiar to the press."

"Of course." Lady Adelaide flashed Ray a genuine smile, winning a slight one from him in return.

While Ray was visibly nervous, Jasper used the opportunity to prove to Merinda exactly how at ease he found himself in a variety of situations. He bowed to Lady Pelham, using the hand not clutching his hat under his arm to take her own hand for a kiss.

"A constable and a gentleman!" Lady Pelham was delighted. She stepped slightly ahead of them and flung her arms out to her wide property. "You must take in as much as you like. You'll find refreshments in the tents yonder, and the gardens are yours to explore. Later, after dinner, I would be pleased to give you a tour of the house itself. Mind, a few wings are yet to be completed* on account of the war. Sir Henry and I want to ensure that Toronto's young men are available for service, and that our industry and resources are available to help the city at large and not just the perfection of our grand estate here."

"That is very generous of you, Lady Pelham," Jasper said.

---

* Skip McCoy had photographed several of these workers in a recent *Hogtown Herald* article.

"One such area is the indoor pool. It will sit right off a tunnel that Sir Henry constructed to lead from the main house to the garages." She inclined her head. "But Sir Henry has decided that is the area of construction of the least importance while we do our part for the war effort, so the poor space goes unused. A shame. It will be one of the first in the city!" Lady Adelaide turned to Ray. "I suppose you would like to see the automobiles? My husband keeps quite a collection."

Merinda caught Ray's eye and nodded her encouragement. *Yes, her cat eyes read, you do want to see the automobiles. One may have crashed into your wife.*

Ray merely smiled at Lady Pelham, who transferred her attention to Jem. "We have just acquired the most darling pair of Indian peacocks," she enthused.

Merinda grabbed Jem's arm tightly. "My friend Jemima is particularly interested in ornithology," Merinda explained.

"Wonderful. Constable Forth and Mr. DeLuca, if you would care to begin with our gun cabinets, I'm sure Sir Henry will be along presently to greet you and tell you all about them. Last I saw him, however, he was engaged in the usual business. Though I tried to encourage him to leave it. For one night. If you will follow me, ladies, I will lead you to the birds. They are outside the conservatory at the front of the house. You will have just enough time before cocktails."

Merinda's and Jem's shoes echoed over the grand threshold and through the great hall, which was ornamented with family crests and a massive Union Jack flag. Above them, the domed ceiling with crisscrossed banners graced balconies rimmed with mahogany rails.

Jem turned her head over her shoulder for a last glimpse of Ray, who stayed near Jasper awaiting Sir Henry's imminent arrival.

Through the conservatory, a glass door led to further gardens and a span of lawn. There Merinda and Jem were introduced to all manner of feathered friend. Beyond their glass-encased shed, the city stretched from the high altitude of the castle's sloping landscape, and the clucks and coos and interspersed music of a rather exotic gathering of birds were splayed on either side of an impressive encased glass shelter. It was not unlike a greenhouse, enshrining all manner of plants and flora.

"We are fortunate to host the magnificent peacock!" said a voice from beyond the door. Another attendant guarding the door gave an indicative nod. Walking further into the shed, Merinda and Jem found chittering ceremonial doves. In other circumstances, pale in comparison to the bright peacocks and parrots, they would have been the least interesting species on display.

"They are specially bred," said a voice with a clipped British accent a moment later. Jem and Merinda straightened from their inspection of the doves and turned to face a man dressed in military attire with an insignia embellishing his shoulders. He approached them and then faced the cage, slipping a finger through the bars to stroke the downy ivory of one of the dove's heads.

"Do they...erm...molt?" Jem asked, while Merinda now inspected their new companion.

"They do! Their cages are usually lined with feathers." He smiled, brightly at Jem and somewhat suspiciously at Merinda, having taken in her odd attire. "I am Philip Carr," he pronounced with a slight bow.

"Merinda Herringford." Merinda pumped his hand. "This is Jemima DeLuca." She cocked her head in a manner akin to one of the inquisitive birds in the cage behind her. "I have heard so much about you. Do you have a particular interest in ornithology?"

"I like birds. They calm me. Do you know the significance of these doves?"

"Messenger birds," Jem provided.

"Feathers that mark cowardice," interceded Merinda, searching Carr's features intently.

"Indeed." He chuckled. "I suppose there is nothing for a layman enthusiast to teach either one of you."

"I have long wanted to meet you, Mr. Carr."

Jem recognized this tone as a rather dangerous one and nudged Merinda that she would make little headway with that attitude.

"Indeed."

"I am likely familiar to you from my escapades in the field of deduction."

But Merinda's self-important assessment of her credentials were interrupted by a rather pompous peacock, who chose that precise moment to flutter down from his perch to shrilly squawk at Merinda, jutting his body, framed by a perfect fan, in front of her.

"Cocky fellow," Carr said, laughing.

Merinda glared at him, which seemed to make the bird more adamant to secure her attention. Unamused by the peacock's intense scrutiny, she pulled Jemima through the glass doors and onto the lawn once more. For a moment, they were blessedly alone, Merinda casting a furtive glance over her shoulder to ensure the bird was encased in his sanctuary, a wall of glass between them.

Jemima attempted to stifle her laughter when the persistent bird escaped through the door in pursuit of Merinda before Mr. Carr could prevent it.

Several feet away, Merinda addressed him, hands on hips and body lurched forward: "Now listen here, you intrusive feathered fiend. Unless you somehow remember a strange man plucking plumage from your dove friend's back, I expect you to turn around and march back to where you came from."

The peacock emitted a little sound and cocked his royal blue head to his side, the tuft of feathers adorning his head swaying with the sudden movement.

"Merinda, he's adorable," Jem cooed, bending down and stretching out her hand to him. The peacock observed her, took two steps forward, and then nipped at her hand with his beak. Jem pulled back just in time.

"You see?" Merinda said. "The fellow is a brute."

The brute, however, was not quite finished with Merinda, strutting after her even as she spun on her heel and led Jemima in the direction of the main house, leaving Philip Carr's laughter in their wake.

Inside, Jasper and Ray feigned interest at the gun cabinets. Certainly Sir Henry had an impressive display. Each rifle and black pistol were gleaming with polish. The man himself had appeared with a few friends in casual entourage. Sir Henry extended his warmest wishes to Jasper and Ray and shook their hands amicably before the trio turned to the gun collection.

"Might this be the same care you take with your impressive collection of automobiles?" Jasper queried.

"You are an astute young man." Sir Henry took a moment to appraise the constable. "I find that I need someone who will treat each with the same amount of special care. I do have one fellow, Graham." He smiled. He turned to the small congregation of gentleman. "If you'll excuse us." He handed off his glass of whiskey to a servant and motioned for Ray and Jasper to follow him. The other gentlemen, Ray and Jasper could only assume, must have previously had the opportunity to view the grand house.

As Sir Henry led them down a set of dark mahogany stairs, Jasper gave Ray a slight smile. *This is exactly where we need to be.*

"The garage is connected to the main house by a rather elaborate tunnel," Sir Henry announced proudly, ushering them forward. "But I must admit that the tunnel and the other wing are still in a rather crude state."

"It's decent of you to allow the men working on your estate to enlist."

"We must all do our part." Sir Henry lifted a lantern from a hook on the wall and led them forward. "My wife will probably have our heads for being tardy for the dinner bell, but I think you two will appreciate my collection."

"We feel quite honored to be shown this part of the mansion," Ray said.

"Nonsense. I saw the way Constable Forth was admiring my firearms. I imagine a man of the law would appreciate seeing how I take care of all of my possessions." The walk thereafter was silent through dank, cement-lined corridors. Then they were met with another staircase. Sir Henry held the lantern in front of him and motioned them forward.

Once they were in the garage, Sir Henry introduced them to Graham, a silver-haired man with a pronounced limp and an oil can, who was attending to one of the many automobiles.

"Graham and I served against the Boers together. Can't go anywhere without him!" Sir Henry said fondly. Jasper and Ray smiled at Graham, who ducked his head sheepishly. "Graham, will you see these fellows back to the main house? Gentlemen, I was not in jest. My wife *will* have my head if I am tardy for the bell. You, however, can be spared a similar fate on account of our hospitality. Graham here can tell you all you need to know."

Jasper and Ray surveyed the latest models of the Ford and Cadillac variety gleaming iridescently through the half-moon windows, their glass panes glistening, their bodies perfectly polished.

"One of the two automobiles we assume responsible for Jem's accident is registered to Sir Henry," Jasper said out of the side of his mouth.

Ray straightened.

Jasper motioned for Ray to follow him toward an impressive model with a green finish. They both examined a scratch above the right headlight. Though it seemed to be newly polished, the tear on the vehicle's finish was quite pronounced.

"A recent accident here, Mr. Graham?" wondered Jasper, taking a look and seeing that there was further damage to the car.

Graham rose slowly and limped in their direction. "That car is so rarely used. The master prefers the Chevrolet Baby Grand for transporting guests and the Silver Ghost for his personal use." Graham inclined his head toward an impressive model of the Rolls Royce family on the opposite side of the garage. "He sometimes allows the head butler to take the roadster on errands."

Ray ran his finger over the jagged edge of the scratch, and Jasper noticed his friend's ears redden, while his right hand shook slowly.

Jasper took command so that Ray could recover himself. "I must disclose that I am off duty, Mr. Graham, but we believe that this automobile was involved in an accident two days ago."

"We are aware that the handle was broken and the vehicle scratched extensively."

"You didn't report it?" asked Ray.

"The butler denied that the damage occurred while he was driving. We're not sure who took the car out, but it was returned, and the master promised leniency if the perpetrator came forward. He assumed the police had enough on their hands during these uncertain days." Mr. Graham shrugged. "I like the challenge of repairing the damage. Sir Henry gave me carte blanche to restore it."

"Sir Henry obviously loves his automobiles." Jasper stated. "Surely he would want to discover who broke his trust."

"He assumed it was an employee on a joy ride. Sir Henry is empathetic enough to remember similar antics in his youth." Mr. Graham tut-tutted. "I have found the perfect finish and am just waiting for a shipment of the correct paint color." His pale finger traced the damage. "I will sand it and polish it good as new. A shame. I never had the chance to test one of this beauties on account of my leg." He stopped a moment, and Jasper and Ray exchanged a glance.

"And no one noticed the car driving out?" Ray asked.

"As I said, the family is used to servants being granted permission to use the automobiles. And so much has been going on, what with Lady Adelaide's attention focused on the auxiliary and Sir Henry in consultation with the war effort." Graham truncated further theory with a shrug.

Jasper and Ray remained a few minutes longer, pretending interest in Graham's extensive knowledge of the other automobiles. Then they asked for his guidance back to the main house.

"Ah!" said Merinda as the gong tolled. "An insipid need for socialization."

As they walked the short distance from the drawing room to the dining room, Merinda sipped champagne while Jem compensated for her silence with an exchange of the usual pleasantries with those around them. Sir Henry suddenly made the room smaller with his entrance. Merinda looked about for Jasper and Ray.

They arrived together from the opposite end of the ballroom attached to the dining room as Martha Kingston appeared at the table.

The lady reporter looked smart in a blue dress with sheer capped sleeves and a flower fastened to her loose red curls.

"Miss Kingston!" Jem said brightly. Her husband came up to stand next to her.

"Mrs. DeLuca." Martha shook Jem's hand warmly. "I am so looking forward to a small audience with your husband." She transferred her cocktail to her left hand, pumping Ray's hand enthusiastically with her right. "A tad hyperbolic," Jem and Merinda heard her assess. "But a voice for the ages."

Dinner was announced, and they all found their assigned seats. Merinda was sandwiched between Jasper and Philip Carr at the end of the table nearest Sir Henry, while Ray and Jemima were in proximity to Martha Kingston.

Their surroundings were resplendent. The wallpaper bore a russet red bear bursting into flame with the incendiary brush of the chandelier's caress. Oil paintings of aged men and women, undoubtedly of the Pelhams' lineage, watched sentry on either side. The table itself was magnificent with tall silver tiers and all manner of polished china and cutlery. Flowers added color and scent, and candlesticks caught the glistening light.

Jem helped Ray get through the meal by selecting the correct utensil for each course and ever so slightly indicating its usage to him.

Dinner was a parade of pretention that would have suffocated a Dickensian feast of the century before. After the distribution of the first course, Lady Adelaide, despite the protestations of her husband, rose.

"I know it is not our custom to toast so early in our evening, but

I really must acknowledge two very special guests." She indicated Jem and Merinda with her champagne flute, and while Jem's cheeks flushed and Merinda beamed, their fame was acknowledged with good cheers from the dozen or so of the city's most illustrious elite.

Each subsequent course was either drenched in rich sauce or candied and colorful in a delicate tableau.

Merinda was bored out of her tree. Jem was savoring every morsel, her appetite strong. Ray assessed each social cue, conversation, and action as if part of a newly discovered civilization.

Martha lifted her wine glass, glanced at Jemima sitting beside her, and then crowded her as she leaned toward Ray. "Mr. DeLuca, I have a proposition for you." She eyed Jem. "Do you mind if we swap seats?"

"I assure you, Miss Kingston, that would be very improper—"

"Grand." Martha was already on her feet.

Jem shuffled over to the reassigned seat, switched plates as unobtrusively as possible, and focused on her food, barely making out the enthusiastic whispers exchanged between Martha and her husband.

Her new dining companion on her other side attempted several times to lure her into conversation, but Jemima merely responded with one-word answers. She looked up and caught Merinda's eyes. Her friend was stifling a yawn into her napkin while Philip Carr prattled on at an astounding rate beside her.

Then the toasts began, tripping over their emphatic words praising the glorious war effort and the men daily heeding its call.

Just as Sir Henry, who had partaken in too many toasts of his favorite scotch, was beginning to slur the opening lines of "The Maple Leaf Forever," the fruit and cheese course was announced. With its entrance, the peacock that had so adamantly kept on Merinda's heels earlier in the evening made an appearance in the dining room.

The guests erupted in excited laughter, but the bird had one intent, and it focused its beady eyes on her. Jasper looked to Merinda, torn between throwing himself in front of her as a barrier against the feathered interloper and laughing.

"Cracker jacks!" Merinda exclaimed with a scowl.

"This is one of our extraordinary Indian peacocks!" Lady Adelaide announced, trying to salvage the indecency of a bird fluttering onto the table and immediately stepping through the display like a prima donna, its unfanned tail trailing saucily.

The bird made its way to its intended party, staring at Merinda before opening its beak and emitting a loud squawk.

Jem was in hysterics, and Jasper was trying to capture his laughter in his napkin. Ray was hoping it would nip her.*

"Oh, for the love…" Merinda said. "Listen here! I don't know why you keep following me."

The peacock squawked again and jutted its neck toward her.

Lady Adelaide, over the commotion of the now feathered table, was desperately trying to get the attention of a maid.

"I've had about enough of you." Merinda's voice rose, causing the others to lapse into an interested silence. "I am particularly fond of Stilton, and your imprint is on it!" she chided, looking the bird in the eye.

It met her glare with unruffled aplomb.

"Merinda, have you met your match?" Jasper whispered.

"Cracker jacks!" Merinda said again. She lunged at the bird and picked it up while rising. Its little feet attempted to claw at her, but she bravely risked being scratched.

Jem was certain now that the audacious creature might take a nip at Merinda. Instead, it burrowed its small head into the crook of her elbow. A servant approached to disentangle it from its one-sided embrace.

Later, with the bird safely returned to its cage, the guests erupted with comments of the peacock so enamored with a lady detective that it followed her in to dinner.

The laughter followed Sir Henry and the men into the study with the promise of brandy and cigars, and it rang with the chime of

---

* Not too painfully. Just a slight nip.

sterling silver spoons against china teacups provided to the ladies in the parlor.

And thus, while Jasper kicked Ray before he could launch into a tirade on the ease of profiteering under the noses of an inadequate city council, Merinda and Jem sat alongside a string of frosted ladies like a chained garland in the uppity parlor.

Merinda tuned out Lady Adelaide's detailed descriptions of every antique and piece of art in the room.

"We want this manor to be a bower in which to hold the finer things. Its purpose will serve my meetings and Sir Henry's enthusiasm and dedication to the war effort."

Merinda was imagining how the grand space, with its turrets and secret passages and hidden wings, was most especially branded with the potential for murder.

An hour later, they spilled into the night. Merinda's fingers tingled with the aftereffect of champagne not abated by the tea she'd sipped in the drawing room. Jem yawned, leaning slightly into Ray. Jasper wondered what it would cost to appropriate this house if only for a night and explore it fully with Merinda. How she would love the adventure of seeking out Sir Henry's gun cabinet! Sneaking into hidden corridors! Speeding off in the automobiles!

So of course they were the last to linger out in the yard.

They stole a moment under the starry canvas of the sky. The world stretched beyond the pinpricks of the city seen from the manor, and Merinda thought, for the first time, that her city seemed small.

"Did you find out anything about your case?" Ray asked Jem quietly while they waited for an automobile in the queue of the fleet charged with seeing their guests safely through the city.

"No," Merinda said. "I didn't even get to see if one of the automobiles here was responsible for the demolition of my roadster."

"My, Jemima, how like your friend you are sounding these days," Ray said sardonically.

"The food was delicious," murmured Jem in an attempt to soften Ray's animosity toward that particular friend.

"And the company more so," Jasper said, smiling at Merinda.

Merinda, unsettled by his nearness, turned her attention to the galaxy. "Oh, look!" she said, her eyes focusing on a bright, flashing dot piercing the navy stretch above. "There's Pyxis."

"Pyxis is best seen in March, Merinda," Jasper said.*

"And Merinda made a new friend!" Jem said brightly.

"Stupid bird!" seethed Merinda, though Jasper and Jem could see her smile in the waning light. She turned to Ray. "DeLuca, a moment."

"Jem," Jasper said, reading a flicker between them, "let's go wait for the car." He took her arm and led her across the yard.

"DeLuca," Merinda entreated.

"I have nothing to say to you, Merinda. Come, the others will be waiting."

"DeLuca, you are being childish!"

"Coming from an expert…" Ray walked several paces ahead of her.

"Argh!" she emitted, sprinting to catch up with him. "I'm sorry!" she exclaimed. "I don't know how to make things right with you."

"Why do you care about making things right with me?" Ray asked innocently, his eyes sweeping over the throng getting into their cars and then the bright lights of the estate sheening over automobiles. Landing on anything but her.

"Because…I just…"

"I lost my job and my typewriter, and I almost lost my wife because you're a lousy driver in pursuit of a mystery you are incapable of solving."

Merinda hid her hurt, though she remained silent on the way home. When Ray told them Martha was interested in loaning him her byline to report on some of the more horrid conditions afforded immigrants like himself, Jem was delighted, Jasper congratulatory, and Merinda lost in the speckle of streetlights like stars lining the road outside the passenger window.

---

* He had begun to learn the constellations a careful reader will remember she always labelled erroneously.

CHAPTER THIRTEEN

In our last exchange, you asked if I would enlist. Because the law needs to be upheld on the homeland, members of the RNWMP are forbidden to do so. In a way I am glad. Not because I am unpatriotic, but because war changes a person, Merinda. It changed my grandfather and my father. There are so many things in life people like us like to control. You follow your guidebooks and your deductive manuals, and I align myself with the rigid rules of the force. But wars change people. They change the rhetoric of a place and the feel of it. If you get caught in the whirlwind, if you find yourself off-kilter in a place and time you cannot quite understand, I want to let you know you are not alone. That from my secondhand experience it is nothing short of normal.

An excerpt from a letter to Merinda Herringford from Benny Citrone

He's safe as houses now."

Merinda overheard Jem talking with Mrs. Malone as she ascended the stairs the next morning. "It was mortifying to have the taxi park at the curb, only to find that the front window in our townhouse had been shattered." Jem shuddered and reached for her tea. "But I am appreciative of your hospitality here, and Ray will stay with Jasper's parents for the time being."

"God save the King!" Merinda pumped her fist in the air. She wouldn't admit, even to Jem, that the grudge Ray was holding against her was nipping at her. That she had spent half of a sleepless night deciding how she could possibly make it right with him. Midway through the pulsing dark, she decided to refocus on the prospect of finally beginning women's rifle practice.

"We are shifting from detective mode to patriotism for the morning," she informed Jem as Mrs. Malone disappeared to retrieve her Turkish coffee.

"Can I perform this task with a bruised rib?" Jem wondered.

Merinda shrugged. "We'll give it the old college try, eh?"

A half hour later, Merinda whistled the "Maple Leaf Rag" as they set in the direction of University from Queen.

Though she had passed the Armories some hundreds of times, Merinda had never been through its turreted doorways. Its grandeur put her in mind of the Coliseum in Chicago, wherein she and Benny Citrone had helped thwart an assassination attempt on Theodore Roosevelt.* The architecture of the previous century molded brick and stone and wheeling arches scoped above the windows and doorways.

Now, it was abuzz with all manner of activity. Men were spilling out from the canvassing tents and along the avenue awaiting their chance to enlist. Soldiers stood guard at each doorway, at attention and with rifles spit-shone and held at the perfect angle.

Jem adjusted her jacket, and Merinda swept her bowler from her head.

Inside, they were nearly overwhelmed with the sleek command of the place: a dizzying whirr of men's voices, heels clacking on the linoleum, stern commands, and messenger boys running to and fro. The ring of numerous telephones clanged from outside administration areas. Men snaked along the walls impatiently waiting for their medicals or to finalize the last bureaucratic steps to see them overseas and into the heart of the war.

Jem and Merinda followed arrows that saw them through broad,

---

* The curious reader will want to follow up with Merinda and Jem's intrepid adventures in Chicago in the case documented as *A Lesson in Love and Murder*.

regal doors and out into the sunny green space of the women's rifle range. Patches of soft grass were interrupted by all manner of callisthenic equipment. To the right, targets erupted from the ground like white statues, their faces circles and numbers around a bull's-eye. Opposite them, men were extended over varied obstacles, positioning their rifles on their shoulders or jabbing at the air with speared bayonets.

Merinda's and Jem's loose-fitting attire was appraised. A sour-faced woman and an overbearing man with a drooping moustache were less than enamored with Merinda's trousers.

Jem watched Merinda's eyes widen as women lay splayed on the ground in a most unladylike fashion—squiggling like worms, adjusting their elbows, and centering their shots before pressing their guns' levers and expelling bullets that whizzed through the air.

"Cracker jacks!" Merinda breathed to Jem as the women reloaded. "A step above Jasper showing us how to fire a pistol in an abandoned warehouse."*

Jem felt at her rib and decided she was well enough to join Merinda as long as she was careful. "If the enemy comes," Jem said, accepting the gun held out to her by the sour-faced woman, "I won't have a moment to stall on account of a slight injury."

Merinda loved the heavy feel of the gun as its stock pressed into her shoulder, the barrel pointing toward the target. She blew a tendril of hair from her forehead and squinted so that her right eye over the gun was directly in line with her target.

Bang! The force of the shot shuddered through her. She took a shaky moment to see if she had hit the intended target before squinting up at the sour-faced woman, who was visibly impressed by Merinda's first effort.

"You're a natural," the overseer begrudgingly admitted as Merinda wiped the dirt from her trousers and turned proudly to Jemima.

Jem, though careful, had also assumed the correct position, and

---

* This experiment was met with near disastrous result on more than one occasion, often because Merinda forgot to empty the barrel of bullets.

while her aim was not as precise as her friend's, the sour-faced overseer hesitantly agreed that with more practice Jem's shots would be as sure.

An hour later, Merinda's arm steadied Jem, who finally admitted her stiff rib was smarting.

"Threaten and point! That's what I always told you. Threaten and point!"

They stood, brushing the dust from their trousers when they heard a familiar voice from the evening before.

"The war on the home front in action," Philip Carr said proudly, removing the folder tucked underneath his elbow to point at them emphatically. "I am impressed." He looked Jem over, appraisingly. "You're more than just a pretty face."

Merinda repurposed her gun as a cane and leaned on it slightly as it stabbed the soft ground. "Mr. Carr."

"Miss Herringford, I trust you have recovered from your encounter with your feathered friend last evening."

"Clearly." Merinda's voice was sardonic.

Jem scraped at civility. "I read in the paper that the ladies' rifle range is one of your particular contributions, Mr. Carr."

"Indeed."

Merinda blinked at him before saying, "As you know, my friend and I are lady detectives, and I was interrupted from my inquiries last evening on account of the peacock."

"Oh? Am I being investigated?"

"I don't like your tone, Mr. Carr."

He ignored Merinda, choosing to extend his arm to Jem. "Come. You seem slightly uneasy on your feet, and the sun is quite bright here. Perhaps we would all be more comfortable at a table under the shade." He indicated a tree nearby.

They had just been seated when Merinda began asking questions. "What sort of operation do you have going on, Mr. Carr?"

"I confess to being at a complete loss as to your meaning, Miss Herringford."

"Oh, really? There you are, knowing about ceremonial doves. Flitting into the city just as men are murdered."

"And why would I murder these men?" he asked while stealing a wink at Jem.

"Because they are covering up something you are trying to hide. Where were you the night of Milbrook's murder?"

"At Mayor Montague's house awaiting the news of the ultimatum on the telephone."

"And not at Spenser's earlier that day, silencing a boy who might have been on to your dastardly war-mongering plans?"

"I enjoy your brand of hyperbole, Miss Herringford. It enlivens you."

"Why, of all the—"

"My friend means well, Mr. Carr," Jem intervened with a silencing look at Merinda.

"Of course. My job is to ensure that, even though factories and munitions operatives of a grander scale are not yet properly outfitted, Canada has yet a way to ensure the munitions needed reach the boys on the frontlines. At least until we have a transparent course of action." He shrugged easily. "Spenser's has an impressive cargo bay, a fleet of its own boats, and a world-class shipping system at its fingertips. With such a shipping system and warehouse, Thad Spenser is a patriot who will see some form of fine recognition once the mess is over. The sacrifice he is making—"

"Sacrifice?"

"The carte blanche usage of his facilities. His dedication to the equipment and shipping needed and available at a moment's notice."

"But we just entered the war," Jem puzzled. "How much equipment and munitions are here?"

"Have you started this industry?" Merinda asked.

"A young man was murdered, as you say," Carr said evasively. "And while I welcome your questions, I fail to see how I could possibly be of assistance."

Merinda wondered if Jem noticed how Carr's eyes flicked to the folder he was carrying now and again.

"Because you are our war agent, and we feel that Milbrook and Waverley were killed because they were looking into illegal means of buying cheap munitions from across the border."

Carr shrugged. "I work for Mayor Montague and I work for Sir Henry. I obey orders."

"Is Sir Henry standing to make the same profit you are?" Merinda barreled on.

"Darling, you're barking up the wrong tree. You're looking for the killer of a *Kraut* boy from the Ward. An enemy. Some ruffian or bully did us all a favor." He cleared his throat. "That fellow from the *Hogtown Herald* has been shadowing me lately for an article."

"You say this proudly," Merinda intoned, wondering if Carr knew that the *Hog*'s reputation suffered even more with the loss of Ray DeLuca.

"I am a person of interest, but not in a murder inquiry. Rather, as a message to the city that we are willing to work with you. That you…all of you…" his eyes looked toward the men still undertaking their exercises around the range, "…are invaluable to our effort."

"You couldn't sound more patronizing if you tried," Merinda grunted.

"I don't know what light you think I might shed." He tipped his chin. "As you say, we have only just entered the war, and to date my role has been…" he paused and worked his teeth over his bottom lip, "…more of a type of surveillance."

"And yet," Jem said, "you have made such close connections that you are a hair's breadth away from Montague and Spenser, two men with a history of trade with anarchist bombs and even aligned with a ring that saw girls sold into the States."

"These things have been proven?"

"As good as," Merinda said.

"Almost," Jem said simultaneously. Chagrined, she murmured, "We haven't ever been able to find quite enough evidence."

"But we know. We just know." Merinda's voice was adamant.

Carr rose and tipped his hat to them. "Ladies, I admire you. As does Mr. Montague. You are emblems of the resilience and fortitude we will need of our women as we step forward into the fray." His accompanying smile held condescension. "But don't steer yourselves off course."

Merinda looked to Jem helplessly. There was something about Carr that set her off. Meeting her friend's eyes, she noticed a slight, mischievous sparkle and waited for the inevitable plan that would follow.

Jem stepped forward and feigned uneasiness, tottering slightly on her heels and falling forward before feeling Carr's steadying arms around her. Merinda pounced on the folder he dropped. Jem flittered her eyes open to watch Merinda rifle through it for anything of importance, rounding her blue eyes to the size of saucers while thanking Carr profusely.

The agent seemed hesitant to release her from his grip once he had assisted her to her feet. Jem looked around his shoulder to receive a slight nod from her friend.

He took his leave the moment Merinda handed him the slightly lighter folder, straightening his shoulders and casting one last appreciative look at Jemima.

"You have an admirer." Merinda beamed as she patted her vest, which covered the tightly folded papers she had managed to pilfer from him.

"Odious man," Jem said, sneering.

"Oh, I wasn't talking about Philip Carr," Merinda joshed, looping Jem's arm with her own. "Come on. We'll take a taxi home to save your rib from more exertion this morning."

"You're more astute than I took you for." Ray assessed Martha appreciatively as Mrs. Malone ushered her into the sitting room of Merinda's townhouse.

"I went to your home address," Martha explained, smoothing her skirt under her on the settee. "And, well, assumed you had the good sense to avoid staying there and wondered where to find you. I know of your particular connection with Constable Forth and was happy when you suggested meeting here." Martha looked around. "It must be nice to be able to appropriate Merinda Herringford's parlor for your personal use."

"She owes me one," Ray said quietly.

"I think you are the person I need in order to be able to make good the faith that Waverley put in me before I came here."

Ray fingered through his notebook and extracted the letter Jasper had given him from the murder scene. "Alexander Waverley left these notes in his desk for a reason."

Martha looked over them. "The munitions smuggling theory." She shrugged. "This will come out eventually."

Ray's expression darkened. "You are a journalist. It is your job to expose the corruption in our higher politics."

She tugged the pencil tucked behind her ear and tapped him playfully on the shoulder. "If you are committed to using the splendor of my byline, I think I have some say in how you use it."

"This is a real story, Miss Kingston."

"So is the lineup at City Hall every Monday morning. Children and their parents clutching cards that label them." She smiled and pointed the pencil at him. "*That* is the story I need."

"Then write it yourself. I am unsure how I can help you."

"Remember what I told you at the Pelhams' last night?"

"It was hard to hear much over the clang of expensive silverware." Ray looked up as Mrs. Malone entered with the tea service and a plate of sandwiches.

"Toronto is a grid of papers. Each daily has its share. The *Globe* is the most respectable. The others teeter off with their own Whig views or liberal nonsense down the rungs of the ladder to rags like the *Hogtown Herald*." Her growing smile was matched by a glint in her eye. "Suppose one paper unified the readership and became the most read daily because it spoke specifically to current events from a perspective that broadly swept the entirety of the Toronto experience." Her smile stretched "Toronto needs a unified voice. One that represents and straddles all worlds. Has a pulse on the political climate and knows the inner workings of the corrupt police force, but also has a decided talent for engaging the lower classes." Martha inclined her chin. "A voice that champions all stations." She poked his shoulder with the end of her pencil. "DeLuca, nothing in the world is as effective as a piece by someone who has lived through prejudice. You have a Canadian wife, and yet you're expected to line up and present yourself every month, while your home country is seen as a stick of dynamite that could blow towards the war?" She slapped his notebook emphatically. "Write that."

Ray had opened his mouth to respond when he heard voices in the foyer.

"Coffee, Mrs. Malone!" a voice unmistakably Merinda's erupted from the foyer.

Ray shot Martha a half smile as the girls removed their hats and stepped into the room.

Jem was patting at her matted hair, Merinda scratching at a smudge on her nose.

"Rifle practice," Merinda said in response to their questioning looks. "What are you doing in my parlor, DeLuca, Miss Kingston?"

But neither were given opportunity to answer. Instead, Merinda reached into her vest for some folded documents, which she then spread on the center table.

"What are these?" Martha wondered.

"We snatched them from Philip Carr," Jem said proudly.

"You suspect the war agent?"

"We've had our best people on him for a while."*

---

* Well, best urchins at the very least. Kat and Mouse always seemed to find time to be at Merinda's beck and call.

"Jem's a pretty good distraction," Merinda said, smoothing their bounty with her palm.

"Blueprints," Ray said.

Merinda rifled through the pile. "Wait." One finger made out the gloss of another sheet further down. "And photographs."

The ring of the telephone from the kitchen set Merinda jogging that way.

When she returned a few moments later, her eyes were cold and her face was drained of color.

"That was Jasper." Her voice was dead, and she swallowed in a rare display of uneasiness. "Jem, we have to go to the King Edward Hotel immediately. Something terrible has happened."

Chapter Fourteen

The careful detective will recognize that little good can come from personal attachment. In order to hone your logic and focus on heightening your skills, you must be willing and able to block out all human feeling. The only empathy you need is the slightest kernel from which to better understand your client's particular situation. All other semblance of affection is little more than a stumbling block.

M.C. Wheaton, *Guide to the Criminal and Commonplace*

The sky matched Jasper's mood, and he hoped the clouds above would soon rumble and split open to reflect the disastrous day. People crowding the street had yet to disperse, and though he and Russell attempted to corral them, they inched in. Three officers pooled traffic on either side of the street, parting a jagged and ineffective path of observers to the tragedy.

Jasper inspected every passing face in the hope that the throng would reveal Merinda. But it was several moments before a black taxi swerved outside the grand hotel and four passengers spilled out.

Merinda dashed over first, elbowing through those in her way.

Jasper intercepted her, holding her back. "Merinda…" he pleaded.

But her wiry frame was strong. "Where is she?"

"The medics are—" Jasper began, but at that moment a familiar figure flew through the commotion and aimed straight at her, crashing into Merinda's chest, encircling her waist, and holding on for dear life.

157

Jem was not two steps behind and gently untangled the slight individual with a gentle grip on her shoulders. "Kat."

For, indeed, it was the girl. Horrified and shivering.

"It's Mouse." Kat's frantic eyes moved from Merinda to Jem to Jasper and then back to Merinda again.

"Jasper said as much on the phone."

"Hit and run," Jasper said quietly, scratching at the back of his neck.

Martha and Ray tried to move in, but Jasper held them back. "There are too many people." He looked at Martha. "I'll give you the story later if you are amenable?"

She nodded.

"Ray?" Jasper motioned him over, and Ray followed suit.

"I have to see how Jem is!"

"I'll take care of her," Jasper said with finality. "Look. She's attending to Merinda."

"Jasper—"

"Just make sure that Martha stays clear away." Jasper squeezed Ray's shoulder. "If there's any news, I will tell you."

"But…Jem…"

"I'll see to Jem. But this is a sensitive issue, and from what we both know about Martha Kingston, she'll be eager for a headline. I want to make sure we have everything we need in order to make a fair assessment."

Ray read between the lines. "You think that this could be the same culprit who has been targeting the Cartiers?"

Jasper shrugged. "It's too early to say. I'll make sure Jem is all right. Believe me."

Ray nodded. "I'll take Martha away from the commotion."

Jasper nodded his thanks and went back to stand next to Jem.

Kat was clinging to Merinda. She looked up at Jasper through the curls curtaining her forehead.

"I…I…the automobile skidded and swerved," Kat hiccupped. "It was like it was…as if…as if it was chasing us…." as she babbled almost incoherently, Jem and Merinda picked up pieces of the fragmented story. The car finally collided with Mouse, who was now on a stretcher being attended to by medics.

"Mouse might be dead, and it's all my fault." Kat looked around. "And look," her shaky hand held up a white feather. "Like in the papers."

Merinda couldn't see straight. She couldn't settle her eyes on Jem even as Jem pulled the urchin to her tightly and kept her still. In her mind's eye, Merinda pulled back a curtain to reveal the horror of what her little Kat had just gulpingly described. And though the constables attempted to prevent her, she maneuvered past them and sprinted the last aching strides until she saw a motionless little Mouse, her perfect pixie face pale with one single ribbon of blood trailing to the pavement. Her arms and legs were crooked under her at a sickeningly still angle.

"Is she dead?" Merinda demanded of an attendant.

"Not yet," he said coldly, transferring Mouse's stretcher to the ambulance.

Merinda pressed her hands into her curls, hunched on her knees. She'd never before felt such a sweeping wave of emotion that made everything tint red and green in her eyes, that twisted her stomach, and that obliterated any rational thought in her brain.

Jem's voice was behind her, but all she could do was stare and tremble and stare. Then she slowly drew in all the breath she could and straightened her shaking shoulders, walking back to the curb where Jem was still holding tightly to Kat.

When Merinda spoke, it was a low gravelly tone foreign to Jasper and Jem. "I will destroy whomever did this."

Jasper told Kat to stay put as he motioned for Jem and Merinda to join him several feet back under the hotel's awning. On any other day, a command to Kat would be akin to catching a slick fish with fingers, but she was too lifeless just now to do anything but obey.

"White feather," Jem said, her eyes red rimmed.

Jasper nodded, taking it from her. He studied Merinda closely.

"I will find out who did this, Jasper." Merinda's voice was a tight wire. "And he had better be prepared."

"Miss Herringford, Mrs. DeLuca, Constable Forth." Skip sidled up. "Quote for the *Hog*?"

"Now is not the time, Skip," Jasper said to the photographer as Merinda lunged at him.

"Get that ruddy camera out of my face, Skip McCoy!"

Jasper restrained her, lest she set off like a rocket. "Easy there, Merinda."

She stared vacantly past his shoulder to where Mouse had lain behind the crowd. "Whoever did this almost slaughtered a child!"

"Merinda, it's disgusting, I know. It's—"

"And if he is willing to do this…if he is willing to…to…" She flung her hand toward the accident. "It's war. He will not *touch* anyone else."

"Merinda. Don't just dart after him—"

She was trying to wriggle out of his arms. "Merinda!" Jasper tightened his hold. It pained him to hurt her, and he watched her wince from the force of his clasp, but he refused to let her go.

CHAPTER FIFTEEN

*A detective learns how to compartmentalize. Use your
brain as a filing system, keeping the most pressing and
imminent facts at the forefront while filing those of not
immediate relevance to the side, no matter how difficult.*

M.C. Wheaton, *Guide to the Criminal and Commonplace*

Later, Merinda paced the Persian carpet in the sitting room.

"Merinda, sit down. Have a cup of coffee. Mrs. Malone made shortbread."

Merinda didn't hear Jem. "The universe is reminding me how clearly I have failed."

"You are going in circles, Merinda. I already told you—"

"Dinner parties and rifle practice. I am playing at detective, aren't I? Just like they always say."

"Who says, Merinda? That Carr fellow? Tertius Montague? You never listen to them anyway."

Merinda stopped a moment, and Jem brightened, hoping her incessant movement would stop. It didn't.

Merinda swerved and walked toward the blackboard. "We haven't solved this white feather nonsense."

"We're pursuing it. We just haven't found our resolution."

"You're not being helpful, Jemima."

"I'm sorry, Merinda. I am as heartbroken as you. I love that little girl, and—"

Merinda spun on her heel and faced Jem. "We can't just sit here."

"Well, what do you propose we do?"

"I don't know. Where's DeLuca?"

"Martha is offering him her byline to write about Montague's war measures. If you think he could help—"

"Nothing can help." She paused and then opened her mouth to continue when a knock at the door distracted her.

A few moments later, Mrs. Malone announced Heidi Mueller.

"Miss Mueller," Jem said with a smile.

"Any news on my brother's killer?" Heidi asked.

Merinda stepped nearer and noticed that the poor girl was shaking, the dark moons under her eyes a testament to too many sleepless nights.

"Unfortunately, no. You see, we've had some terrible news," Jem explained.

Merinda shook her head. "But we are not giving up."

"It's bad enough I have to humiliate myself at city hall," Heidi said. "Checking in, answering drivel. Tedious."

"Has the vandalism in the Ward stopped?" Jem asked.

Heidi shook her head.

Merinda bit her lip. "Tonight." She decided boldly, grasping at the opportunity it afforded to put the awful day behind her. "We'll solve this once and for all tonight."

In *The Adventure of Charles Augustus Milverton*, Holmes and Watson make use of silk masks and rubber-soled shoes in order to break into Milverton's house and subsequently his safe. Jem, donning black trousers, shirt, and cap, couldn't help but think of one of Merinda's favorite stories.

"It needs to be someone who can fit into any situation," Merinda said as they set off into the breezy evening, the darkness falling portentously around them. "Someone who can flitter in and out of the Ward like a ghost at night with no one stopping him."

"Someone they are familiar with," Jem added.

"Exactly." A smirk flirted with Merinda's mouth, and Jem was thrilled to see her friend act a little more like herself.

"Someone who has such a deeply ingrained hatred of so many that he would act on his own and not hesitate to distribute his particular sense of justice," Jem continued as they walked in the direction of St. John's Ward.

Merinda's eyes flew wide. "You really are a remarkable conductor of light,"* she squealed, taking Jem's arm. "That's it, Jemima! The man we are looking for tonight has every reason to be patrolling the Ward."

"You can't mean…"

"What if it *is* Russell St. Clair? Jasper hasn't stopped harping on this fellow's brand of prejudice. He can maneuver in and out of the Ward because he is a police officer. He is meant to be a beacon of protection, yet he can use the same influence to threaten and bully."

"Is he the murderer, then?" A chill tingled Jem's shoulders.

Merinda shrugged. "I can't be sure. But I'm willing to put my bottom dollar on his skulking around tonight. No wonder he fought to keep poor Lars behind bars!"

A slight breeze fluttered around them as they crossed Center Street. Mellow light spilled from ramshackle cottages, dogs yelped, and chickens clucked. Merinda and Jem kept to one side of the dirt road, Merinda rapping her crowbar-walking stick silently on her open palm. Her pistol was tucked safely in the waistband of her trousers. The murky light from the sputtering streetlamps did little to brighten the din of a night whose moon was hidden by latticelike clouds.

They slowly crept along, Jem jumping at every noise, be it a squirrel, a fox's errant footfall, or the raucous voices of men engaged in a ribald rhyme as they stumbled home from the tavern.

A chiming *clink* sound drew their attention northward. They crouched and crept across the street, hiding behind a shrub while the *clink* began again. A shadowy figure was tossing pebbles, but not to

---

* This particular Sherlock Holmes paraphrase from *The Hound of the Baskervilles* was one Merinda had attributed to Jemima before in an adventure documented as *Conductor of Light*.

rouse a sweetheart from slumber. Rather, he was doing so to plague and terrorize.

Just then a trio of giggling young men stumbled into view. A lanky kid appeared under the swath of light.

The black figure moved toward them, and Merinda and Jem saw one kid stumble back, most likely on account of unexpected collision with another man.

Then they recognized a large, familiar figure as Lars Hult calmly crossed the road to confront the situation. Merinda and Jem edged closer, abandoning the hedge and watching in plain sight. If their hypothesis was correct and the man was indeed Russell, he would be too preoccupied with the situation swarming around him to make them out in the dim light.

"These men were not causing any trouble." Lars's heavily accented voice cut through the darkness.

"You again! I should've insisted you remain locked up!"

Merinda snickered. "Well, well. It is Russell."

"And never once recognized." Jem clucked her tongue as they watched Lars with rapt interest.

"Of course not. He could easily rough up whatever kids he wanted, throw a few bricks, ransack a few properties, and then collect his uniform from a nearby location. Then he would return on the beat and convince the neighborhood he was keeping watch." Merinda looked around as if expecting to find the uniform he must have discarded.

They watched a few moments more, Lars's physical presence controlling the situation. The kids scattered homeward while St. Clair attempted to stand his ground.

Finally, Merinda motioned to Jem as she extracted her torch from her pocket and shone it in St. Clair's direction.

"Russell St. Clair!" she called as she illuminated him. "Take off that ridiculous cap." When he failed to obey, instead gaping at her, she passed the torch to Jem and swiped it off his head. "You're the lowest sort of cad."

"Merinda Herringford!" Russell said in surprise.

Lars beamed, recognizing them both, most likely from their exploits in the *Hog*.

"You will never bother the Muellers again!" Merinda threatened, her hands on her hips.

"Or what? A girl will attack me with her walking stick?"

"No," Lars interjected with a knowing nod at Merinda. "But I will."

At his silent behest, Merinda passed Lars her walking stick, and he held it at an ominous angle. "You are fighting a war against people who would rather be left in peace. These boys are joining every day."

"Why do you hate so much?" Jem interjected.

"I hate because I know." Russell eyed Jem. "I know that we are better without this degradation to humanity."

"Spare me!" Merinda was seething. "So you would see men murdered with white feathers beside them to compensate for your own cowardice?"

"What?"

"You're telling us you didn't murder Hans Mueller?" Merinda queried, with a flick of a look in Lars's direction. Lars raised the walking stick and pressed it into Russell's neck. With Merinda's slight nod, he pressed harder.

"What?" St. Clair repeated, sounding as if he were choking.

"Harder!" Merinda bellowed to Lars.

"Wait! I'm no m-murderer! You think I went and m-murdered Milbrook? *Take this off me or I can't answer you!* You think I murdered Milbrook and Waverley and then stuck around to question them?"

"But Mueller?" Merinda asked, while sending another pointed look at their unexpected ally.

Lars leaned back and took the weight of his bulk with him. St. Clair was diminished in forced recline. Jem saw that St. Clair's Adam's apple bobbed as he swallowed uneasily, and his eyes under the dingy streetlight were fearful. "I-I didn't mean to! It was an accident…"

"An accident?"

"I-I wanted to teach him a lesson. He was hiding something. I knew he was."

"So it had been another night," Merinda began. "And you applied yourself to a patrol of your own making as you had many times before. But Hans evaded you, and Lars stepped in and you were angry. You never finished what you started. You knew that Hans worked at Spenser's—you had seen him en route before. The station is not that far from there. So you followed him, wanting to teach him a lesson. You found him, tired and a little beaten down from the night before, which made him easier to corner…"

"I didn't mean to kill him. All right? It wasn't my fault that he kept fighting back and that…I accidentally…" St. Clair cursed. "My only crime is wanting to drive these people away. I didn't mean to kill him." He swallowed, an act made difficult by the pressure of Merinda's stick on his throat. "And I wasn't the only person at Spenser's that night."

"Who else was there?" Jem asked.

"You think I know?"

Lars released the walking stick and pinned Russell's elbow behind his back. "What do we do now, Miss Herringford?"

Merinda clucked her tongue and tapped her brogan. "Well, three people have heard him confess to murder, so we had best take him into the station and let the police deal with him."

Jasper was startled to see Jem and Merinda lead Lars into the station house, a dirty, bleary-eyed St. Clair holding his sore neck and muttering a string of curses.

"What are you doing?" Jasper said to Merinda.

"Solving Hans Mueller's murder." Merinda shoved her finger into St. Clair's shoulder. "He may not be our white feather murderer, but he killed an innocent kid at Spenser's."

"It was an accident," St. Clair said through gritted teeth.

"Really? I was also there at the scene," Jasper said, coldly. "Didn't look much like an accident to me." He ran his hand over his face.

"Then you had the audacity to go and inform the family that…" He squeezed his eyes shut. "Never mind. It doesn't bear thinking about."

Jasper turned to Merinda, Jem, and Lars. "We can take it from here," he said, grabbing St. Clair's arm and leading him in the direction of his office for questioning. "You all had best be off home. It's late."

Merinda nodded, and the trio set out into the night, leaving Jasper disgruntled, shocked, and perplexed. His first thought was most likely the one running through Merinda's head. If St. Clair was Hans's murderer and the white feather found with him presumably an accident, their pattern was off.

Not twenty minutes later, St. Clair was moved to a holding cell with Tipton arriving due to the emergency phone call that dispatched him.

By the time the chief met with Jasper, his eyes were bleary, and he muttered several curses under his breath.

"I wouldn't have called for you, sir, if it wasn't an emergency," Jasper said, following Tipton into his office and watching the chief pour a finger of strong liquid from his decanter.

"Forth, you can't hold St. Clair."

"He admitted to killing the Mueller kid! There were witnesses. He's also the man prowling in the Ward and making the lives of these innocent people a living hell!"

"He says it was an accident."

"Some accident." Jasper ignored the chief's insistence that he take a seat.

"Can you imagine how this will look in the papers?" Tipton asked. "It's hard enough for us to scrape up some credibility as is. Let's just write it off as St. Clair being a little too rough. I'll give him a slap on the wrist and the public will never know."

Jasper's eyes widened "You can't be serious. He *killed* a boy, sir! An innocent boy! He's been smashing windows, probably getting in and around on account of being in uniform."

"He has a lot to learn, granted. But I am ordering you to keep quiet."

Jasper stood a moment, gripping his hands behind his back. They shook slightly. This was an order he wouldn't listen to, and it ran through his ears and buzzed through his fingers. He was stepping away from something deeply inherent in him, the response to a command.

"No, sir," Jasper said evenly.

"Excuse me, Forth? Are you disobeying my direct order?"

"Yes, I am, sir. I am going to let Toronto know there is no unseen terror. That there is a man responsible for the actions in the Ward, and that Hans Mueller died innocently as a result of the brutish tactics of a prejudiced officer."

"I will have your badge, Forth, so quickly that—"

Jasper reached into his pocket and flung it onto Tipton's desk. "Spare me, sir. I give it freely. I want nothing to do with your tyrannical brigade." He turned toward the door, his breath heaving and a cold sweat sheening his face. What had he done? Then, settled with a strange certainty, he turned. "I don't know what justice you're peddling here, but I can't believe in it anymore."

"You're a fool, Forth. You have a great career ahead of you. I am only doing what is best for the station."

"You are doing what is best for *you*. And *you* are not the law. And I will not subscribe to your skewed view of justice anymore."

"Forth, if you—"

But Jasper was gone, slamming the door behind him. He bounded into his office and then bounded out, grabbed a canvas sack from evidence, and returned to his office, collecting all of his trinkets and knickknacks and photographs—one of his parents, one of himself and Merinda—and he shoved them all in. When he left, he clicked closed the door of his office reverently, tipped his head in acknowledgment of Kirk, and set out into the night.

"Constable Forth!" Skip McCoy intercepted him on the station steps. "I heard of some sort of ruckus in the Ward."

"What are you doing sulking around the Ward at this time of night, Skip?" Jasper growled. He couldn't plaster even a semblance of amicability for the photographer this evening.

"Always following a story," Skip said, shoving his glasses up his nose. "Quote for the *Hog*?"

"I miss Ray," Jasper said sourly, taking the last steps of the station house without looking back.

"You have a lot of stuff there, Constable Forth," Skip said thoughtfully, looking at the sack Jasper was clutching.

"I just quit."

Skip came closer. "You quit the police? Now, *there* is a story." Skip proclaimed a headline: "*Tipton Loses His Finest.* What are you going to do now?"

"Besides sidestep nosy photographers?" Jasper smirked. "I haven't yet decided."

CHAPTER SIXTEEN

The boats lap into Toronto Harbor, and the trains belch smoke from Union Station, and droves of men in khaki filter in and out to the shrill of the train whistles while a band plays "The Maple Leaf Forever" in the corner. Mothers and sweethearts and wives wave handkerchiefs in white surrender to the change coursing through their world.

Newsies sell out within the first hours of the new day. Any news that would bring the victory that is promised us by Christmas.

The city empties of men young and middling, whose boots scrape the promenade of Yonge, heavy under its swinging Union Jacks in a mournful parade, before leaving for a world that might never release them.

In Britain, the men who have not yet enlisted find white feathers of cowardice slipped to them in shame.

And yet there is another layer to the corruption even as families wring their sorrows with their damp handkerchiefs: the self-same that waved their lads off to the fray. Those Torontonians who had the audacity to be born of a country that is pitted against Great Britain as we answer the piper's call.

Martha Kingston,* the *Globe and Mail*

---

* Ray DeLuca.

Time crawled. September arrived, and the newspapers were so preoccupied with the escalating conflict that the white feather murders took a back burner. Mayor Montague himself expressed solidarity with Chief Tipton, who was adamant police efforts were more productively charged in keeping the peace of the city.

"We must put these unfortunate events behind us," Montague was quoted as saying. "Violence in the Ward. Perceived notions of police neglect. We must move forward. We are all doing what we can."

Even though St. Clair had been deported back to his post in Hamilton, the vandalism in the Ward trolled onward. It seemed to come mostly from street kids now, but also from some grown men with an agenda. Tipton finally caved and saw that junior officers were put on double patrol. There was no one as able to elude detection as St. Clair had been. Not possessing his police disguise, it was easier to catch vandals and tyrants in the act.

Merinda visited Mouse almost daily, Jem sometimes at her side. Mrs. Malone was at the ready with baskets of her favorite treats. The doctors assumed something was pressing onto the little girl's brain, locking her in a slumber they were unsure would give way to eventual waking.

Martha Kingston's editorials in the *Globe* were so well received that when she pulled back the curtain on their true source, the staff at the city's most popular paper decided to hire Ray DeLuca themselves. The interim managing editor told Ray that it was unanimous. The whole staff, from the typesetters to researchers, had nothing but respect for his expositions. In Waverley's honor, Ray was assured, they were taking the paper in a new direction—and what better voice to lead the way?

Merinda rang to congratulate him, but he remained curt to her. Frustrated, she slammed down the receiver and returned to the blackboard.

"Obstinate!" she repeated over and over even as Mrs. Malone announced a visitor. "Are you settled into your new domestic bower?" Merinda was feeling surly as Jem walked into the parlor.

"Merinda, I thought you would be happy that we are closer and that we have working electricity and a telephone!" Jem couldn't stifle her smile. "I will be at your beck and call."

"Much good it will do us on this case," Merinda huffed.

"Perhaps this is not the most suitable hour for you to receive me." Jem's tone was sarcastic.

"What have we accomplished?"

"Merinda, please don't. You have done so much. What happened to Mouse is not your fault."

"What have we accomplished?"

"There are so many people whose lives are better because of your adamancy that a woman can pursue a man's profession. Our empathy and our resilience and our stubbornness have all contributed." She accepted the china cup Mrs. Malone handed her, exchanging a sympathetic nod with the housekeeper. When Jem wasn't in close proximity, she knew the dear lady was on the receiving end of many of Merinda's barbs. "Look at Heidi Mueller. Her brother's killer has been identified and is no longer in Toronto. There is one less insect prowling on the weak in St. John's Ward."

"And justice?" Merinda hedged.

"We have to believe that there will be final justice for him, Merinda," Jem said somberly. "If not here, then in the next life."

Merinda paced silently before flopping into her chair, stretching out her trouser-clad legs in front of her. "My world is changing. I don't want this autumn wind to come any closer and bewilder what is left of this summer. Is it our last summer, Jemima?"

"I-I can't say. Merinda, you need something to hold on to. Some fixed point."

"You're my fixed point, Jem." Her voice was tremulous.

"No. I cannot be. You know that. Once I was here, but then I met Ray and had Hamish and our world has changed. And it might keep evolving. You need to believe in something. Something beyond me."

Merinda shook her head at the empty hearth. "Don't."

"Merinda—"

"I believe in you and Jasper and DeLuca. But now..." She clutched the sides of her armchair and faced Jem straight on, her green eyes blazing. "DeLuca is no longer at the *Hog*, Jasper quit his job, Mouse is in the hospital, and you...I don't know what to believe in."

"I know," Jem said softly.

"I'm not ready."

"Maybe not. But you will be. Someday. I have faith in that. For now..." Jem raised an I-have-an-idea finger and turned toward the bureau. A moment later, she returned with the papers they had snapped from Philip Carr before Mouse's accident. "Keep your mind occupied. It *rebels at stagnation*." Jem laughed at her Holmes's paraphrase.

Merinda flipped through the papers with a fresh eye. "If we take this incriminating evidence to the police, what do you think they will do?" Merinda worked her teeth over her bottom lip. "Arrest Carr? Spenser? Montague?"

Jem shook her head. "Probably not, but I know you still believe that the white feather murderer is tied to the potential of this munitions smuggling. Someone who knew we would be on its trail."

Merinda studied the blackboard. "But who?"

"I have to go," Jem said, rising. "But I know we'll figure it out, Merinda. And now," she leaned forward to grip Merinda's hand a moment, "I am an easy telephone call away."

Merinda bellowed for Mrs. Malone to see Jemima out and then redirected her attention to the papers in front of her. She loomed over the photographs. One had a jagged tear at its right corner. She held it up to the light. It was grainy and somewhat underdeveloped, but she made out the familiar logo of "Spenser's" on the barrels and crates piled in a corner documented in the scene.

Merinda set it aside and studied the next picture. This one was harder to make out. The photographer had spent little time processing it. Only a slight imperfection blemished the top in a black smudge, but the rim of the photograph had been lazily clipped. The scene was rather bland—tiled walls and a cement floor, without the recognizable evidence the other photograph provided.

Merinda turned it over a few more times, losing herself in a dozen possibilities as to its whereabouts, when a knock at the door roused her.

A moment later, Mrs. Malone admitted Jasper.

Though dressed in civilian clothes, his bearing was the same as it had been on the police force. "I am at your disposal, Merinda."

"My disposal?"

"You needed me as your connection to the police force. I can't morally align myself with it anymore. So I will do what you need me to do to bring about the conclusion of this outstanding case, but I cannot apologize for acting on my convictions. Even those acted on regardless of your own selfish gain."

"Jasper, please."

"Merinda, I shall go mad without some occupation. Think of the freedom I have." He tapped his forehead. "Before, Tipton wouldn't sign off on my pursuing the white feather murders, but now..." He shrugged and settled easily onto the sofa. "Besides, Jemima is busy playing house."

"Hans Mueller's murder is solved." Merinda motioned in the direction of the blackboard. "Then why did I find a white feather at his resting place?"

"You said St. Clair thought he heard someone else."

Merinda nodded. "I thought I did too. The night of the ultimatum. Maybe I imagined it...or it could have been a raccoon...but..." Merinda exhaled and moved her gaze over the photographs. "Then there are these. They were in Carr's possession." She handed them to him. "One is clearly a layout of Spenser's. I have the blueprint of the warehouse as well." She bit her lip, watching Jasper study the print. "But the other? If this is an indication as to where they might smuggle their illegal weapons, then it would do well for us to determine the second location."

Merinda watched Jasper squint at the print before holding it up to the light.

While he perused it, Merinda pulled her knees to her chest, staring at no central point in the parlor. It was the same as ever: mismatched furniture of high value, crystal decanters and knickknacks from her parents' house at a dissonant clash with cushions and drapes and a Persian carpet of the same affluent history. All stamped with objects of the profession she was never sure she would excel at.

For Merinda Herringford was one of those rare people believed unflappable and ensconced by a heavy shell, and yet whose center was far more easily rattled than she would ever admit. Even to someone as close as Jasper.

She straightened her shoulders with a confidence she didn't feel and wondered what modicum of control she could exert. Outside the window, beyond the fluttering shadows of the falling light, the moon was harvest bright, foreshadowing the season slowly unfurling. It shrouded the edge of the Herringford and Watts sign, peeking up from its sentry at the front of the townhouse.

Simultaneously, she and Jasper spoke.

"Merinda, I have an idea…"

"Jasper, I have an idea…"

"Ladies first."

"I want to do something for Jem and DeLuca."

"That's rather benevolent of you," he said drily.

"And you'll help me? As you said, you have plenty of time on your hands."

He nodded.

"And you?"

"I know the location in this photograph."

Merinda jolted up. "Where?"

"The night of the Pelham dinner, Ray and I were given a tour of the automobiles in Sir Henry's extensive garage." He nudged the photo toward her. "The tile. Merinda, this photo was taken at Pelham Park."

Merinda brightened. "Of course!" She clapped. Then her brow furrowed. "I just need to find a way back in."

"Lemon everything!" Merinda instructed Mrs. Malone. "Tarts, sandwiches." She threw her hands in the air. "Even lemonade!"

Merinda surveyed the room and the large frame covered with a black dust sheet perched atop the easel that usually held her blackboard. After Jasper had recognized the Pelham mansion in one of Carr's photographs, Merinda put good use to Jem's new telephone and instructed her to find some way to return to Pelham Park. "Make up something about our canvassing for a hospital ship."

Jem acquiesced, and now Merinda awaited her first guest.

When Mrs. Malone ushered Ray into the sitting room, he turned his hat over in his hands. "Merinda, sometimes I say stupid things."

She cocked her head to the side. "Is this an apology?"

"I just…"

"Never you mind, DeLuca. You'll just trip over a bunch of sentences in a hybrid of languages and then end up telling me I was right."

"That was not exactly—"

"Besides, if you prattle on, I cannot give you your present. Come!" She tugged him into the dining room, where a shiny new typewriter sat proudly on the lace tablecloth.

"I can't accept this," Ray said, admiring the smooth veneer of the new Underwood. "There's no missing *H* key! My fingers wouldn't be able to find their way around." He winked.

"It's the latest model," Merinda said shortly. "You'll need it for your new job."

"I can't accept it."

"It's a birthday present."

"It's not my birthday."

"Well, it was, wasn't it?" she said, huffing. "Cracker jacks! And I clearly failed to give you a present, and…DeLuca! Don't stand there smirking at me. Just take the stupid typewriter." She ran her index finger over the side of the apparatus. "I don't like it when we get to blows." Her voice was soft.

"I don't either." He grimaced. "Merinda…"

"I told you," she said snarkily. "I don't want to hear you mumble an apology."

Ray smiled, pressing at the keys with his dark fingers. "I should make you take it back." He caressed the *H* key while raising his head so their eyes locked. "But I am far too fond of it."

Merinda's Cheshire grin spread wide.

Jem arrived not two moments later, her smile radiant as the marquee at the Elgin. "Jasper's straight behind!" she said, admiring Mrs. Malone's liberal spread of sandwiches, cheese, and fairy cakes.

Jasper then appeared, bearing something whose value outshined Merinda's typewriter. Hamish peeked out from under the large police hat Jasper had placed on his head.

"He can hardly see!" Ray said with feigned annoyance, scooping up Hamish, removing the hat, and kissing the boy heartily on each cheek. "Where did you come from, Hamish?" he asked, studying his son's big blue eyes.

Hamish just smiled and repeated the word "hat" a few times.

"There's no sense in living in fear, Ray DeLuca," Jem said, sidling beside him and running her fingers through Hamish's curls. "Besides, we both missed him something fierce. Mrs. Malone has offered to help where she can during the remainder of the case, as has Jasper's mother. Indeed, it was the wonderful Mrs. Forth who arranged to pick up Hamish in London on a return trip from visiting her sister."

When the baby had been kissed, cuddled, and hugged by one and all and then tucked into bed in Mrs. Malone's quarters behind the kitchen, the quartet settled comfortably into chairs. Merinda popped up to retrieve a bottle of champagne from the sideboard in the adjoining dining room and poured it into four flutes.

Ray watched the bubbles pop and fizz through the amber liquid, while Jem tipped up a sip that tickled her nose.

"You may think we are here to celebrate DeLuca's well-deserved transfer to the *Globe*," Merinda began. "Or Jasper's foolish and rash decision to quit the police."

Jasper swallowed his champagne too quickly and choked. "A very optimistic way to put it." He moved to clink glasses, but Merinda stalled him.

"But we are toasting *neither of those things*."

"The glorious war effort?" Jem asked.

"Too many auxiliary meetings for Merinda's taste," Ray quipped.

"I had a very enlightened idea, and I wanted to show you the fruits of my labor."*

She rose and inclined her champagne glass. "You may notice something amiss in this room."

"Your blackboard is gone," Ray surmised, wondering if he should forgo the toast and just taste the champagne.

"Indeed, DeLuca, and in its stead is something I believe you and Jem will appreciate."

Jem rose slightly in her seat. "You have my interest."

"And mine," Ray agreed.

Merinda tugged the dust sheet away with the flair of a matador and then awaited the inevitable excitement that would follow the unveiling.

The inevitable excitement, however, was not to be found on Jem's and Ray's stunned expressions.

"What?" Merinda waved at the newly created sign reading *Herringford and DeLuca* in an ornamented font. "It's the same specifications of the previous sign, just a little less weather-beaten and more reflective of our practice."

"Merinda..." Jem began. "I don't know what..." She rose and threw her arms around Merinda's neck. Merinda returned the embrace by patting her awkwardly on the head.

"I think you should put the old sign back," Ray said in a low voice.

Merinda swerved to face Ray so quickly she sloshed the champagne in her glass. She locked eyes with him. "I will not sit here and let this city continue to praise Jem and me for establishing a symbol of

---

* Read: Merinda picked up the telephone and dialed a carpenter.

feminine fortitude and resilience while treating others so abominably. Women like Heidi Mueller." Her eyes drifted to the sign a moment and then went back to Ray. She waved to Jasper. "He helped!"

Jasper nodded. "Merinda thinks we can all do better. For everyone." He looked at Jem kindly. "And I agree."

"Why aren't you saying anything, DeLuca?" Merinda chided. "I thought…"

Ray exchanged a look with Jem and then focused on Merinda. "I always thought she should have one part of her life separate from me."

Jem shook her head, laughing softly. "Really? Ray, I can cite plenty of arguments we have had that contradict that statement." She gave him a knowing wink. "That's not how marriage works."

"I'm not finished, Jemima." He cleared his throat. "I always thought it would protect you. That my name might hinder where you could go or what you could do."

"I won't give into them, DeLuca." Merinda stood her ground. "And neither should you. Your name and your voice recently found you a promotion you had dreamed about. Jem, you need to stop being something you are not."

Jem nodded. "I know."

"So a toast, finally?" Jasper rose extending his arm.

"There is one thing I appreciate about the war," Jasper said before biting into a lemon sandwich. "It's been rather romantic to watch."

Merinda answered with a combination of vowels that failed to make up a proper word.

"I am serious, Merinda. The ladies who see their young men off put in all the effort in the world. These young men are stepping into some brave frontier, and we cannot comprehend what awaits them, and they are rewarded by women who give them a picture to come home for."

"A picture to come home for," Jem repeated softly. "I like that."

"The ladies do their hair and put on their Sunday best and wear flowers and…" Jasper sighed. "I just think it's wonderful for those young men to know it's worth it and they have that memory to carry. And all of our strict rules about propriety? Well, the Morality Squad can go hang the moment those young uniformed men take their best girl in their arms and give her a kiss…"

Ray laughed.

Merinda cocked her head to one side. "You've been spending a lot of time thinking about the war, Jasper Forth."

He shrugged. "It's of interest to all of us these days."

"Indeed," Merinda said evasively, setting down her half-finished champagne and watching Jasper with renewed interest.

Jasper finished his sandwich.

"I never want this to change." Jem's eyes glistened. "Us. Sitting here. Toasting. That gorgeous new sign. There is nothing better in all the world."

"Everything changes, Jemima," Ray said quietly.

"But I want to bottle this moment, Ray. Merinda giving Jasper a hard time! You admiring your new typewriter. When we are safe and we are *here*. And I worry that tomorrow or next week or next month I will be angry with myself for not holding on as tightly as I should have. For not clinging to and savoring every solitary second!"

The mood decidedly changed. Jasper silently nibbled at another sandwich, while Ray inspected first his new Underwood and then the new sign. Jem dabbed at her eyes.

"This is unbearable!" Merinda pierced the silence after a moment. "There have been so few opportunities for fun lately. Come, Jasper." She took a sip of her champagne with gusto. "Let's go into the sitting room, where I'll beat you at checkers."

Merinda cheated her way through a round and then contentedly sighed. "I challenge you to another! Best two out of three."

"You'll win three out of three if you keep cheating like that," Jasper teased.

Merinda didn't hear him and concentrated on setting up the board for another match.

"I passed my medical exam, Merinda."

"Hmm?"

"Early this afternoon when you were finalizing things for our little soiree. I passed."

Merinda stared at him a moment, and then realization came over her face. Just as quickly she moved her eyes back to the checkerboard. "I don't know why you're telling me this. Surely you don't mean to enlist."

"I already have," he said gravely.

Merinda shook her head. Slowly at first, and then faster. "No. No, you didn't. You didn't consult with me."

"I'm no longer on the police force. I need to do something."

She shook her head a few more times, her curls bouncing in the firelight. "You said *our* world needed changing first. You said…"

Jasper smiled ruefully, touched by her strong reaction. "It's the right thing to do."

"It's *not*! I need someone to rely on…I need…"

"You have Jem," he reminded her gently.

"I don't have Jem for chemical experiments on Saturday afternoons. I don't have her when she needs to go running after DeLuca and Hamish. *You* are my unconditional, Jasper."

He snapped at the opportunity and took her hand across the board. "Merinda, I will always be your unconditional." He tightened his grip, and his eyes bored into hers. "I will always be there for you. You will always be the first thing in my life. What I am fighting for." He smiled, the words he'd longed to say finally unfettered. "You know I love you. I have always loved you, and I always will. And I believe in you. As my equal. I believe in you because we are the same. We share a passion for truth and an innate sense of justice. When I am over there in those European fields, I will be willing to die daily if it means that your world will be a better place. A place where you can pursue any-thing you wish and be respected for the remarkable woman you are."

She shook her head. "No." Her eyes glistened. "No, you can't go. Jasper, I don't want you to go."

"I can't stay, but I will be yours. Forever, Merinda. It would take so little on your part. Everything on my own. I would tilt the world over if it meant you would be mine. I will come back. The slightest word will make me face anything with a strength only you can give me." He tightened his hold. While her knuckles were white, she didn't pull away.

"Jasper, if only…"

"You hang the moon for me. But what's more, you're my dearest, dearest friend. There is no one I can talk or laugh with the way I can with you." He leaned forward, and though his breath on the tendrils of her bobbed hair made them move in a whisper across her cheek, she didn't pull away. "Merinda, I have saved money. For you…for a life…when I get back."

"I have my father's money," she said weakly.

"But you don't need it. Do you see how happy Jem and Ray make each other?"

Merinda couldn't say anything without stepping on dynamite. "Jasper, I just can't be the woman you need. And I never, ever will be. Never be one of those girls you talked about that you can use to paint a picture in your mind." She rose, almost tipping the board with the sudden movement. "But that doesn't mean I will let you go."

"You say that now—"

"No more!"

"I'm persistent, Merinda."

"I know. It's one of the many things I admire about you." She slumped in the direction of the dining room, where she could hear Jem and Ray's quiet laughter rippling in the low light.

Chapter Seventeen

*Cases are meant to confound us. If they were tied into
neat, predictable bows, the clever detective would
have nothing on which to cut his deductive teeth. In
order to better learn about the world around us and
to better understand the hidden depths of ourselves,
we have to be foiled, to come to a fork in the road, to
be muddled. It is only as we work through the tenets
of uncertainty that we are able to truly understand
the experience gained from moments of confusion.*

M.C. Wheaton, *Guide to the Criminal and Commonplace*

Merinda shot and reloaded and shot and reloaded, and at the *swooshing* of each bullet, a piece of her was reconciled. She imagined him: the faceless person, the white feather murderer who had preyed on her friends, and she imagined hitting him on impact. The sour-faced overseer was visibly impressed by Merinda's efforts but kindly chided her to take the rest of the morning off to save powder for the other participants and for the greater war at large. Merinda saw the first crack of a smile on the coarse woman's pasty face.

"It's not just your accuracy," the overseer said. "It's the confidence in your bearing. If the enemy saw you, they might take one look at the steel glint in your eyes and run for cover!"

The rifle fell to Merinda's side. She stared after the overseer a moment and then turned to Jem. "'What you do in this world is a matter of no consequence,'" Merinda said, quoting Holmes. "'The question is what you can make people believe you have done.'"

"I'm working to be proficient enough to blast the initials V.R. into our sitting room, much as Sherlock Holmes did at Baker Street," Jem said proudly, raising the rifle to her shoulder.

"You're improving," the overseer said.

Once they finished at the range, Jem stretched. "Rib is getting better every day!" she announced. "And there's something about this— about our practice here, hoisting a rifle over my shoulder that makes me believe I can do anything."

Merinda chewed on this a moment. "And what is 'anything'?"

Jem shrugged easily. "Finish settling. Invite my parents to tea. Make them see how my life really is and how I have made a home for myself, albeit a nontraditional one. Maybe I could tuck all my insecurities behind the door when they arrived, just like I do with the gun! Maybe I could straighten my shoulders and make them believe, as Holmes says, that I am something that…"

Merinda grabbed Jem's arm so tightly that her friend's sentence cut off. "And it will be more than a question of what you can make them believe you have done," Merinda paraphrased. "Jem, that's it!"

"Pardon?"

"What you can make people *believe* you have done."

"You're speaking in riddles, Merinda. Otherwise it's your golden moment. Either way, they are interchangeable and—"

"When is our meeting with Lady Adelaide?" Merinda consulted the timepiece attached to her shirtwaist.

"Not for another hour."

"We don't have an hour to lose!" Merinda announced, returning their rifles to storage and dragging Jemima through the range and out to the street. A short taxi ride later, they arrived at Sir Henry and Lady Adelaide's grand estate.

Pelham Park courted the sunny day well. Bright rays shone over the manicured lawn, and the many gleaming windows in the mansion's turrets beautifully mirrored the cloudless sky's reflection.

Merinda and Jem crossed over the tiles as they followed the maid into the library. Jem gasped at volumes and volumes settled cozily on dark mahogany shelves, while Merinda's eyes drank in the gleaming rifles and swords ornamenting the library, her gaze ever upward even as women lowered themselves into red-leather chairs.

"So pleased you could come early." Lady Adelaide smiled kindly at them. "I would have received you in the conservatory, but we have a fellow working on the indoor swimming pool. Some form of water sanitization, and the smell is something pungent. Here we have dark coolness. The perfect place to conspire." She gave them a friendly wink. "And fear not, Miss Herringford. I have been assured that our illustrious peacock is restrained."

Jem made a noise between a cough and a snort.

Lady Pelham pretended not to hear her. "When our construction is finished, I will ensure you have a tour. My husband has hired Canada's most prominent architects from Montreal to oversee the completion of a second building of sorts. You see, underneath Pelham Park is a tunnel that leads through the coal stores, but then further still to a staircase that leads up to a grand structure and garages the distance of a few city blocks away."

Jem emitted an interested "ahh..."

Merinda didn't seem to hear at all. "And what are we conspiring about today?" she asked, eyeing the many-tiered tray displaying numerous delicacies a maid carried in, while another with pristine gloves poured strong-looking coffee into their cups.

"Miss Herringford, I hear you are quite fond of Turkish coffee."

"I am!" Merinda said, her eyes as round as saucers, greedily watching her china cup filled with dark liquid.

"I wondered if you had ever tried Viennese coffee. My husband special orders it." Lady Pelham waved an inviting hand, and Merinda raised the cup to her lips.

She closed her eyes as the strong, bitter tang washed over her taste buds and lingered on her tongue. There was an almost burnt aftertaste, reminiscent of the Turkish coffee she was so fond of, but with a slightly different note.

"That is delicious!" she exclaimed.

"I am having Cook package some of it for you to take home. As a little thank-you for all of your assistance."

"We feel we could do more," Jem said. "We have been canvassing with the other women, and we think we have been able to raise as much as anyone for the hospital ship, but with more and more men shipping out every day…" Jem didn't need to finish her sentence. All three knew the ramifications of a city drained of able young men. Sons, husbands, fathers. Would their city become a tap of men that drained away to the faraway fields of Europe, never to return?

Lady Adelaide sighed in acknowledgment and then began to list several of the ideas she had. Everything from tearing bandages to knitting socks.

"Lady Adelaide," Merinda said, interrupting her.

"Hmm?" Lady Adelaide's attention was still on Jem, her fingers still splayed, counting off some of the budgetary results of the last auxiliary meeting.

"Might I freshen up?"

"Of course, my dear. You will find the facilities at the end of the hall."

Merinda gave Jem a quick nod, and Jem continued holding Lady Adelaide's attention with questions about the war effort. Like an overturned vessel, Lady Adelaide's desire to speak of all of her grand ideas would likely spill for several minutes, especially when prompted by Jemima's interest and enthusiasm.

Merinda walked through the doorway toward the modern lavatory to the end of the hallway. During their visit to Pelham Park for dinner, she had noted Sir Henry's study. Its door had slightly creaked open as Sir Henry entertained a gentleman whose face and voice Merinda had been unable to make out through the slight slit. While Sir Henry had returned to the dinner table mere moments after Merinda, the figure he had conversed with was nowhere to be seen.

Now Merinda was met with a locked door. She reached into her pocket and extracted her set of picklocks, the second she tried fixing its way into the latch and opening the lock. Merinda closed the door gingerly behind her and looked around the rich study. Its coloring was the same dark mahogany as the library, its chairs and sofa the identical red leather.

On Sir Henry's desk, framed photographs of his family set off a modern typewriter that had pride of place amid various documents, ledgers, and knickknacks. A meerschaum pipe and gold-plated tobacco box sat atop a stack of papers. Merinda looked about instinctively and was met with silence. Nothing shifted in the quiet room save the slight breeze ruffling the curtains from the slightly open window.

Merinda carefully moved the pipe and tobacco box. The papers were blueprints and requisition orders for all manner of ammunition. Beneath them were a few photographs of a warehouse she assumed was Spenser's—a theory confirmed a second later when she made out the familiar insignia on some of the crates. She ran her fingers around the perimeter of the photograph. It was taken at a strange angle, fuzzy at the top. Jagged too. She realized that the photograph had been doctored and the top cut off.

Merinda was in the process of folding the papers and tucking them into the hidden pocket in her vest* when the clang of the telephone at the edge of the desk startled her. She fell against the desk, and one of the framed photographs toppled over, facedown. She caught her breath as the jangling chime of the telephone's ringing finally desisted. She gently righted the photograph, mortified that a jagged crack marred its shiny glass.

"Miss Herringford, however did you get into my office?"

Merinda jumped at Sir Henry's appearance. Then she smoothed her trousers and tilted her chin forward. "I believe you are in league with the white feather murderer."

Sir Henry chuckled. "You sound like a dreadful in a dime serial."

"I have reason to suspect, sir, that your premises have been scouted

---

* The longer Merinda pursued the detective trade, the more she relied on Mrs. Malone's proficiency with a needle to supplement her wardrobe with all manner of hidden pockets and compartments.

as a possible way of transporting illegal weapons and arms alongside Thaddeus Spenser's retail establishment."

Sir Henry cocked a bushy eyebrow. "Indeed? Well, do sit down, Miss Herringford." He settled behind his desk and motioned to a chair directly across from him.

"The papers you have on your desk are nearly identical to plans I confiscated from Philip Carr. Photographs were included in those documents. One of the photos boasts the same tile used at the edge of the tunnel that leads to your garage."

"And my swimming pool. You *are* bright. But you are misguided."

"How so?"

"I cannot speak for Philip Carr, but for my own part, my park is being outfitted not for the transportation of weapons but of the wounded."

"The wounded?" Merinda gasped.

"This will be a conflict unlike any we have seen before." Sir Henry opened the gold-plated tobacco box on his desk, filled the bowl of the meerschaum pipe, and then struck a match. After a few puffs, he studied Merinda amicably. "All manner of warfare is being created and experiments run on it. It will kill and maim and destroy, and if there is the slightest chance that the grand space with which I have been blessed could potentially save lives, then I mean to offer it."

"I had no idea that—"

"The modern age is a fascinating conflict all its own, Miss Herringford. While there is progress and automobiles and transportation unlike any we have ever seen, there is also the potential for us to use the great strides we have made in the realms of science and machinery for devious end." Sir Henry smiled. "And I wish to ensure that we are champions of progress. Such conflict can only set us backward. I yearn to go forward."

"So you are not on a committee with Spenser and Montague to smuggle munitions and other implements of warfare?"

"Absolutely not. I have too much respect for your country and for my homeland."

Merinda rose. "I should return to Lady Pelham. I am truly sorry for barging in."

Sir Henry shook his head. "All is forgiven."

"And…I cracked your picture frame," she added, backing toward the door. "I'm sorry about that too."

"Easily fixed. A bit like Lincoln, eh?"

"Pardon?"

"The famous photograph." Sir Henry picked up the frame and ran a finger over the crack in the glass. "I suppose it must have been a faulty camera. There's old Abe sitting prim and stoic as can be, and a crack runs right over the top of his head in the portrait. When you think of it…" Sir Henry looked up to an empty office. "Miss Herringford? Miss Herringford!"

"I am an atrocious knitter," Jem informed Lady Adelaide. "I could no more knit socks for our glorious troops than I could coax that metallic knight over there into a dance."

Lady Adelaide laughed, pinching a fairy cake from the tray. "My dear, of course. My husband calls him Herbert in jest. Did you find him at arms again?"

Jem laughed and then abruptly stopped when she heard Merinda's voice shrieking for her even before she appeared breathless in the door of the library. "Jemima! I need you!" She clapped her hands jubilantly. "I think I know who the white feather murderer is!"

"Excuse me?" gasped Lady Adelaide. "The murderer? What does she mean?" Lady Adelaide's eyes darted between Jem and Merinda and then back to Jem again.

Jem gingerly set her china cup on her saucer and kept her voice even. "I am certain Merinda is just having a revelation. She is renowned for these outbursts." Jem feigned a smile. "She calls them her 'golden moments.'"

"Is the murderer here, Miss Herringford?"

Merinda stood silently ruminating.

Jem flashed her friend a dagger look. "Sometimes my friend forsakes propriety. Especially when she has a big idea."

"So there is nothing to fear?" Lady Adelaide asked tentatively, her fairy cake hovering in midair.

"Not in the least," Jem assured her, rising. "But…if you'll excuse me?"

Chapter Eighteen

Every criminal will leave some signature, for as much as he wants to duck justice, his ego finds a balm in recognition.

M.C. Wheaton, *Guide to the Criminal and Commonplace*

Once Jem had left Lady Adelaide to her tea with as much decorum as she could muster in the face of her friend's revelation, it was all she could do not to dash after her. She matched Merinda's determined stride across the grand foyer.

"At first I thought it was that quote. Something about what you could make people believe you had done." Merinda waved her hand about in the air. "Here are all these men auspiciously contributing to the war effort who stand to make a profit. But Sir Henry is a man I feel I can take at his word."

"So who is the murderer?"

"Jemima, the most beguiling aspect of having a golden moment* is having someone to explain it to. Piece by piece."

"Piece by piece," Jem gritted out impatiently.

"I supposed it could have been that Carr fellow. He's just the sort of ridiculous chap I would attribute something like this to. But he has a solid alibi the night of Milbrook's murder. He was with Mayor Montague."

"I suppose."

---

* Readers familiar with Merinda Herringford's previous (mis)adventures in murder and mystery will recall this as the term she ascribes to her moments of particular brilliance.

"And while he is doubtless involved in some underhanded enterprise with Montague and Spenser, he is not responsible for the deaths we are investigating. It wasn't until I saw the photograph—"

"The photograph?"

"In Sir Henry's study," Merinda explained airily before barreling onward. "We would need someone who could be at all levels of society. Who could borrow an automobile from a friend he'd made at a grand estate or slip in and out of a crime scene nearly undetected. Someone who knew what was going on in the Ward at night, could trail a policeman to Spenser's, and then frame said policeman with a white feather. Someone who had access to the Pelham doves. Someone who knew where we might be headed after Waverley's death. Someone right under our noses." Merinda looked over her shoulder to see if Jem was catching up. While a flicker of something crossed her friend's face, Jem remained silent, and Merinda carried on. "Then I saw the photograph in Sir Henry's study. The frame cracked when I accidentally knocked it over. Sir Henry mentioned that famous final portrait of President Lincoln and how—"

Jem suddenly gasped, clearly following her friend's train of thought.

Merinda nodded. "That line that overruns the stoic portrait. Cuts right through." She grinned. "There must have been something. Something about the…" Merinda snapped her fingers while searching for a word, "…exposure! First there was that day at the *Hog* when he was snipping off the tops of the photographs. He could have been removing the fractured line from the pictures: a result of his camera being jostled that night at the ultimatum. Then the photographs I found in Pelham's study and the ones we found on Philip Carr." Merinda was beaming. "It's been Skip McCoy all along!" She grabbed Jem's forearm.

"He can work through all levels of society," Jem conceded. "But why?"

Merinda looked around the broad foyer. "Because he stands to gain from something greater than Sir Henry's benevolent plans for his grand house."

"May I fetch you ladies a taxi or a ride home?" a servant asked.

"Yes, thank you." Merinda patted around her vest, praising Mrs. Malone's latest ingenuity in hidden pockets. But not feeling the weight of her pistol therein, she scowled.

"I didn't suppose you would find yourself armed so easily," Jem said as they crossed the lawn toward the waiting taxi.

"I cannot believe I left my own pistol in the bureau," Merinda replied, rebuking herself.

"I cannot believe Sir Henry loaned one of his pistols to you with no questions asked." Jem watched Merinda secure the gun at the back of her vest.

"I suppose we developed quite a rapport while he was telling me about his charitable plans and I was unravelling the last threads of our mystery."

"And you think Skip will just be sitting at the *Hog* snipping pictures?"

"If he isn't there, we will await his return and intercept him. A criminal will always return to the scene of the crime, and a criminal always wants to be caught on some base level, and—"

"Now you're just taking all of your Wheaton quotes and sewing them together."

"Jemima! What if he's *here*?"

"At Pelham Park?"

"Lady Adelaide mentioned someone working on the pool, but Skip's *Hog* articles and information given to us the night of the party both mentioned that the pool construction was halted in order to loan men to the war effort. Sir Henry decided it was the last part of the mansion that needed completion." Merinda spun on her heel back in the direction of the main house, and Jem followed suit. "When I showed Jasper the photograph, he recognized the tile. Sir Henry thought it was part of the plans he is pursuing in preparing an emergency hospital. But what if something else is happening right under his nose?"

"Philip Carr and Skip?" Jem wondered.

"There's only one way to find out." Merinda grabbed Jem's arm and tugged her over the green lawn and up the walk of the estate. Inside, they shoved past the butler and several uniformed servants in pursuit of the back staircase. "A shame we only made it this far on our tour!" Merinda said wryly as they dashed down the stairs to the lower level, skidding out of the way of the staff.

"Please excuse us," Jemima entreated of a young woman affixing a white cap to red curls. "We are lady detectives in pursuit of a criminal, and we are wondering if you might indicate the way to the underground tunnels."

The girl held up a pale finger and pointed.

Jemima kept a hand to her rib as Merinda hurried them through the corridor and then farther and farther below the grandeur of Pelham Park.

The stairs leading to the underground tunnel were dank and slick, but the coolness of the lanterned passage was still a fine reprieve from the heat of September mugginess. They slowed at the sound of belches and gulps from the furnace and boilers, tiptoeing over the grate and then peeking into the dark coals and incendiary sparks. Soot-faced workers were providing the grand estate with hot water even as they toiled and scraped with the coals below.

A little farther in the tunnel, Merinda assessed its resourcefulness. It was a perfect place to store and redistribute any type of munitions needed for profit. She half recalled Lady Pelham's rather innocent explanation of its resourcefulness. A place to store coal and heat the house! Ha! All that was needed was a quick trip into Hamilton or the Niagara region to pick up ammunition at a discounted price from still neutral America, slice a bit of the profit, and then divide evenly. The factories being built at the edge of the city would wonder why their product, no matter how quickly produced once everything was in full swing, wasn't as much of a necessity. A nation at war would pay little attention to what was sent over to the brave men in the front lines. A nation at war would load the cargo, uncaring as to where the weapons came from and concerned only that they make swift voyage across the sea and into the hands of the lads who needed them to battle the German enemies on the front lines.

Merinda motioned for Jem to get behind her as they approached the light at the end of the tunnel. They walked across slowly toward it and noted the interruption of the darkness by ascension into light. If Merinda were of the philosophical type, she might have admitted that a staircase leading toward a lighter, cleaner prospect was some sort of emblem. As it was, she was just happy to have a way out of the constricting underground passage.

They knew that at the top they would come to the grand stables and garage. A faint tang of bleaching powder tickled Merinda's nostrils—a welcome reprieve from the coal- and soot-infested tunnel underneath. Jem's breath was close behind her as they went up, pausing to grip the railing, the natural daylight flickering finally through a window overhead. Merinda reached behind her back to the hidden pocket and patted her borrowed pistol. She then passed her walking stick to Jem, who held it aloft.

"Skip McCoy!" Merinda shouted, her echo reverberating through the stairwell.

A moment later, Skip's shadow filled the doorway at the top of the stairs. "Isn't the security here a travesty?" he asked as he nudged his glasses up on his nose and directed a pistol at Jem's chest.

Chapter Nineteen

Jem yelped slightly.

"Did you really kill all those people just for a profit made from the sale of munitions?" Merinda asked levelly, her eyes never leaving Skip's gun.

Skip smiled and waved them up the rest of the way. As they reluctantly joined him on the landing, he grabbed Jem's arm and pressed his gun into her side. Then he said casually, "Munitions?" His voice echoed somewhat in the corridor running along the side of the garage.

"Tell me! You had access to the Pelhams' cars."

"Sir Henry trusted a friend to do some work for him nearby. I merely *intercepted* the friend."

"And promised him what?"

"I promised him a cut. I took the green automobile with the express purpose of a quick getaway after dealing with poor Waverley, but then you two came sniffing around."

Merinda took a step forward. "How much is your cut? Are you working with Philip Carr?"

"You ask a lot of questions." Skip straightened. He wasn't a prepossessing figure, but Merinda knew he was wiry and fast.

"Come," he said, moving slowly, Jem walking alongside him out of necessity and Merinda attempting to formulate a plan. "See where all of the war effort is happening."

He led them through the corridor to a door that opened up into a different building. There sat the not-yet-finished indoor swimming pool.

"They're such nice people, these Pelhams, that they've delayed construction on the estate so that young men can enlist." Skip gave a dark laugh. "Not that their building plans make much sense. Stables and a swimming pool and a garage all connected to the main house by an underground tunnel?" He looked around and shrugged. "Cleaner to be working with bleach powders than shot in a trench."

Jem and Merinda peeked into the dug-out marble rectangle.

"So it's a quiet and unsuspecting place." Skip's voice rumbled back at them in an echo. "And far enough from the main house to avoid any real suspicion. Even from Lady Adelaide, who keeps taking me at my word that I am merely surveying here."

"I don't understand," Jem said, watching Skip look to the far side of the pool, where a set of silver stairs leaned against the side for eventual installation.

"You think I want to spend the rest of my life at the *Hogtown Herald*, Mrs. DeLuca?"

"I suppose not."

"It's always been a perfect ruse. I can move around. No one suspects me of doing anything. I'm smarter than they think too. And polite. Timid." He shot a look at Merinda. "DeLuca would leave his Cartier Club minutes in a drawer in his desk. And despite all his careful organization, if a telephone call came from his wife that he had forgotten supper or that his young son was running a temperature, forcing him home early, he would sometimes forget to lock that drawer. I confess to orchestrating ways to get him out of the office. I started reading about how all of you reformers were redirecting your thoughts from curing tuberculosis to monitoring our new British war agent. By that point we had already developed a bit of a connection. Then I went to Milbrook's office to interview him, and some politician he is. He immediately started talking about his first days in office and how he would commission a report on Spenser's conduct. He always thought we were too lenient when it came to monitoring Spenser's shipments." He transferred the gun to his other hand and scratched his neck.

"So you killed him," Merinda summarized with a quick glance back to Jem.

"He made me think he had more on Spenser than I thought he had a right to."

"Then Alexander Waverley?"

"The *Globe* was fine as long as it was in Montague's pocket, but Waverley was going rogue. I knew he was plotting something. I knew because I read the changing tone of the articles." He laughed. "I suppose I was more engaged in journalistic competition than I had right to be. He really enjoyed running pieces on Carr. Carr's job was to ensure we were ready for war. And *I* was making sure we were ready for war. Some people were readying themselves by throwing their lot in with the conflict. I was ensuring we had the resources."

"Very selfless of you, I am sure," Merinda said, scowling.

Skip shrugged.

"Why the white feathers?" Jem asked.

"I think most of the police are incompetent. They just follow Tipton around. Then there was that lout, St. Clair. It was something I heard him say on assignment in the Ward one night, preaching on about the glorious war against the Boers. I decided if I was going to keep everyone off my trail, I should make it a bit of a game."

"A terrible, deadly game," interpreted Jem.

"But some are bright. Even Jasper Forth. I wanted to give him a bit of a run about." Here Skip's eyes shone on Merinda. "And by him, I also mean you, because you know you are smarter than most of the lot of them."

"Strange your complimenting me." Merinda shifted her weight, feeling the familiar steel of her gun against her light cotton shirt.

"You have foiled every plan I have ever had." He looked between them. "I thought you would have caught on by now. But even though you're brighter, you must still have your blinders on. So expound, Merinda Herringford. I have time."

"I don't care to expound," Merinda said calmly, even as the wheels in her brain instinctively chugged.

Skip moved the gun from Jem's side to her temple and pulled back the hammer. "I think you care to expound on this."

Merinda, flustered, stared at Jem, who was calmly terrified and then blinked at the reflection of the sun through the grated windows, which flowed over the green of the tile in a sickly emerald glimmer.

"All right." Merinda squeezed her eyes shut. "Skip McCoy, the photographer who has a broken plate. Skip McCoy, the *Hog* photographer who knows the tunnels and traps of Toronto. Who bored me several times with urban legends about a tunnel built from underneath the bank and exiting at Massey Hall…" Merinda opened her eyes and stared, the rhythm of her realization picking up pace. "Skip McCoy, who could easily have been involved with Spenser and Montague in a gambling ring that—"

"That you mucked up, thanks to your trailing after things that are none of your business!"

Merinda's eyes opened wider. She saw Skip now as if encountering him for the first time, and the longer she stared at him, his white knuckles straining on the pistol he held to Jemima's head, the curtain peeled back further. "The night of the Emma Goldman rally!" she continued. "I was at the *Hog*, and I saw a maple syrup requisition form, and…you were involved. You were involved with Spenser somehow, ensuring that the anarchists got their explosives and you got a cut."*

"There are so many hidden nooks and crannies at the *Hog*," Skip

---

* The careful reader familiar with *The Bachelor Girl's Guide to Murder* and *A Lesson in Love and Murder* will recall these instances.

explained easily. "I doubt even DeLuca has ever gone up to that rickety old attic." He shrugged. "Spenser needed another ally."

"And now…munitions," Merinda concluded.

"I didn't just wake up one day and decide to be involved. I built a trajectory, and somehow you found a way to stop all of my payments." He shook his head. "In a million years I never suspected you would be the one in Chicago."

"We weren't there for you!"

"Of course not. This is peripheral. But then I decided to play with you. Because I could easily have just knocked each one of these men off. But it was more fun if you trailed me. Sometimes DeLuca would quote that silly guidebook of yours. Wheaton something or other. Something about how there is a part of the criminal that needs recognition."

Skip turned to Jem and watched her for a few moments. She breathed slowly, the slight movement through her parted lips flickering the tendrils grazing her cheek. "Then Mr. DeLuca started sniffing around. The night after the ultimatum, he told McCormick and me that he was going to start redeeming Milbrook's name. I knew where that would lead." He smiled at Jem. "Nothing would have set Mr. DeLuca further off course. I didn't plan on killing you. I just thought I would distract him for a bit."

"In that much we were right," Merinda grumbled, mostly to herself. Then, "Mouse!"

"You sent those urchins trolling around Carr. But that was a by-the-way. At that point, I wanted to do everything I could to make the most impact." He shrugged again.

Merinda looked at him and then to Jem. If she reached for her gun, Skip would do heaven knows what. Jem still had a loose grip on the walking stick, but Skip followed Merinda's eyes and ripped it out of Jem's hand, flinging it across the tile.

"So I suppose you'll drown us in an empty pool," Merinda decided.

"Even after everything, I like you, Merinda. I always have. We have had such a good rapport. The interviews. The photographs. We're the same in so many ways."

"How?" Jem wondered aloud, even as Merinda shrieked, "I am *nothing* like you!" Jem had rarely heard her friend so moved.

"Are you not? You work for your own self-interest. Your promotion. To keep your little detective business chugging away. You do it for the game and the pursuit. And as much as I want my paycheck and ticket out of here before my conscience, or what is left of it, shoves me in the army, I enjoyed this game with you." He focused on Jem. "She's so quiet."

"You have a pistol pointed to my head," Jem said, shakily. "There's little I can say or do."*

"You've never been as much fun as your friend here." Skip nudged the gun emphatically. "You're still learning how to play detective, but in some ways you are strides ahead of her."

Merinda scowled. There it was again. *Playing detective.* Even Skip thought it. Was she just some part of ironic justice and solutions she stepped into? Now, playing detective meant that a strange and angry photographer, someone as much a part of her Toronto landscape as Big Ben at City Hall or the Wellington, was pressing the barrel of his gun to Jemima's temple. Her eyes flittered over the pool. She had no way out. No Plan B. "So you got me to expound on your brilliance, Skip," she said after a moment, the first prickles of entrapment encircling her. "How does this end?"

"It could end with me shooting Jem. But I've spent enough time with DeLuca to know that is the usual trajectory of these stories. Jem needing to be rescued! Jem in peril!" He snickered. "She's good collateral, wouldn't you say?"

"I would say you're a foolish and horrible human being."

"And I would say that may be true." Skip waited in the stretching silence for Merinda to do something.

---

* Other than review mental images of her perfect life with a man who spoke in voice equal parts chocolate and moonlight, a little boy whose slightest smile constricted her heart.

Could she run and draw his fire, distracting him from Jem?
Then she could reach into her pocket and extract the pistol.

"We seem to be at a standstill," he said. "I'll let one of you—"

"Jem," Merinda stomped on Skip's sentence.

"Merinda," Jem said simultaneously

"Oh, shut up, Jem! You know it has to be you."

"I can't..." Jem shook her head.

Merinda thought and she thought and she thought, and if the only answer was Jem leaving this wretched place and escaping through the tunnel and back to the safety of the house, then that was the only possible scenario.

"You're not Sherlock Holmes at all. Loving something more than yourself."

Merinda narrowed her eyes at him. "Cracker jacks! Take that gun off her and point it at me. And don't you dare go back on your word. You can have me, but she goes free."

"Merinda!" Jem attempted.

Merinda shot her a look. "You know and I know that this is the only way this can end, Jemima. You have people who need you."

"I need *you*!"

"It's not the same."

Skip nodded. "And she keeps quiet."

"Or what?" Jem's voice was tremulous.

"You have a husband you adore and a little boy." Jem shuddered as Skip swerved back to Merinda. And with his turn he transferred the gun from Jem's temple to Merinda's. The final adventure. Merinda supposed she should have anticipated a moment where she had stepped too far. But she confessed to herself even as she anticipated his clicking the trigger that it was an infuriatingly dull way to go.

More infuriating still because Jem was not turning and running as promised. Rather, she was inching nearer.

"Jemima," Merinda said between clenched teeth. "Run far away!"

"You have to let me hug her goodbye," Jem told Skip calmly.

Skip looked between the two of them. "I know she keeps files and picklocks in her vest. And an ivory-handled pistol."

Jem opened Merinda's vest and showed the file to Skip. She pinched it between two fingers and tossed it across the tiles. "And her picklocks!" Skip instructed. Jem obeyed and passed them over. Skip skipped them over the tiles so that their echo ricocheted across the pool.

"I love you so much, Merinda," Jem said, her arms encircling, a whisper of her breath against Merinda's bobbed hair. "You are my very best friend."

Merinda shifted uncomfortably. Even seconds from death, she wrinkled her nose and assumed Jem knew precisely where the flap in the back of her vest exposed the pistol they had earlier procured. "There, there," she said.

And as Jem backed away, Merinda noticed a considerable weight lifted from underneath her vest even as Skip pressed the muzzle of the gun harder against her temple.

"Goodbye, Merinda!" Jem started a slow move toward the door. "I will uphold your sacrifice and honor you for what you have done in order to send me back to my family."

"Oh, for heaven's sake!" Skip exclaimed.

"And I shall always regard you as the best and wisest woman I have ever known."

"You sound ridiculous," Skip continued. "Leave before I shoot both of you."

Jem turned toward the door before backtracking slowly and shoving Sir Henry's pistol into Skip's spine. "You're stupid, Skip McCoy." Skip recovered quickly and shoved her away, swinging his own gun in the air and expelling a shot as she kicked him. Merinda pounced on him, wrestling for the weapon and momentarily grabbing it. She clung to it even as he recovered and grabbed her around the neck, pressing the gun to her head again with renewed dedication. "You shoot me, Jem, and I will kill her."

Jem slowly rose and extended her arm, the sinews of her muscles tight with a new energy. She expected to see a flutter of fear across her friend's face, but Merinda was merely amused. She watched, she encouraged, she nodded. Jem saw the brightness in her friend's cat eyes. She wanted Jem to do it. She wanted Jem to draw on everything that was within her and steal a moment and become the heroine of this story.

Jem inhaled. *Threaten and point.* She just had to adjust her gaze, shut one eye, and compensate with the invigorated focus of the other. Jem saw where Skip ended and Merinda began, and there was but a slice. There was a good chance she could miss. Skip gripped Merinda tightly. Jem held out the gun, took a fluttering breath, and pulled the trigger.

At first she couldn't look, pressing her palm over her eyes. Then, slowly, she unclutched her fingers, assuming the weapon would clatter to the floor with the movement. Instead, it clung to her index finger.

"Jem!"

Jem's eyes flew open with a wave of nausea. "Did I kill you?"

"Jemima!" Merinda—a very much alive Merinda—crossed over from where Skip was slumped on the tiles, the blood draining from him.

"Jemima!" Merinda said one more time, closing the space between them. She held up her shirt and Jem's eyes rounded at the graze of the bullet on the sleeve. "You are one cracker jacks shot!" Merinda flung her arms around Jem's neck and pressed her nose into her shoulder. "The best shot in all of Toronto."

"I suppose it's not enough to just threaten and point," Jem said dazedly.

"I suppose not," Merinda said with a chuckle, pulling her friend closer.

CHAPTER
TWENTY

Herringford and Watts contribute to the
war effort. Lady Adelaide and Sir Henry
Pelham offer particular commendation.
The white feather murderer has met justice
at last, thanks to the considerable efforts
of Toronto's celebrated lady detectives.*

An excerpt from the *Globe and Mail*

Merinda expressed her delight with a sound caught between a giggle and a snort. "I knew that muckraker would be good for something someday."

"Ha!" said Jem.

Jemima thought Ray's attention to their efforts in the *Globe* showed a bias not befitting a journalist of his new caliber, but he was adamant that much of his success was a result of his paying particular attention to the bachelor girl detectives on their first case four years previously.

But beyond the bold print of the dailies, the world was changing before her. Anytime Merinda strolled passed Big Ben at City Hall, the bell's toll startled her.

When Jem passed her the paper for her own inspection, she tossed it aside. She was in a lousy mood. Jasper was leaving, Mouse was still in the hospital under careful observation, and even rifle practice

---

* Ray's habit of referring to the duo as Herringford and Watts proved a habit difficult to break, no matter how long the new sign flourished in Merinda's townhouse window.

couldn't distract her. Skip was dead, the mystery solved, and yet there remained a portentous shadow that something was off-kilter. That while they had been able to stop Russell St. Clair and keep Skip from harming anyone further with his skewed view of justice and revenge, a darkness hovered.

Indeed, when a message boy arrived with a pristine, cream-colored envelope bearing the insignia of City Hall, Merinda ripped it open and read the note within it aloud to Jem. The sheet of paper bore Mayor Tertius Montague's gold-embossed and overly designed monogram.

"He wants to see us?" Jem said, her eyes wide.

"I highly doubt it's to give us the key to the city."

At the appointed time that afternoon, they alighted outside City Hall and stared out at the commotion spread over the span of green. There were kiosks and banners, recruiters standing sentry, and women who recognized the duo, looking up from their careful formation and offering waves and small salutes in solidarity.

Once they had reached the top of the stairs leading to the massive redbrick building, Jem took a deep breath while Merinda pushed open the heavy wooden door.

"I'm nervous," Jem admitted.

Merinda chuckled. "Oh, please! We have encountered far more imposing foes than Tertius Montague!"

They reported at a desk on one side of the grand foyer. Upon direction, at the very end of the corridor, they arrived at Mayor Montague's large suite of offices. His name was set in gold font not unlike the embellishment of his signature.

Montague's secretary's was perched behind a desk. "His Honor will be with you presently." Her voice was clipped.

Jem and Merinda waited. The toe of Merinda's brogan impatiently tapped on the linoleum. The secretary emitted a vehement "Hush!"

Jemima was taking in the walls around her: the photographs and framed news clippings, the campaign slogans, the unending promenade dedicated to Tertius Montague's pomp and power.

Finally, the heavy door to his personal office creaked open, and they were admitted into his bower.

The first thing Jemima noticed was the incredible view. Huge windows provided a large cityscape of Osgoode Hall and beyond to University Avenue. Beyond the manicured trees and bushes, however, was the persistent thought that this grand Gothic structure stood sentinel while garishly facing the Ward. A dissonant chord clashing against the poverty and squalor stretched in City Hall's boisterous shadow.

"Mrs. DeLuca, Miss Herringford." Their names seethed through Montague's clenched smile. Merinda had never actually seen him up close. He wasn't as large as she'd anticipated. Maybe that was because he always found a platform, podium, or even staircase on which to ascend.

He motioned for them to sit, and seconds later they occupied the leather wingback chairs in front of his large desk.

"How do you do?" Jem's voice warbled slightly. She folded her hands in her lap.

"What do you want?" Merinda asked at the same time.

Montague assessed them, one triangular eyebrow raised.

"Mrs. DeLuca, might I presume that your husband is enjoying his…erm…unexpected advancement?"

Jem's smile cut through Montague's condescension. "He certainly is."

"Hmm. Miss Herringford…" His watery gray eyes appraised her. "Have you found your way back to earth after your not inconsiderable efforts in bringing Skip McCoy, our sensational white feather murderer, to justice?"

"Sir, we would love to know why it was so important for us to meet you here."

"You think that McCoy was your Moriarty." Merinda shifted ever so slightly, though Montague noticed all the same. "Ah, yes. My son is quite a fan of Mr. Doyle. I am familiar with the great detective whom you emulate in your *little* adventures."*

---

* Merinda yearned to shake him so as to rattle the italics from his head. Instead, she sat patiently with a pasted-on smile.

"I think Skip McCoy was the white feather murderer," Merinda said evasively.

"And he was, wasn't he? So the city is safe, isn't it? With you at the helm?"

"I didn't say anything of the kind, Your *Honor*." Merinda tried on her own italics for size.

"But I know that's what you feel in that womanly heart of yours. Oh, don't give me that look, Miss Herringford. McCoy wasn't your *Moriarty*. But I am."

Though her pulse skipped, Merinda guffawed. "What are you talking about?"

"I play your game, but I loathe you. I play your game because my approval ratings go up. But you are against every modicum of order I intend to eke out in our city during this most inconvenient conflict."

"Inconvenient!" Merinda spat. "You are probably receiving a cut of the munitions' profit. You have probably won another turn. Skip did you a favor by eliminating any potential conflict."

"I will always win."

"What is it you want so badly?" Jem intervened.

"Control, Mrs. DeLuca. I want control. The world is in upheaval. *Toronto* is in upheaval. I need some safe, sane certainty—"

"That you will provide," Merinda said, cutting in.

"You are not God." Jem's voice was low. "You cannot control, and you cannot decide. There is a higher power than you even in this country, and reporters will stomp out your corruption, and people like us will fight it."

Montague watched Jem with interest. "And I thought you were the silent, subservient one."

"What *is* the point of our meeting, Mr. Montague?" Merinda asked again.

"You have solved the white feather murders. You have seen a young man sent to his grave for crimes he committed. Those were the *only* crimes committed. A man driven by power he knew he would never have."

"We all know that is only one layer of your treacherous cake!" Merinda cried.

"I am warning you, Miss Herringford. Play by my rules, and I will keep my Morality Squad off your backs. But don't think I am not inspired by McCoy's ingenuity."

"Ingenuity?" Jem repeated.

While Montague addressed Jem, his eyes coldly sought Merinda's. "Picking off those Miss Herringford holds dear one by one."

Canadian men, in smart berets with crisp khaki uniforms and shimmering bronze buttons, shipped out daily as they had since the first regiment proudly marched from Exhibition Place through the downtown core, Jem and Merinda joining the witnessing throng.

The collective fervor stirred a proud community, but all too soon the streets emptied, and the men left on trains to Halifax before crossing the Atlantic, and the world chugged on behind them.

Merinda and Jem canvassed for Lady Adelaide's hospital ship, capitalizing on their minor celebrity, posing with bowler hats while change jangled in their labeled tins.

You are not God. Merinda remembered Jem saying that to Montague. She chewed on this. She didn't share her friends' faith, but she saw the way it coursed through them, saw the way that it glistened in the eyes of the women sending their men away, saw the way it rippled through the national consciousness. This something higher than any understanding she would hammer away at. Merinda didn't pretend to know much about God, but she knew that Montague was wrong. So she would saunter forth and arm herself against her own war. Her contribution beyond strips of bandages and canvassing for coins to contribute to a hospital ship.

"I am my own special brand of different," Merinda decided, tilting her bowler at a jaunty angle. "And that's all right with me."

Merinda was told to go to the last bed, near the grated window. She tugged at her shirtwaist, straightened her back, and entered the large room.

The patient practically blended in with the starched ivory sheets. She seemed smaller than she ever had before. It would still be several weeks before she was released, the orderly had informed her.

"Hello, Mouse!" she said brightly. The girl's wide brown eyes watched with interest as she lowered herself into a chair.

"Hello, Miss Herringford."

"Mouse, you're awake and alert!" Merinda inspected the bandage under Mouse's hairline. Her right arm was in a cast. "You right scared me."

"I knew I'd be all right. I'm more worried for Kat. She was in a state."

"Where is she now?" Merinda looked about, as if Kat might pop out from behind a screen or curtain.

"She went to rustle up something to eat."

"Well, you must be bored out of your socks. So I am here to keep you company. I brought a deck of cards." Merinda reached into her trouser pocket and splayed the hand over the bedcover. "I can teach you something. Go Fish! Or—" Merinda reached into her other pocket and pulled out a folded *Strand* magazine. She unrolled its pages and opened it up. "I can read you a story."

"What kind of story?"

"A ghost story. A horror story. You might get scared."

"I won't get scared."

"Scared as a mouse!"

Mouse shook her head with a slight smile at the pun.

"Very well." Merinda thumbed to the beginning of the greatest ghost story she had ever read and knew nearly by heart (with dramatic looks up from the well-worn pages now and then alongside a rather terrible attempt at dramatic recitation). "'Mr. Sherlock Holmes,'" she read, "'who was usually very late in the mornings, save upon those not infrequent occasions when he was up all night, was seated at the breakfast table. I stood upon the hearth rug and picked up the stick which our visitor had left behind him the night before.'"

Beginning with *The House of the Baskervilles,* she read Sherlock Holmes serials well into the night.

The invitation arrived on the peeling paint of the porch beyond the overgrown shrubs. A hand unfamiliar to Jemima scrawled on pearl-colored stationery, which clashed with their dusty furniture. Sure, they had moved to a new place with windows intact and a few extra rooms,* but some things, such as Jem's attention to domestic detail, had not been transferred with their boxes and furniture on moving day.

"Ray?" she called. "I think we've been invited to a wedding..."

Ray bit his lip and rubbed at a smudge of ink on his ear. He shifted in his arm chair, watching Jemima as she traded one frock for the next, adjusted the pearls or brooch affixed to her collar, and kicked off one pair of heels before stepping into another. He had offered to buy her a new outfit with his increased salary, but she maintained that she had plenty of lovely things she could wear to Viola's wedding. She wanted to make a good impression. She didn't want to stand out too much.

Canada will experience pockets of prejudice my family never antici-pated when we scraped together our fare for passage to our promised land. We will never learn who throws rocks through windows or smashes a print-ing press. The battle for our home front...

Ray chewed on the end of his pen. Those last words would make a corker of a headline.

"We can't be late," Jem chided, having apparently decided on a lemon-hued organdy.

"I recognize the color of that dress, but it is... it is different somehow."

"I had Mrs. Malone take off the sleeves and move the waist line."

---

* One room Jem was secretly certain would soon need to be outfitted in either pink or blue.

She spun in front of the mirror. "You like it? It's the more modern style and yet quite frugal!"

Ray smiled, struggling into his pin-striped jacket and two-toned shoes.

His *Globe* salary afforded him a sudden splurge on a rather sharp made-to-wear suit from the Spenser's discount rack. He did up the top button of his collar. But not a moment later, his finger hooked, tugging at it, and he undid the button again. Then he wrestled out of the jacket.

Jem giggled at the transformation. A bit of something new fringing some irrepressible part of him that could never change. She edged toward him, and he felt the rustle of lace on his collar bone, the light scent of lavender tickling his nostrils. She ran her fingers over the back of his hair line. "It's too short."

"It looks smart. Professional." He smoothed his hair down at the part line.

"Still too short."

He combed it away from his face. "It's not falling over my eyes."

"I know!" She pouted. "Too short."

"But dashing, right?" Ray tilted his head to the side.

"I suppose."

Ray couldn't keep his stomach from fluttering at the prospect of seeing his sister again. And Luca too. Ten minutes later, they stepped into the September sun tinged with the warmth of leftover August, yet pinged with a portentous hint of a chill to settle in. Jem looped her arm in his. After they deposited Hamish with Mrs. Malone, Jem smiled into the waning sunshine.

"Now admit to me, Ray DeLuca, that it is nice to have a night out. Just the two of us. We must allow ourselves one night now and then. Our son will be safe under the watch of Mrs. Malone."

A smile tickled Ray's cheek. "For one night. Now and then."

She fell into him, and he took her hand in his, marred with ink, in momentary reprieve of any tremor.

It was a short jaunt of a trolley ride before they alighted at the mouth of the Ward. Evening was just flirting with the sunlight still staining the sky like a swath of butter from an uneven knife.

Jem had rarely experienced St. John's Ward in broad daylight or on happy terms. So many of the clients she and Merinda received, especially during the first years of their practice, were residents of some of the ramshackle cottages. Ray tugged her hand gently into a side alleyway and through a shortcut to the Community Center. He explained that the hall was a prime example of the mosaic they were trying to achieve. Differences were left at the door, and despite barriers of language and tradition, a community was burgeoning.

Jem and Ray heard merry voices, a fiddle, and the tinny chords of an out-of-tune piano even before they entered the door.

Once inside, Viola was in Ray's arms in a moment.

"It's bad luck to cry on your wedding day, Vi," he said, his voice cracking.

"Ray! I could hardly wait for you to get here."

Viola then turned to Jem with a smile that lit up her entire face. "Welcome." She pulled Jem close and kissed her on both cheeks.

A moment later Lars appeared with Luca at his side.

Ray shook Lars's hand and was nearly bowled over by Luca's quick embrace. His nephew remembered him. And fondly.

While they found their seats, Ray examined Lars, who looked at Viola as if she were a piece of fine china. Luca remained nearby, inquisitively looking up at the bear of a man with wide black eyes and expectant smile.

The ceremony was brief. Incense permeated the cedar pews and week-old communion wafers. Viola's dress was secondhand: a yellowed ivory that smelt of mothballs when one was up close. Yet she was radiant underneath her makepiece veil and too-long skirt.

Lars's voice was brusque as they tripped through their vows in a hybrid of Italian and Swedish and the English they were determined to master.

Then their new life officially began, and they led the procession to the basement, where the ladies of the neighborhood had laid out a feast days in the making.

Rickety boards in the unstable floor were whitewashed clean, though they were subject to the scrape of scuffed shoes.

A violinist played a tune in the corner, a pint of ale beside him.

Ray recognized a number of people, many from his intimate acquaintance with Toronto, who smiled and raised their glasses. And all the while Jem held tightly to his hand.

Food was piled high, and the sparse orchestra was in full swing.

On each side of the room, plaques and banners and poorly framed photographs displayed the Ward Boys, a mélange of dialects and nationalities strewn together by common cause all proving themselves to Canada. *We will be home by Christmas. We will be home.*

Lars towered over Viola. The DeLucas were never known for their prominence or stature. Viola smiled happily as Luca grabbed at her skirt and Lars tugged at her hand.

Ray, satisfied, let his eyes roam over the scene.

This was his Toronto. This hodgepodge, potluck crew of overlong hair and rehemmed dresses. Every person possessing a tapestry of stories, carrying his or her past like a rucksack on sunken shoulders. Not crushed by the weight, but instead hopeful for eventual rest.

Now they proudly gave their sons and fathers to the European conflict, aligning themselves to the Union Jack, embracing the tenuous jingoism of their appropriated home. A few tears were shed in remembrance of the fields and plains across the Atlantic, but Canada was branded on their hearts now.

Jem politely nodded and smiled at a man whose broken English was tinged with a Yiddish dialect, promising to save him a dance.

Ray tightened his grip on her hand and tugged her toward the center of the whirling crowd. Then he pulled her tightly to him. "I don't know…" he paused, his breath momentarily stolen by her nearness, "…if I have ever properly asked you to dance."

"You haven't." Her smile was giddy. "I didn't know you knew how to dance! Yet you have your arms around me. You are holding me close…"

Very close. The lace at her neck tickled the space at his open collar again. "But I don't want to hurt you," he said, his eyes shifting down to her rib.

"I'll take the risk. It's just a little stiff. Almost as right as rain."

The band struck up a familiar ditty known to both from Merinda's gramophone. It spilled out in three-quarter time and Ray, to Jem's surprise, turned her to the floor.

"I didn't know you could waltz!" Jem sounded joyfully surprised.

"My little sister and I learned from our mother. I always anticipated a situation wherein I would want to spin the most beautiful woman in the city around a crowded room."

Jem smiled, and they continued through several dances more.

"May I cut in?"

Jem turned her flushed face and met Viola's kind gaze directly. "Of course," she said, making her way to the side of the room.

Jem watched brother and sister dance, and her heart rose and then rested. Viola was a missing puzzle piece. Ray would never have quite been the same without her near. She was his connection to his life before Canada. *She* was his homeland.

Once the dance ended, Jem saw Ray looking for her in the crowd. She wondered if she would ever stop blushing when his gaze sought hers and then decided she didn't care if she didn't.

He strolled over, took her hand, and led her back to the dance floor.

His breath tickled a stray strand of hair from her chignon, his long fingers stayed at the small of her back, and she couldn't tell right from left or her hat from her glove, and she didn't care.

"We deserve a little magic," she whispered into his right ear, his *good ear*, when she could manage enough of a voice to speak.

"A little?" he said with a sly grin, spinning her again.

Jasper peered out the lace curtains of his childhood bedroom over a neighborhood of picket fences and redbrick houses in row upon congenial row.

Then he stood back, his eyes languorously moving over the varsity pennant on his wall and then the toy soldiers on his dresser. The sounds of an everyday morning came in through the slightly open window: the trolley bell, the clip-clop of horses' hooves, the creaking wagon bottles clanging as the milkman continued on his run.

It had been years since Jasper had occupied the now-made bed. It didn't really fit him anymore. His feet draped over its edge. But he wanted to make sure he spent the last night with his mother and father. After supper his mother had taken the clock off the parlor wall so her eyes wouldn't be drawn to the time, so the rhythm of its tick wouldn't toll the hours till morning.

Hearing his mother's stern-sweet beckoning coming from downstairs, Jasper donned his robe over his pajamas and tied the belt.

He held on to the bannister, following the scent of breakfast with a slow stride. *Might this be the last time I will descend from my bedroom to the wafting smell of syrup and pancakes?*

His mother's smile wavered, but the pancakes were hot, the syrup a sticky river through tasty fluff.

Everything was as it was when Jasper was a boy, his greatest worry losing a round of marbles to the school bully.

"I want to make this morning last!" he said.

His mother nodded, piling another stack of pancakes on stoneware whose design he used to make out with his fork on meatloaf night.*

"Why has every morning of my life dragged, while the one morning I want to keep forever rushes by?" his mother wondered in an uneven voice.

---

* Jasper never fancied meatloaf.

Lemon light pierced through the homemade gingham curtains.

"You'll come back, though," his father said gruffly, following Jasper's gaze to the window. "And we're proud of you."

"Have you seen your friends, then?" Jasper's mother's hand trembled around her teacup, and Jasper was pained to see her trying so hard to keep herself in check.

"I have."

"Well, we'll see you off."

Jasper swallowed a bite of pancake, shaking his head. "No. I don't want to remember you there, me looking back and you unable to keep your heart from breaking in front of me." He took his mother's hand and squeezed gently. "I won't look back at all. Like Lot's wife from the Sunday school story." He cracked a smile. "I want to remember you here, waving from the front door like you did when I would head off to school."

"And you will write."

"And I will write."

Jasper didn't know what stretched before him. He didn't know if his life would be truncated in the trenches or his heart be stolen by a chance encounter with a doe-eyed French girl. He didn't know if he would be scared or homesick or sad, nor if he would ever see the four walls that embraced him now again.

But he had a certainty beyond his mother's tears and his father's averted eyes.

Beyond any law inscribed by Toronto's police force.

Beyond.

A line from a verse in Habakkuk, one he'd heard Ethan Talbot quote numerous times.

I will work a work in your days...

Jasper Forth knew he would be just fine.

Epilogue

*Our world moves on, and our transient city welcomes
some and waves goodbye to others in a consistent state
of uncertainty. Our enduring constant is change. We
will be ready for it, armed against it, and welcome it.
Perhaps Toronto's limitless quality is the inability for
it to be pigeonholed into one thought or idea. You
cannot impress upon it a label or description. You
cannot ascribe to it one culture or tradition. It
is all of these things, strong and supple and
welcoming. A revolving door. A welcome mat.
Ultimately worth fighting for.*

Ray DeLuca, the *Globe and Mail*

J*emima,*
    *We arrive by the 12:15 train on Thursday. While we have made
arrangement for accommodation at the King Edward, we have not
yet arranged transportation from Union Station to the hotel. Your father
is unaware I am writing you, but I am assured he would be placated
by an opportunity to see his grandson again—however unexpected such
opportunity may be.*

Jem clutched the note from her mother to her heart.

"You're nervous," Ray said, tugging a sweater over Hamish's head.

"Not for myself. For you."

"Jem…"

"It slays me that they haven't taken the time to get to know you."

"Jem, while I would dearly love your parents' approval, I have never expected it."

"I know, but you deserve it. You have mine."

Ray smiled. "Come, then."

A short, sunny walk later they arrived at Union Station, Ray fiddling with the button on his collar. Jem let Hamish walk a few steps before his "up, up!" had her hoisting him into her arms.

"Ray…"

"My love, we are doing this right."

Jem repositioned Hamish in one arm and reached for Ray's hand as they crossed through the station lobby to the tracks. A group of soldiers meandered by, their rucksacks over their shoulders, their girls at their heels, handkerchiefs balled in their hands.

Ray's fist, too, was balled to stop its shaking. Jem turned to him with a smile. "I never wanted anything but you, even before I knew you were *you*. My heart knew before my head could catch up."

The 12:15 train rumbled over the track with sparks and smoke, and then it screeched to a stop.

Jem's stomach was doing somersaults as she watched the doors to the first-class compartments creak open. She didn't want Ray to see her nervousness, so she studied his profile under his smart new bowler. He wasn't completely handsome, of course. She would have found him boring if he were. But he looked rather smart in his new clothes, and she had always loved the way his long eyelashes nearly swept his cheeks and his ears stuck out just a little and his hair (even newly cut) rebelliously curled a bit at the back of his collar.

She set Hamish down a moment, relishing the way his strong little grip held tightly to her skirt, and then she reached over and began unbuttoning Ray's collar button.

"Jem! What are you doing?"

"There." She leaned in and kissed him on the cheek before stepping back and taking his free hand. "I see them!" she announced a moment later, her eyes flickering over the platform.

She loosened Hamish's hand from her skirt and placed it on Ray's pant leg. He felt a small tug and looked down. For a moment he only had eyes for Hamish, who was chewing on the string affixed to his sweater. But once he looked up again, his father-in-law's stony face stalled his delight.

He was, however, mercifully silent.

Ray watched Jem slowly straighten her spine and saunter ahead. She kissed her mother on both cheeks and took her father's hand. "Mother, Father," she effused cordially. Then she walked back to her husband and child and picked up Hamish. Ray watched her eyes glisten.

Jem's mother observed her grandson, smiling with undisguised joy when the baby seemed to recognize her and began babbling a string of happy, chattering sounds. She leaned over him and kissed him.

"He is almost speaking." Jem's mother's voice wavered slightly. Ray couldn't tell if it was from emotion or pride.

"Darling, take him a moment?" Jemima turned to Ray and winked.

"Mother," Jem said proudly, knowing neither of her parents would lash at Ray while he held their precious grandson in his arms. Her heart skipped several beats watching the reverence with which he hoisted Hamish higher on his shoulder, caressed his cheek, and allowed his sometimes-stalled half-moon smile to tickle wider across his cheek. "I believe you have yet to meet my husband."

Ray found something in himself there, with this beautiful, beaming girl beside him and her father's moustache the latest thing of interest to his beautiful little son. He gave Mrs. Watts a bow, taking her hand and kissing it. "A pleasure!" he said and upon rising, conjured up the brightest, most luminous smile he could, full-teeth flashing, black eyes twinkling, and he watched as her breath caught a little.

Mrs. Beatrice Watts melted into the platform.

They dress in their Sunday best and give their men something to picture on the battlefield. Merinda recalled a line from a recent *Globe*

article that had reminded her of Jasper's desire for a "picture to come home for."

Before this moment, the closest Merinda Herringford had come to cosmetics were soot and grime on a case. She stared at the mirror in the foyer, dabbing her lips with rose color, working the slightest line to her eyes, impressed at how even the minimal smudge of gray at her lashes made her green eyes look brighter.

Then she took a sparkly bandeau borrowed from Jem, flouncing her bobbed blond curls around it so the beaded ornamentation caught the light.

She tugged at the skirt falling away from a ribbon accentuating her waist and then at the gossamer tulip-shaped sleeves scalloped over her arms.

Perhaps Merinda Herringford wasn't able to give Jasper Forth the kind of send-off he desired or deserved, but she could give him a farewell worthy of his sacrifice.

She arrived at Union Station as it erupted in an uproar of goodbyes. In a few moments the platform would empty of its cacophony and chaos, and then it would be relatively quiet and peaceful until another regiment would pull in like a gruesome tide.

And she wondered as she scoured the crowd for a sight of him why she wasn't made like Jem, who was happy with the knowledge that a man lived and died for the prospect of holding her near.

A moment later she spotted him, just under the clock, every other man surrounding him diminished by Jasper in uniform.

Merinda straightened her own shoulders, exhaled, and seized the moment, parting the crowd and tapping Jasper on the shoulder. Swerving, he took in her glossed lips and lined eyes and bandeau and feminine shape. His intense gaze made her feel as if she were her blackboard and his eyes a piece of chalk.

"Jasper."

"Mer—" His voice tried to wrap around her name but failed. "You came."

He adjusted his rucksack, removed his highlander beret, and then ran his hand through his regulation length hair.

"Jasper, I need to—"

"Tell me you're here because you love me," he pleaded. "Please tell me, Merinda, that you're here to make everything I have ever wanted appear in thin air. Tell me that every dream I—"

Merinda's voice was like broken glass. "I can't. I don't feel that way, Jasper."

"What is it, Merinda? What is it you feel? It has to be me."

"It's not you." She grabbed at his uniform.

"Don't say it."

"I'm sorry, Jasper."

"Please, Merinda."

Merinda—nose running, splotchy, frantic, afraid Merinda—held him tightly. "Stop it!" she shrieked. "Jasper…I don't know how."

"To love? Rubbish!"

"You want all of me. You want all of me, and I am not meant to give that to you. But you are one part of my heart, and it's likely to rip if you keep talking like this." She rose on her tiptoes to bring them eye level. "I'd trade my life for yours in a moment." She spoke through the milling soldiers, the din of farewells. "I'd fight in your place. You know I would because I do love you. Just not in the way you need." She drew in a long breath. "But I can give you one cracker jacks of a send-off!"

She tilted his head down and kissed him, hard and strong. He fell into it desperately, his arms encircling her and every breath traded with her. He gave in longingly, pulling her more tightly against him. He gave in hungrily to grasp the second-rate stars he was being offered, the edge of a complicated dream. He ferociously kissed her and then pulled back to plant a few more kisses over her tear-stained face and into the bobbed curls under her fashionable bandeau and into the nape of her neck and over her collar bone. She knew it wasn't meant to be, but she tasted it.

When they stupidly drew back, tears stained his face as well.

She punched him, beat against him. "You have to come back for me. You have to come back for me."

"I will. You know I will." He touched her cheek. "What you did today...for me...I didn't think you were listening that night."

"I am always listening to you, Jasper."

"No, you're not. You don't even know how I take my coffee—"

"Black. One sugar."

"Merinda, I'll write you."

She punched his arm again. Her words were gone. She nodded as she watched him turn at the shrill of the whistle.

Time peeled back, revealing moments when Jasper and Merinda skipped class to wander the Philosopher's Walk, taste the tingle of ice cream or the first warm summer rain on outstretched tongues, balance test tubes and test theories. Then Jasper passed the police exam, and Merinda found the city a puzzle she would never fully solve.

The shrieking train's whistle pulled them back to the present. Merinda heard Jasper's last farewell, and then he was lost in a depth of khaki uniforms.

The crowd swarmed around her in a wave of noise, some sobbing, others cheering. A reflection of a city on the brink of something momentous. But she knew the light would come, eventually. She knew that while Toronto might find itself wading in a darkness it had never known, it would emerge stronger. It was resilient.

She shouldered through a mass of people, hope surging through her. With Union Station behind her, she tilted her chin in the direction of Yonge Street. Though autumn was actually just beginning to make its presence felt on the year, to Merinda it seemed this moment that winter was whipping through the air, its first portentous chill blasting September in with a harbinger of darkness and frost.

Merinda crossed Front Street at a diagonal, in the opposite direction of the driving wind humming over the lake and nipping at her heels.

She didn't look back. She passed another swarm of service men in khaki kits, their rucksacks full of bully beef and regulation socks, their eyes under their peaked knit hats full of the promise of victory and adventure. Their sweethearts, in painted lips and spit-shone Sunday best, were draped on their arms, tripping along to the promise of *We will be home. We will be home by Christmas. We will be home.*

Merinda breathed in her city, drawing strength from its pulse. It was her own, this ragtag, mismatched quilt of a place with its Tower of Babel dialects and soot-stained buildings and cadence of progress and reform.

Her city.

And she took it alone. No man on her arm, no family awaiting her. Just the promise of Turkish coffee and problems to be solved, an empty blackboard, a small magnifying glass, and years' worth of Wheaton and Holmes quotes.

Merinda drew a deep breath and straightened her shoulders. She took the city in her stride, the trumbling street cars, the horses' hooves, the whistles of the constables on patrol, the screech of an automobile's tires. Merinda waded through the collage and maze of a world that might, at any moment, leave her behind.

Above, a few saucy clouds puffed out their presence in a cerulean sky. Towering buildings scraped to heaven alongside steeples and trees and the ornamented outlines of large structures in marble and stone.

Toronto wasn't just a city. Rather, it was a starring character in the nickelodeon of her life. She matched the rhythm of the pulse of its people, their steps a heartbeat, the tangy breeze and whistling music of the street musicians their lifeblood.

This is your great romance, she thought with a growing smile. *The one true love of your life.* And for Merinda Herringford, jauntily swinging her arms as she quickened her pace toward Wellington Street, flirting with the bustling enterprise of Yonge, she knew that was all she would ever need.